Ambitious: Love

& Hustle

By

Danielle Grant

Ambitious: Love & Hustle

Copyright © 2016 Danielle Grant

This is a work of fiction. It is not meant to depict, portray or represent any particular real persons. All the characters, incidents and dialogues are the products of the author's imagination and are not to be constructed as real. Any resemblance to actual events or person living or dead is coincidental and is not intended by the author.

Dedication

I dedicate this novel to all my readers who has supported me on this wonderful writing journey. I have come a long way from where I first started and I owe that to everyone who has pushed me to go harder than I ever did before. I would also like to take this time to thank Cedes and Jassy for letting me use them as inspiration for the two leading lady characters. Y'all are hilarious and keep me laughing nonstop. To my support system, you all know who you are. Thank you so much for the love and support. ♥

Table of Contents

Prologue

~Three Years Prior~

"*Something* is going to have to give soon. I don't think I will be able to work at the home healthcare agency for much longer." Jasmine sighed.

Her best friend Mercedes sat down on the couch next to her. "I'm tired of working for other people period. If these chicks call off one more time, I'm going to slap the shit out of them." She said looking at her phone frustrated.

"They called off again? Damn how many days is that in one week?"

Mercedes looked at her and rolled her eyes. "Girl, that makes three days already and the week not even over yet. I'm really losing my patience with them and this damn job."

"I feel you on that. Between work and school I barely have enough time for a social life." Jasmine said mentally exhausted.

"Oh, speaking of a social life. I went out with Cree last night and all these clubs are the same. The music wasn't that good. They kept playing the same shit over and over again. The liquor was watered down, but the prices were high as hell."

"I haven't been to a club in a long time, but I could just imagine everything you just said. It's always been like that." Jasmine said.

"Well, you ain't missing anything special because it's still the same. I just wish for once we could go to a nice club with good music, great drinks, and just an all around dope atmosphere." Mercedes said leaning back on the couch.

Jasmine sat there and thought about everything she just said. "What if we opened up our own club?" she blurted out.

Mercedes glanced over at her with a raised eyebrow. "You want to open up a night club?"

"Yes, but not just any kind of night club. During the day we could host different kinds of events. At night it could be a place where everyone from different ethnic groups can come and enjoy themselves. We could do like different areas and rooms where people could choose the type of music they want to hear."

She sat up and looked her in the eyes. "You're serious about this?" Mercedes asked.

"Yes! I really think we could do this. It will be a new experience for the both of us. We won't have to worry about going back to work for someone else ever again. We will be our own boss. I have a nice size egg nest that I could use to help us with the start up." Jasmine stated getting excited just thinking about it.

"Okay, I like the sound of that. I never heard of any clubs being like that before. If we going to pull in all kinds of crowds then we need to figure out how to pull in the women that don't usually go to clubs."

Jasmine stood up and started pacing the floor. "You mean like the cougars who usually roam country clubs? The ones who wait until their husbands are gone to flirt and sleep with the pool boys?"

"Yes. Let's not forget the shy women with all that pent up sexual frustration because they're too shy to speak to men. We can't forget about the men who love men as well." Mercedes said smiling.

They shared a laugh. "Okay, maybe we could do a dating service during the day?" Jasmine suggested.

"Naw, that won't work. A lot of those people don't want others to know what they do behind closed doors." They sat and thought for a moment until Mercedes hopped up off the couch abruptly.

"The night club could be a front for the real club that we run!" She shouted.

"Girl, what are you talking about?" Jasmine asked looking at her as if she was crazy.

"Okay, hear me out. Let's say we do the club and events thing during the day and at night like you mentioned. That's where we will find our clients for the secret club that we will run." She said.

"What secret club?"

"The secret club where we help women find or create their perfect fantasy guy. If they're looking for a guy to take them on a romantic date, they come to us. If they're looking for a guy that they just want to have the best fuck of their life with, they come to us. If they're in need of a guy to take home for the holidays so their parents could stop trying to play match maker, they come to us. We could make a shit load of money just by helping women who are undercover freaks live out their fantasies." Mercedes explained.

They stood there staring at each other for a moment. Neither one said a word as they let their imagination run wild. After a few minutes Jasmine finally spoke up.

"Okay, if we do this, where are we going to find the men that is willing to let us pimp them out?" She chuckled.

Mercedes placed her finger on her chin as she thought about that for a second. "I think I have the person that could help us with that." She walked back over to the couch and grabbed her phone off of the coffee table. She started typing away on her phone before placing it back down.

"Now we just wait." She said sitting back on the couch. Jasmine stared at her with her arms folded across her chest before returning to her spot on the couch as well.

~An Hour Later~

The doorbell rang causing Mercedes to jump up and head towards the front door. She looked through the peephole and smiled at the visitor. She wiped the smile off her face as she opened the door.

"You said give you thirty minutes it's been an hour now." She said with an attitude.

"Man listen, either you fix that fucking attitude right now or I'm walking my black ass back to my car and pulling off." He snapped back at her.

"Is there a problem?" Jasmine asked turning the corner with her .22 gripped tightly in her hand.

When she saw it was Cree, Mercedes's boyfriend she smiled. "Ohhh, hey Cree! I thought you was somebody else that was anxious to meet their maker." She said tucking her gun in the back of her waist.

"What's up, baby thug." He said calling her by the nickname he gave her even though he knew she hated it.

She rolled her eyes. "Don't make me pull back out on you fool." She walked back into the living room, but not before flipping him the bird.

"Oh, so just because it's him you wasn't going to shoot? What if he was trying to whoop my ass? I see how you be... with your fake ass!" Mercedes yelled after her.

"Girl shut the hell up! You know I'll shoot his ass for you!" Jasmine yelled out from the living room.

"Oh, okay. I was just making sure!" Mercedes then turned her attention back to her man.

"So, y'all just going to plan my murder like I ain't standing right here?" Cree asked looking at her.

She shrugged her shoulders. "You are either with us or against us. If you against us then your ass is fair game at getting shot. We can't take any chances." She said, and he knew she was serious.

He shook his head before snatching her up in his arms. He kissed her a few times on the lips before placing her back on her feet. "I love that you ain't afraid of me or any other nigga, but don't get fucked up." He whispered in her ear. He walked passed, smacked her on the ass, and headed towards the living room.

"Chill out Cedes, you got company. You can't be freaking on him while your girl sitting in the living room." She gave herself a pet talk and then closed the front door.

When she got to the living room, Cree wasted no time getting to the point. "Okay, so tell me about this plan you two have come up with." He said sitting on the couch with his elbows resting on his knees.

Mercedes repeated everything that she and Jasmine had come up with. She and Jasmine watched him closely to see what his reaction would be. To their surprise, he didn't show any emotion.

"What you need me to do? I could help y'all find a starting spot for the club and pay on it for you." He said shocking them.

They looked at each other and then back at him. "We could use that help as well, but that's not what I really called you for." Mercedes said a little nervous.

"What's up? What you need?" He asked again.

"We need help with finding employees for both clubs." She revealed.

Cree chuckled. "You want me to find dudes that's willing to make money by fucking different women?"

"Yes." They both said at once.

He thought on it for a second before agreeing. "Alright. I have a few dudes in mind already that won't mind doing that. Let me see what I can do to help and get back to y'all."

"Aww thanks baby!" Mercedes squealed before falling into his lap. She wrapped her arms around his neck and kissed him.

Jasmine smiled then glanced at her watch. "I have to get going, but call me so that we could finish mapping everything out." She said grabbing her things.

"I'll call you tonight. We're actually going to do this." Mercedes said smiling at her.

"I know I can't believe it. Okay, bye y'all." She said walking out the door.

Cree looked at his woman and shook his head. "What?" She asked.

"You two are not your typical women. Other females are planning shopping trips with their niggas' money or opening up salons and bakeries. Not you and Jassy though. Y'all are trying to make some serious money. Opening up a club and pimping niggas." They shared a laugh.

"Right, and just think this only the beginning for us. We're going to build our business into something great." She said excitedly.

He stared her in the eyes. "I'm here to support you through it all."

"That's all I ask for right now." She kissed him.

Cree picked her up and carried her towards the bedroom.

"Where are we going?" She laughed.

"Oh, you thought I forgot about that attitude you had when you answered the door? I'm about to tear that ass up. You know I don't play that shit." He said serious as a heart attack.

Mercedes knew she was in for a long night, but she had no complaints. If he thought she was just going to take it, he had another thing coming. He better be prepared for a serious rumble between the sheets. She knows that the bond they share will only help their relationship grow stronger as time goes on.

Chapter 1

~Fast Forward Three Years~

Jasmine walked into Retro Fitness ready to get a good work out in. She hadn't been to the gym in over three months. Even though she had been a little tense and stressed out from her breakup with her now ex-boyfriend Davon. She kept busy by overworking herself. That had seemed to only make it worse. They had been together for a year and half. Things started off good for them until he found out she owned a few night clubs around town. The night he found out they had argued for hours. Well, he argued, and she ignored him. He felt that she was keeping secrets from him. She had explained to him that she didn't feel a need to tell him every move she made because they weren't married. Once he got over that it seemed as if things changed. Jasmine thought it had something to do with the fact she made more money than he did. Whatever the case may have been, she wasn't allowing any man to cheat on her while she stayed faithful to him. After she broke it off with him, he had been calling her and popping up at her house nonstop. Her patience with him ran out quick. She had to threaten to shoot his dick off for him to realize she wanted nothing to do with him. After that she hadn't had any more problems out of him.

After she placed her things in the locker, she looked herself over in the mirrors that lined up against the back of the wall. Jasmine thought she looked cute in her green and black workout outfit. From the stares she received from some of the men when she entered the gym, she knew she wasn't the only one who thought so. Once she finished her warm-ups, she started off her workout on the bike machine. She spent thirty minutes on there before heading over to the treadmill. She placed her ear buds in and let the music take her to another place.

Forty-five minutes later and she was still going. She was so lost in her workout that she didn't see the guy standing next to her watching her until he decided to get her attention.

"Excuse me shorty." He said tapping her on the shoulder.

Jasmine jumped a little as she looked to see who had touched her. When her eyes landed on the guy standing by the treadmill next to her, she let her eyes roam over him. He looked to be about six feet tall, freshly done dreads that come a little pass his shoulders, tattoos covering his arms and upper chest, chocolate colored eyes, and deep dimples on both cheeks with a killer smile.

"Damn he fine." She thought to herself.

He smiled as he watched her check him out. When their eyes connected he knew he made the right decision to come over and talk to her. She was beautiful to him.

Compared to his six feet height she had to be around 5'3. She was thick with smooth chocolate brown skin that made him want to lick her all over. Her shoulder length dark reddish brown hair fit her face perfectly.

"Can I help you?" She asked bringing him out of his thoughts. She stepped off of the treadmill and stood in front of him.

"As a matter of fact you can." He said grinning at her.

"Oookay." She dragged out.

"I just had to come over here and introduce myself to the beautiful woman in the green and black workout fit. The name is Kasim." He greeted with his hand held out.

She placed her hand in his and shook it while trying to keep a straight face.

"I was wondering if you would like to go grab some coffee or something after your workout." He offered.

Jasmine smiled at him. "How do you know I'm a coffee drinker? I probably hate it." She teased.

He chuckled. "I don't, but I'm willing to drink water as long as I have you to keep me company." He flirted.

She laughed at the corny game he was spitting. "What did you say your name was again?"

"Kasim. What's yours?"

"Jasmine."

"Well, Jasmine it's a pleasure to meet you. So, what do you say about that drink?"

She bit down on her bottom lip. "I don't know. Once I leave here I have plans, but maybe I could take you up on that coffee some other time." She said letting him down easy. She wasn't ready to get into another meaningless relationship at the moment.

He nodded his head. "I can respect that. So, can I get your number to call you some time? I just want to get to know the lady behind the beautiful smile." He smirked at her.

She looked around the gym before glancing up into his eyes. "Okay." She agreed and gave him her number. After they talked for a little while longer they said their goodbyes. Jasmine left the gym with a smile on her face that she couldn't seem to get rid of.

"Maybe I could give him a try. Maybe." She said as she got in her car and pulled off.

By the time eleven o'clock hit Jasmine and Mercedes were three drinks in while chilling at one of their clubs out in New York. They were celebrating their three year anniversary of being successful club owners. It wasn't easy for them when they first started because no one believed that two women would succeed in the business. They proved all their haters wrong and tonight were living proof of that.

"I'm just so damn happy!" Mercedes yelled over the loud music.

"Me too. We did what a lot of people said we couldn't." Jasmine co-signed.

"Fuck them!"

Jasmine laughed. She knew her girl was twisted, and she wasn't too far behind. "Is Cree still coming out tonight?" She asked taking another sip of her drink.

"Yeah, he said he would be here around one." Mercedes replied.

"I'm so happy for you guys. You're still going strong. I need to find me someone that can handle my lifestyle without acting like a bitch about it."

"You will find the right person or he will find you."

"I hope so."

"I think I'm going to ask Cree to have my baby." She blurted out causing Jasmine to crack up laughing.

"You mean you going to have his baby." She corrected her.

"Noooo, he's going to have my baby. I'm not carrying a damn baby for all those months. Why do men think they can just get the woman pregnant and we do all the work? Oh hell naw, I ain't going out like that." She said drunkenly.

"You don't even want kids!" Jasmine was laughing so hard she spilled some of her drink.

"Well, I might want one someday with him. He's going to do all the carrying though." She looked over at her girl and started laughing.

"You crazy as hell. Give me this you done had enough." Jasmine said snatching her drink out of her hand and finishing it off.

"Heifer, I wasn't done with that." She frowned. She flagged the waitress down to order another drink.

She looked towards the entrance and noticed a drunken man scanning the room. "Who is that?" She asked.

Jasmine followed her eyesight and shrugged when her eyes landed on the man. "I don't know, but he looks as if he's searching for someone." She said as she watched the man make his way towards them.

"Yo... you!" He shouted while pointing and shaking his finger at them.

"Oh here we go! Who are you?" Mercedes asked looking him up and down.

"You two bitches are the ones who set my wife up on a date to get fucked!" He shouted at them.

Jasmine and Mercedes looked at each other before they both reached for their purses. "Who are you?" She asked again while discreetly pulling her .22 out and sitting it on her lap. She glanced over at Jasmine and noticed she did the same.

"I'm John, Kelsey's husband. She confessed about cheating on me with some guy you fixed her up with!"

Jasmine waved him off. "Look here Johnny boy. You can't blame us because you weren't fucking your wife right, so she went elsewhere. Stop blaming others for what you were lacking. Now, if you were putting it down in the bedroom like she likes it she wouldn't have to go find someone else to break her back in." She said with a chuckle.

"Right! You should be at home with your wife right now tearing that ass up. Showing her why she married you and that you still got it. Instead, you're standing here in front of us drunk and whining about your wife getting fucked." Mercedes added.

He looked pissed off as he balled his fist up. "You bitches are going to pay for disrespecting me and ruining my marriage!" He took a step forward, but stopped.

Jasmine and Mercedes both placed their guns on the table in front of them. They glared at him and waited for him to make a move. When he didn't Jasmine spoke again.

"Next time you call us bitches I'm sending a bullet directly between those bushy ass eyebrows. We didn't ruin your marriage. If your wife was out seeking new dick then your marriage was already fucked up. Now, I'm going to ask you nicely to get the fuck out of my club before I have those two big guys standing behind you toss your ass out. You're ruining my buzz." She dismissed him.

John looked behind him and for the first time noticed two huge guys standing three feet behind him. He glanced back out the women and walked away with his head held down. The two security guards followed him to make sure he left out of the club without any problems.

"It's crazy how we always get the blame for someone else's actions." Mercedes said shaking her head.

"They're going to learn that we don't play that shit. Everyone we deal with is grown and does things on their own free will. Now, I need another drink." Jasmine said as the waitress brought their drinks to the table.

Even after that incident both ladies still enjoyed their night out. Jasmine left when Mercedes and Cree disappeared to her office. She knew what those two had planned and that they wouldn't be back anytime soon. During most of the night she had been busy texting Kasim.

Jasmine hoped by morning she didn't wake up and realized she drunk texted him some crazy shit.

Chapter 2

Mercedes walked into her office and took a seat at her desk. She placed her purse in the bottom draw before shuffling through the notes her assistant handed her on her way through the door. She glanced up when she heard a knock at the door.

"Come in!" She called out.

Her assistant Stacy poked her head inside. "Miss. Taylor your four o'clock is here. Would you like for me to send her in or have her wait for a moment until you get settled?" She asked.

"No, go ahead and send her in." She waved.

"Okay." Stacy closed the door and walked back in a few minutes later with a woman behind her. The lady looked a little nervous as she stood in the middle of the room while taking in her surroundings.

"Please, have a seat." Mercedes offered.

"Thank you. I'm a little nervous. I have never done anything like this before." She said shyly.

Mercedes chuckled as she looked her over. She saw plenty women like the one before her come into her office saying the same things. Once they get to talking she learns that they are nothing but undercover freaks wanting to be released. That's where her and her best friend Jasmine comes in. They run many nightclubs from New Jersey to New York. Even though their nightclubs are very successful, it's what goes on underneath them that bring in the most money.

"Okay... Amy is it?" Mercedes looked over the papers with her information on it.

"Yes, it's Amy."

"Okay, well let's get started shall we? What kind of date are you looking for?" She turned her chair slightly, so that she got a good view of the large flat screen behind her.

"We have all types of men here for the picking. Describe to me your type." She turned the TV on and a lot of pictures of different men of different races and sizes popped up.

"Well, I was looking for a tall, dark handsome man." She said getting all excited.

"Oh okay, so little Miss. Amy likes black men." Mercedes thought to herself.

"Okay, we have a lot of men fitting that description." She clicked on a few things until pictures of men in business suits popped up on the screen.

"Oh, no that's not really what I want." Amy said shaking her head.

"Well, tell me more about the kind of man that you are looking for."

Amy smiled at her before speaking. "Sure. What I want is a strong man that can pick me up and toss me around a little. I need a man that will pull my hair and smack me on the ass while demanding me to tell him who's is it."

Mercedes looked at her with a stone face before breaking out into a laugh. "Oh okay, so you want a thug Amy?"

"Yes!" She shouted then covered her mouth when she realized she got a little carried away.

"Say no more. I got you." She clicked some more until she pulled up pictures of guys who looked as if they did years in the state penitentiary. She handed Amy the remote control and told her to look through the different bios on the men and see which one she likes most.

While Amy did that she pulled out the contract that she's going to have her sign and go over it. There was a slight knock at the door before the door came open. Mercedes smiled as her man of over four years, Cree walked into the office with his swagger on a million. At twenty-six years old, 6'2 in height, slim build, tatted from the bottom of his neck down to his waist; front and back.

His deep waves, amber colored eyes, brown pecan skin tone, and kissable lips drove women crazy. Mercedes was just the lucky one who called him her man. Before he made it over to her she could smell his enticing cologne.

"Hey baby, what are you doing here?" She asked as he stood in front of her.

He leaned in close to her ear so that only she could make out what he was going to say. "I'm about to head out to Jersey for a little while. I wanted to leave you with some encouraging words before I go." She could feel his warm jolly rancher scented breath on her ear as she listened to every word he spoke.

"Tonight when I get home I want a good meal waiting for me. That means you better be waiting for me ass naked on the kitchen table with your legs spread eagle style. After you're done feeding me, I'm going to bend you over that table and fuck you until your legs give out. Then I'm going to carry you to the bedroom and fuck you some more until you pass out. Once I feel you can't take any more of the dick, I'll let you get some sleep while I clean you up. Now, if you play like you don't know what's up, there will be consequences for that. You got me?"

Mercedes clenched her legs together as tight as she could. He lifted her head up by her chin and stared into her eyes. She nodded her head, but didn't speak. She couldn't even if she wanted to her voice was stuck in her throat. He smirked and kissed her lips before walking back out the door and closing it behind him.

"Ahem." She cleared her throat and placed her attention back on Amy, who was staring at her with admiration.

"I want a man like that!" She said excitedly while bouncing a little in her seat. She looked back at the closed door then back at Mercedes.

"I'm sure we can find someone who might come close." She assured her.

Amy frowned. "He's not available? I would whether have him."

"No sweetie, he's off limits. That's my nigga and messing with him will get your ass whooped. Now, we don't want that so let's find you someone that you can have your way with for a night. That fine specimen that just walked out the door ain't it."

Amy looked as if she now had an attitude. Mercedes calmly opened her top draw and pulled out her baby .22. She placed it on top of the desk and glared at Amy.

"Amy, we don't have a problem now do we?"

Amy eyed the gun while shaking her head. "No, of course not. I think I found the guy I want." She said pointing to the TV with a shaky hand.

"Oh, that's great!" Mercedes said clapping her hands together. After they got everything squared away, she called her assistant in to escort Amy out.

She placed her gun back in the draw and smiled. "Never thought I would've had to come close to shooting a bitch about my man." She shook her head and continued on about her day.

Chapter 3

Jasmine had been talking to Kasim for about a week now. She finally gave in and decided to go out on a date with him after he asked for what seemed like the millionth time. He had told her to dress in something comfortable, so she went with some tight skinny leg blue jeans with rips in the front, a white long sleeve fitting shirt, and white blazer. She finished her look off with some white flats. She grabbed her purse off the bed and headed for the door when she heard a knock at the door. At the same time she got a text from Mercedes.

Cedes: What are you doing?

Jassy: I'm about to go out with the guy I been telling you about.

Cedes: Oh, okay. Call me when it's over. I want all the details.

Jassy: You know I got you.

She threw her phone in her purse and headed for the door. "Hey." She greeted him when she opened it up.

"Hey beautiful. You look good." He said licking his lips.

Jasmine gave him a small smile. "Thank you."

"So, you ready to go?" He asked.

"Yes, just let me lock my door." She stepped outside then locked the door.

"Okay, I'm ready."

He led her to a 2015 all blacked out Benz. *"Damn he rolling like this? Okay, one point for him. He's going to have to come better than that to impress me though."* She thought as she got into the car.

They talked a little as they drove to their destination. He kept stealing glances of her and grinning. "Why do you keep looking over here and grinning at me?"

"I can't look over there at you?" He asked still grinning.

"You making me nervous. It's one thing to look, but you over there grinning like you up to something. Please don't ruin our first date by making me tase you." She looked at him seriously.

He chuckled. "You'll really tase me?"

"Hell yeah! If you try anything slick you getting fried my nigga." She said pulling a taser out of her purse and pressing down on it.

"Oh shit! You're serious." He glanced at her in shock.

"Hey, what can I say? Mama didn't raise any fools." Jasmine shrugged.

He nodded his head. "Okay... okay. I like you Jasmine. You a little pretty ass thug." They shared a laugh.

When they pulled up to their destination she looked over at him confused. He undid his seatbelt and got out of the car. He walked around to the passenger side and opened the door for her. They held hands as they walked to the entrance of Barnes and Noble. He opened the door for her to walk inside ahead of him.

"This is just the first stop on our date. I remembered how you mentioned that you love reading different kind of books. So, I got this for you to pick out whatever you want." He handed her a gift card.

She looked at him suspiciously. "What's your motive?" She questioned.

"I just want to show you that I'm really trying to get to know you as a person. I want to feed your mind before I even attempt to try to feed your body. That card has a two hundred dollar limit on it." He said licking his lips and placing his hands in his pocket.

Jasmine took a step back and looked him up and down. "Would you excuse me for a moment, I have to use the restroom."

"Sure go head and handle your business. I'll be over there at that table." He pointed to a table located across the store.

"Okay, I'll be right back." She made a beeline straight for the ladies' restroom. When she walked inside she sat her purse on the sink and looked around to see if anyone was in there with her. When she saw that it was empty she pulled her phone out and called Cedes.

"Why the hell are you calling me while you on your date? Don't tell me that nigga was wack, and you dipped on him." She said as soon as she answered the phone.

"Girl no, this is an emergency call." Jasmine said hyped up.

"Oh shit! Okay, tell me what happened. Do I need to bring the big gun or my baby .22 would be enough?" She asked jumping up off of her couch and heading to her closet to grab her gun. No matter what the situation was right or wrong they were always down to ride for each other.

"Noooo it's not that type of emergency!" She stressed.

Cedes stopped and walked back to the couch. "Okay, so what's wrong then?" She asked plopping back down in her spot.

"I think this nigga trying to get laid. He ain't playing fair." She told her.

Cedes scrunched her face up. "Why you say that?"

"Because he brought me to a bookstore for the first half of our date. He even gave me a gift card with a two hundred dollar limit on it."

The next thing she heard was the sound of Cedes cracking up laughing on the other end of the phone. "Girl this shit not funny!" She yelled, only causing her to laugh harder.

"Yeah girl, that nigga trying to get into the panties. How does he know you love books like that?" She asked once her laughter calmed down a little.

"I guess he was actually paying attention when I was telling him I love to read different kind of books. Also, how I wanted to build my own personal library inside my house." She replied.

"Oh girl, you went and told him the secret to your heart and panties." Cedes laughed again.

"Okay, I'm done talking to your ass for the day." She was about to hang up.

"No wait!"

"What?" Jasmine rolled her eyes.

"Are you going to give him some?" She asked trying hard not to laugh.

"Byeee!" She yelled before hanging up. Cedes was at home falling on the floor laughing her ass off.

Jasmine fixed herself up before walking out of the restroom. She looked around until she spotted him sitting at the table reading a book. "Damn he likes to read too? He ain't playing fair at all." She mumbled.

He looked up when he saw her walking towards the table. "Are you okay?" He asked standing to his feet.

"Yeah, why you ask me that?"

"You was in the restroom for a little minute. Don't tell me you was in there taking a shit?"

Jasmine tried to stop it but she couldn't help it. She busted out laughing real loud. Other customers started looking over at her. She glared back at them.

"You real funny, but no I was not taking a shit. Let's go pick me out some books to read while you tell me more about yourself." She said walking towards the romance section.

As they scanned shelves after shelves of books, she got to know more about him. She couldn't help but to think that he would be a nice distraction from her everyday hustle.

"Who wouldn't love a fine ass man who likes to read just as much as I do? Shit I might have just found

my future baby daddy. " She joked to herself as she eyed him with a devious grin plastered on her face.

Chapter 4

Five months had passed and all of their businesses were booming. Jasmine and Mercedes were living out their dreams as successful business women. Almost everything in their lives was going smoothly. Everything except their love lives. Mercedes and Cree relationship was growing stronger by the day. They got each other. They just clicked. The only problem was Cree started hinting around about starting a family. Mercedes joked about having kids all the time with him, but she wasn't sure that she was ready to be a mother. She also threw around that she would like to be a wife before she became anybody's mother. That was the first biggest disagreement they ever had since they started dating.

Jasmine's relationship problem wasn't at that level just yet. She and Kasim had been getting really close lately. They had created a special bond, but there was just one problem. Jasmine had started to pull away from him. He noticed it about a month ago after they shared their first intimate moment. He still hadn't penetrated her but what they shared was nothing less than amazing. She had finally let him near her secret valley and he took his time enjoying her waterfall. After that night he sensed a change in her behavior. For a moment he doubted himself, but then he shook it off. He knew his head game was bananas and from the way she called out his name he knew she enjoyed every suck and flick of his tongue. He couldn't understand why she was acting weird. Every time he brought it up she would brush it off. Now he got a feeling that she was trying to friend zone him, and he would be damned if he let that happen. She was the first woman he ever thought about taking things serious with. She meant a lot to him and he refused to let her throw what they were building in the friend zone.

That was what brought him to her house unannounced. He knew if he called first she would have made up some lame ass excuse why they couldn't talk. He got out of his car and walked swiftly up the steps to the front door. He was getting ready to knock on her door when it came open.

Jasmine looked up at him surprised to see him standing on her porch. "What are you doing here?" She asked holding a trash bag in her hand.

"Hold that thought." He said before taking the trash bag out of her hand and taking it to the trash bin on the side of her garage. When he came back she was standing on the porch with her arms folded tightly across her chest.

"What are you doing here Kasim?" She asked again. This time she had a serious tone in her voice. He smirked at her acting all tough. He learned from the few months they been spending together that she tries to put up a tough front all the time to protect herself from being hurt by anyone. He had been trying like hell to show her that she didn't need to act tough around him. She could let her guard down and just be herself.

"I came here because we need to talk. I would have called you first, but I didn't feel like listening to any of the excuses you probably would have made." He said staring her straight in the eyes.

Jasmine leaned her head back and frowned at him. "Excuse me? I don't make excuses about anything." She said with a lot of attitude.

Kasim grinned. "Oh is that so?"

"Yes it is." She rolled her eyes and looked away. If she continued to stare in his eyes she was going to get lost in them. His eyes always made her feel weak in the knees.

"Can I come in so we can talk?" He asked.

She shrugged her shoulders and stepped to the side to grant him entrance inside her home. After locking the door she led him to the living room.

"Okay so what is it that you wanted to talk about?" Jasmine asked taking a seat next to him on the couch.

Kasim reached over, grabbed her left hand, and pulled her up off the couch and in between his legs. He then sat her on top of her coffee table in front of him. Staring into her brown eyes he smiled.

"You was pushing me away and I want to know why?"

"I haven't been..." She started, but he placed a finger to her lips. She moved her head back and frowned at him again.

"Your damn finger better be clean while you putting it all on my lip and stuff."

Kasim pressed his lips together to get from laughing. When he got himself under control he spoke again. "Nope, I just got done scratching my balls with this finger." He wiggled it at her.

Jasmine threw her head back and laughed. "I promise if that's true I'm going to tase you in the balls."

He started laughing too. "You know I'm just playing. You ain't slick though. Stop trying to take me off subject. Now, tell me why are you pushing what we're trying to build away?"

Jasmine sighed. "I'm just... I'm just not sure if I'm ready to actually be in a relationship. I like you Kasim... a lot. I don't want to ruin the friendship that we created. I feel like if we were to really take it there something is going to come along and destroy it. Most likely it would be something that I do or say. I don't want that. I like you being a part of my life and I don't want to picture you not in it."

He took both her hands in his. "Listen to me. I doubt that anything you do or say would ever cause me to walk away from what we share. Whoever in your past that caused you to feel this way, I'm not him. He wasn't man enough to realize and treasure what he had in you. I'm not going to make that mistake and I'm also not going to let you push me away. I want to be with you and I can tell that you want the same thing. We not about to let anyone who doesn't matter interfere with that. Plus, after I had a taste of that waterfall that flows between your legs, there is no way I am letting you get away. We go together now." He said with a chuckle. He watched as she looked at him and laughed.

"So, what you are saying is we go together now whether I agree or not?"

"Naw, we had already been going together. Your stubborn ass was just acting like you didn't already know this."

Jasmine giggled. "You can't force me to be your girlfriend."

"Trust me when I say baby I don't have to force you to do anything. You will willingly do it on your own."

They just sat there staring in each other's eyes. Jasmine sighed. "Before we go any farther I have to tell you something."

"What's up?"

She just came right out and said it. "I own a few businesses with my best friend Mercedes. A few of those businesses are night clubs. Can you handle your woman making moves like that?"

"Mercedes is the one we had hung out with a few times right?" He asked.

"Yes."

"That's impressive. You two are doing your thing. To answer your question, I can handle anything that has to do with you. I'm trying to build a relationship with you. That means as your man I will support anything you do within reasonable doubt and you would have to be able to do the same for me." Kasim said brushing his hand down the side of her face.

She smiled sweetly at him. "Well, it looks like we are boyfriend and girlfriend."

"Ahhhhhhhh!" She squealed when he jumped up and picked her up into a tight hug. He then kissed her passionately on the lips. She had never been kissed like that before. She wrapped her arms around his neck and deepened the kiss.

They were so into each other that they didn't hear anyone knock on the door until they knocked for the eighth time.

"I should get that." She said softly while biting down on the corner of her bottom lip.

"You do that." He kissed her again before placing her on her feet.

Jasmine took a deep breath then headed to the door. She was still swooning from the intense kissed that they just shared that she forgot to check the peephole before opening the door. She swung the door open and set eyes on the last person she expected to see at that moment.

"Well, are you going to let me in?" The visitor asked.

"Mom, what are you doing here?" Jasmine asked looking at her mother confused.

"Is that really how you're going to greet your mother?" Her mother Shia asked with her hands on her hips.

Jasmine sighed then smiled at her mom. "Hey mom... how are you doing? Great I truly hope. Now what do I owe for this pop up visit?"

Shia rolled her eyes and made her way inside the house. She kept walking towards the living room. "You need to fix that attitude of yours and remember the same person that God sent you too, can also send you back to him." She said over her shoulder.

She paused when she found a handsome young man sitting on the couch. He glanced at her and smiled before standing to his feet. "Who may I ask are you?" She asked grinning at him.

Jasmine smacked her forehead and shook her head. Kasim smirked as he took her hand in his. He kissed it softly. "My name is Kasim. I'm Jasmine's boyfriend."

She looked over at her daughter than back at him. "Well, it is nice to finally meet you Kasim. I'm Jasmine's mother. You can call me Shia."

"The pleasure is all mines." He said kissing her hand again before releasing it.

Shia glanced over at her daughter again. "Oh, he really knows how to lay it on thick."

"Mom, you never told me what your visit was all about." Jasmine said walking towards them.

"Oh, yes. Is there somewhere we can talk?"

"There is no need. I was just about to tell Jasmine I needed to go. I have some errands to run. I will call you later." He said walking up to her and kissing her gently on the lips before making his way to the door.

When they heard the door close Shia smiled at her daughter. "He seems like a very nice guy. I like him so far. He doesn't give off bad vibes like that other guy you were dating." She sat down on the couch.

Jasmine rolled her eyes and made her way over to the couch as well. "So, what's going on mom?"

"I got a visit earlier from your ex." She said as if she's annoyed.

"Davon came to your house?" Jasmine asked shocked. She didn't think after she threatened to shoot his dick off that he would have the balls to show up at her mother's house.

"Yes. He came there begging for me to talk to you."

"Talk to me about what?"

"He wanted me to convince you to give him another chance. I told him that you are your own person and no one can talk you into doing anything. Not that I would have anyway. I don't like his ass and I told him just that too. He had been calling my house nonstop lately I had to block him. For him to show up at my house that's just doing too much."

"I can't believe he had the nerve to do that."

"Yeah, he crazy as hell. I just wanted to give you a heads up that he not over you. I told him if he shows up at my house again, I was going to put something hot in him." She said seriously.

Jasmine laughed. If people ever wondered where she got her temper and ain't shit attitude from, all they had to do was be around her mother for a few minutes and they would get the answer they seek.

"I will take care of it mommy."

"Just be careful. You know men have a hard time getting us out of their systems once they get a taste of the goods."

"Oh my God! Mom, I do not want to hear that!" She shouted jumping up off the couch.

"Oh girl please! We are both grown. I still can't keep them men off me and I'm a married woman."

"What am I going to do with you?" Jasmine asked with a smile.

"Baby there ain't anything you can do with me. I'm about to get out of here. Remember what I said Jasmine. Be careful when it comes to these men. Nowadays they don't take rejections too well." She said standing to her feet.

"I will be careful mom." She assured her.

She led her to the door and said their goodbyes. After she waved her off she then shut and lock the door behind her. Jasmine headed for her bedroom. She had some things she needed to take care of and someone to see. Apparently, she didn't make herself very clear the last time they saw each other.

Chapter 5

Day had just turned into night and everyone was out and about. The streets were live with the everyday hustle and bustle. On the corner of Avon and Tenth Street the usual misfits were out trying to make a come up. There were dudes standing all around while a dice game was going on. There was always one person in a crowd who was louder than everyone else. Tonight that person just so happened to be Davon.

"That's right! Show me the money!" He yelled as he threw the dice down on the ground.

"Aw hell naw! Somebody check those dice. There ain't no way this nigga keep hitting like this without cheating!" One of the other dudes yelled out with a frown on his face.

"Shut your bitch ass up! I don't need to cheat. I'm good luck nigga." Davon said collecting his money from the ground.

"Damn who is that? Shorty bad." Someone said a few feet away from him. After he grabbed all his money he placed it in his pocket. He then turned his attention to the person who seemed to have caught every other nigga's attention that was standing out there. A grin spread across his face when he saw who it was.

"Chill out nigga that's all me." He said confident that she was there to take him back.

"Come here Davon let me talk to you for a minute." Jasmine waved him over with a finger.

He smiled and looked back at the guys. "I'll be right back I'm about to holla at my girl right quick."

He walked over to where she stood a few feet away from the crowd. "What's up baby?" He nodded while licking his lips.

Jasmine rolled her eyes already annoyed being in his presence. "Why are you popping up at my mother's house and calling her? She told me you showed up there begging her to convince me to take you back."

He scrunched his face up. "I wasn't begging her for shit. I just asked her for your number. She said no so I asked her to tell you to call me." He lied trying to save face in front of the guys who could hear them.

"Whatever Davon. This is my last time telling you to stop calling my mother and showing up at her house. Next time I won't be so calm or nice about it."

They heard a few of the guys laughing behind him. He looked her up and down. "Bitch, you act as if you are God's gift to man. You came all the way over here to act stuck up and shit like you don't miss daddy's dick. Quit playing with yourself Jasmine and come back to daddy. You probably frustrated because I haven't laid the pipe down on you in a while. I tell you what... we can go in the cut and I can give you a sample of what you missing." He grabbed his dick and licked his lips. He then turned around to some of the guys that was laughing and smirked at them.

Jasmine was so quick with her movements that no one had time to warn him of what was about to happen. She quickly took her taser out of her jacket pocket and placed it to his dick. She pressed down on the button and sent a high volt electric shock to his little member. She kept it there for a few seconds until she got the reaction she was looking for. He fell to the ground shaking and holding his hands between his legs. She bent down close to his left ear.

"Next time you feel like talking shit and not following the boundaries that I set, I will shoot your dick off. Please don't try me Davon. You would be better off trying one of these niggas out here than trying me." She then stood up straight and looked at all the dudes who stood around staring at her in shock.

She looked down as a stench started to assault her nostrils "Y'all might want to help him out. I think he shitted on himself." She said before making her way back to her car. When she got in her cell phone rung.

"Hello..." She sang into the phone.

"Girl, why the hell you sound so happy?" Cedes asked from the other end of the phone.

"I can't be happy about life?" She asked starting her car up after putting Cedes on speaker.

"You must have gotten some dick today." She laughed.

Jasmine laughed along with her. "Nope, but I did just tase Davon dumb ass." She revealed.

"Why?"

Jasmine told her everything that happened leading up to her tasing him. "Wait! He really shitted on himself?"

"Girl yes!" They shared another laugh.

"That's what his shitty booty ass gets. Anyway, I was calling you to see if you and Kasim wanted to go out with me and Cree tomorrow night?"

"Y'all on good terms now?" She asked her.

Cedes sighed. "We're as good as we're going to get for now. We won't be completely good until we come to some agreement."

"Cedes give that man a damn baby!" Jasmine giggled.

"Tell that man to give me a damn ring and I'll think about it shit." She rolled her eyes.

"You something else. Anyway, I'm going to talk to Kasim and see if he wants to go."

"Okay, I see y'all getting real close."

"Yeah, he told me today that we go together." She laughed.

"Good because I bet your ass was probably about to friend zone that man."

"You know me so well, but he shut that shit down quick."

"If the head game was as good as you said it was I don't know why you was trying to put him in the friend zone anyway. You know good head is hard to come by nowadays." Cedes said.

"You see… this is exactly why I don't talk to you on the phone for long periods of time. You don't know how to act."

She laughed. "You know it's true."

"I'm hanging up now!" Jasmine yelled.

"You can deny it all you want to, but you know I'm telling the truth!" Cedes yelled through the phone.

"Byeee!" Jasmine pressed the end button and shook her head with a smile on her face.

"What am I going to do with that girl?" She mumbled.

Mercedes hung up the phone still laughing. When she turned around to walk out of the kitchen, she bumped into a hard sweaty chest. Taking a step back she looked up into the eyes of her man. He stared down at her with a curious expression. He looked as if he had just come from the gym or playing ball with his boys.

"Why you all up on me like that?" She asked with her hands on her hips.

Cree smirked at her. "Did Jassy say she was coming to hang out with us tomorrow?" He asked completely ignoring her question.

"Yes, but she said she has to check with Kasim to see if he wants to come too. Now, back to my question…"

"Naw, I'm not really interested in your question. Why you keep playing with me Cedes?"

She rolled her eyes. "How am I playing with you Cree? You're the one standing behind me breathing all on my damn neck." She tried to walk pass him but he grabbed her by the back of her neck and pulled her close to him. He then merged his lips with hers and slid his tongue into her mouth. The kiss was so intense that Cedes thought her legs were going to give out on her at any minute. When Cree pulled his lips away from hers, he stared deep into her eyes with his hand still gripping the back of her neck.

"You know there is no question about how much I love you. I would do anything for your little stubborn ass. I know for a fact that there is no other woman out there for me. You're it for me baby. All I want is to be able to use that love and create something that has a piece of both of us in it. You acting as if having my baby would be the worst thing in the world." He chuckled a little, but it wasn't a funny chuckle. It was more of a confused one.

"That's not true. I just don't see what the big rush is for us to have a baby. Not to mention I would love to be somebody's wife before I'm somebody's mother. You know the love is mutual and I would do anything for you as well. All I ask is that you give me time. We're still knee deep in the business we started. Before I start making babies I want to be settled to where I don't have to leave my house unless I truly want to." She said rubbing the side of his face with her right hand.

Cree sighed. "You don't have to leave the house now if you choose not to."

"Cree…"

"Okay… look I understand what you saying. We'll come back to this conversation at a later date." He kissed her again before walking away.

Cedes stood there staring at his back as he disappeared up the stairs. She didn't know what had brought this on. One day out of the blue he just started talking about having a baby. She knew something had to happen for him to be coming at her hard about the subject. She made a mental note to go have a chat with his mother soon. Maybe she could give her some insight about what's going on with him.

She got ready to make another exit out of the kitchen when her cell phone rung in her hand. She looked at the screen and saw that it was her assistant calling.

"Yes Stacy?" She answered on the third ring.

"Hello, Miss. Taylor. I was calling to remind you of your meeting that you have this evening with all the staff."

"Oh yeah, I almost forgot about that. I need you to reschedule that meeting for me. I have some personal business that I need to take care of."

"Sure thing Miss. Taylor. Would there be anything else?" Stacy asked taking down notes on her notepad.

"No, that's it. Thanks Stacy."

"No problem. I will text you the time for the new meeting."

"Okay." They disconnected the call.

Cedes walked out of the kitchen and headed for the stairs. When she got to the bedroom she could hear the shower still going. She debated on whether she should join Cree in the shower or head out to take care of some business. A smirk covered her face as she started getting undressed.

"Business can wait for a little while longer." She mumbled as she walked inside the bathroom and climbed into the shower with her man.

Cree turned around to face her with a smirk on his face. He wasted no time snatching her up. She wrapped her legs around his waist as he threw her up against the wall kissing her roughly on the neck then the lips.

Cedes smiled inside as she bit down on her bottom lip. "Yes, business can definitely wait."

Chapter 6

"Shiiiiit! Cree wait!" Cedes screamed out as he pounded in and out of her with force.

"Don't play with me baby. You know when I'm in the honey pot ain't no way in hell I'm stopping." He whispered in her ear.

"Damn!" He grunted as he thrust in her. He could feel her nails digging into his back.

"I'm about to cum baby!"

"Do what you got to do baby. Come for daddy!" He encouraged.

Within seconds she was cumming all over his dick. She still had her legs wrapped around his waist as she leaned against the shower wall. Cree grabbed the back of her neck and brought her lips to his. He tongued her down as he came long and hard inside her. She wasn't too worried about it since she was on birth control.

Cree pulled out of her before placing her on her feet. He then grabbed her body wash and sponge. He proceeded to wash her from head to toe. After he was finished he let her return the favor.

After they both dried off, they climbed into bed naked. She laid her head on his chest. As they lay there in the dark listening to each other's breathing, she could feel herself slowly falling asleep. The last thing she remembered was Cree kissing her on the top of her head and pulling her into a tight hug.

~The following morning~

Mercedes told Cree that she was going to be running a few errands and would meet up with him tonight before they go out. She left out the part that one of those errands was going to see his mother. She needed to find out what was going on with him. Who better to know that than his own mother? Cree was very close with his mother. He talked to her at least two to three times a day. She and Mercedes had also gotten close over the years. That's why it was no big deal for her to pop up over her house without calling first.

She pulled up to a blue and white two story house on a quiet street. After parking and getting out the car she made her way to the front door. Before she could even knock the door swung open.

"It's about time you brought your ass over here to see me." Cheryl said with one hand on the door knob and the other on her hip.

Mercedes smiled at the woman. She was the female version of her son. They could double as twins. "I came to see you two weeks ago." She resorted.

"Girl, please! That was two long weeks ago. You know I need to have my weekly girl chat with you. God didn't see it fit for me to have any girls so he sent you to me. Now get in here."

Mercedes laughed as she walked inside the house. She made her way straight to the kitchen. From the smell she could tell that's where Cheryl was at before she answered the door.

"How you know I was at the door?" She asked walking over to the stove.

"I heard a car door shut. Plus, last night I had a dream that you were going to come see me soon."

"Mhmmm, it smells so good in here." She went to lift the top off one of the pots, but Cheryl popped her hand.

"You worse than my damn son. Stop touching my damn pots and you ain't washed your hands. I swear the two of you are made for each other." She fussed.

"Cree worse than me and you know it." She said walking over to the sink.

"Yeah, you right. His tall lanky ass would have stuck his hands in my shit. Sit down and I'll make us a plate. Then you can tell me what your visit is all about."

"Don't be talking about my man. You know those fighting words. He is not lanky. How you know I didn't just come over here to chill with you for a minute?" She asked her with a half smirk.

"Mercedes, who the hell you think you fooling? Don't come over here to get your ass whooped for Cree big head ass." They shared a laugh before she continued speaking.

"You like a daughter to me so that means I know how your ass is. Something is on your mind and I got a feeling that it has to do with my son." She gave her a knowing look.

"Ms. Cheryl, don't be over there reading me." She chuckled.

Cheryl sat a plate of fried chicken, homemade baked mac & cheese, collard greens, yams, and a buttery roll in front of her. After fixing her own plate she sat down across from her. "Okay, so tell me what's going on?"

Mercedes placed a forkful of mac & cheese in her mouth. After chewing and swallowing she looked over at Cheryl. "One day out of the blue Cree comes to me talking about us having a baby. We even got into a huge argument about it." She explained to her everything they talked about and her feelings on the subject.

"Umm, I see. Around what time did this argument occur?" Cheryl asked.

"I don't know the exact date but it was a few months ago."

"Damn." Cheryl mumbled but Mercedes still ended up hearing her.

"What?"

"I think I know why he's been talking about having a baby." She said sadly.

"Why? What's going on Ms. Cheryl?"

"Hold on a minute." She got up and walked out of the kitchen. When she came back she had a piece of paper in her hand. She took her seat and slid the paper across the table to her.

"What's this?"

"Just read it and then I will explain it to you more." She said as she continued to eat her food.

Mercedes picked the paper up and begun to read it. As she read each word her mouth dropped open and her eyes got bigger. She glanced across the table at Cheryl with sad eyes.

"Wh... why didn't you tell me?" She asked.

"I didn't tell anyone actually. Cree only found out because I had forgotten I left it out and his nosey ass was going through my shit." She laughed to try to change the mood, but the look on Mercedes' face showed that she didn't find a damn thing funny.

"Look Mercedes, I was having a hard time dealing with it myself. I was going to wait to get everyone together and then break the news." She said.

"You said it was months ago that Cree found out. How much longer were you going to wait before you told people?" She asked. Cheryl could see the hurt in her eyes.

"I don't know. I'm scared okay. I don't know how to tell my family that I have a bad heart and it's a possibility that I could die from this shit. I need a new heart, but there's no telling when my turn for the surgery will be. I had been waiting a long time already. A part of me is kind of glad Cree found the results because I won't have to deal with this alone anymore." She then looked over at Mercedes with tears in her eyes.

"As you know, none of my three sons have any children. I think Cree is so hell bent on having a baby so that I could be here to see my grandchild before I…" Her voice trailed off as she looked passed her.

"Mama, what's going on?" Mercedes turned around to see Cree's younger brother Cortez standing there. She grabbed the paper off the table and slid it into her pocket.

"Uh, nothing. We're just having some girl talk." Cheryl said standing to her feet.

Cortez looked from her to Mercedes then shrugged his shoulders. "Y'all in here looking all sad and shit. Mercedes looks as if she on the verge of tears. That would be a first though. She a thug and thugs don't cry." He cracked up laughing at his own joke.

"Boy you better stop cursing like I'm not standing right here!" She disciplined.

"Sorry mama."

Mercedes got up and smacked him upside the head. "Ouch! What you do that for?" He asked rubbing the back of his head.

"Baby cause I'm a thug." She sang. She and Cheryl laughed at his expense.

"I'm telling my brother." He joked.

"Boy she'll whoop his ass too. You ain't helping your situation." Cheryl said over her shoulder while she fixed him a plate.

"Right, Ms. Cheryl you know what's up. He be like, baby why you thug me like that." She cracked up laughing.

Cortez looked over at her and shook his head. He couldn't help but laugh too. Mercedes was like a big sister to him. They cracked jokes on each other all the time.

"Y'all just teaming up on me because my brothers not here. Cedes know that Cree running things. She just putting on a front for you mama."

"Boy, please! Cree knows I'm running things. He knows that I'm the HBIC." She popped her collar.

"Oh is that right?" She froze at the sound of his voice.

Cortez smirked at her. "Naw don't freeze up now gangsta. Finish telling us how you be thugging Cree."

Cree came around the table where he could see her face. "Oh so you tell people that you be thugging me?"

She looked around at everyone then shrugged. "I'm just saying we all know the truth." She said before picking her fork up and continued eating.

"Yeah, we do. That you don't be running shit!" Cortez teased. Cheryl placed his food in front of him then smacked the back of his head.

"I told your black ass to quit all that damn cursing in front of me. With your disrespectful ass."

"Ouch, mama that hurt." He complained.

"Not as worse as this ass whooping I'm going to give you if you keep playing with me." She walked back over to the stove.

"Cree, you want a plate?" She asked.

"Yeah mama." He said never taking his eyes off of Mercedes. He sat down in the chair next to her. He watched as she continued to eat her food as if she had no worries in the world.

"What are you looking at?" She asked glancing over at him.

"I'm looking at you. You got a problem with that?" He asked with a raised eyebrow.

"Ms. Cheryl why your sons keep bothering me? Why they won't just let me eat my food in peace. Geez, you would think they never been around a woman other than they mama." Cheryl laughed.

"I had been around a lot of women. I got a whole stable of hoes." Cortez said. He ducked when Cheryl threw a spatula at him.

"Mama, you gotta stop abusing me like this! They are going to lock you up."

"Boy shut the hell up! You nineteen, they not going to give a damn about me beating your ass." She rolled her eyes before sitting Cree's plate in front of him.

"Thanks mama."

"You're welcome baby." She sat back down in her seat next to Cortez.

They continued to eat their food and crack jokes on each other. Mercedes and Cheryl kept stealing glances of each other. Each time Mercedes would smile letting her know that she didn't have to worry. Her secret was safe with her. Now she knew why Cree was pressuring her for a baby. She still wasn't ready, but they had some more talking to do. She glanced over at him and smiled. He seemed to be so happy, but she now knew he was harboring a lot of pain.

"Ouch! Damn mama why you... ouch!" She was brought out of her thoughts by Cortez whining.

"Hit him again." She instigated. She smirked when he looked at her with his eyes narrowed.

Cree pinched her thigh causing her to scream out. She punched him in the arm. "That hurt fool!"

"I know something else that will hurt but you'll enjoy the pain." He whispered in her ear.

She blushed and leaned into him with her shoulder. "Look at them over there being nasty. Go hit on them." Cortez said to his mother. She slapped him upside the head again.

"Ouch!" He yelled out. Everyone at the table laughed again at his expense.

Chapter 7

Play Time night club was packed and jumping. Everyone was having a good time letting loose after the hectic week they just had. Amongst the party goers were the two owners of the club along with their men. They were posted in the V.I.P section enjoying each other's company.

"That song will never get old." Jasmine said as she and Mercedes made their way back to their seats.

"Right! Every time females hear Juvie say, cash money taking over for the 99' and 2000s women run to the dance floor." Mercedes said sitting next to Cree.

"You lucky I don't get jealous over little shit. If I did I'll have to shoot this damn club up. All these thirsty ass niggas watching y'all every move." Cree said kissing her on the cheek.

"Cree if you shoot up our shit I'll be forced to shoot your ass too." Jasmine joked.

"I believe you too lady thug." He smiled at her.

"You so damn violent, but that shit turns me on." Kasim said wrapping his arm around her waist.

Jasmine didn't respond she just blushed. They ordered more drinks as they talked amongst themselves.

"Aye the party man has arrived!" They all looked up at the same time.

Cree stood up to give his brother a half hug. "What's up man?"

"I see y'all started the party without me. Y'all a bunch of rude muthafuckas." He joked.

"Cordell shut your ass up and sit down somewhere. I don't know who worse you or Cortez." Cedes said laughing.

"Cedes you might be punking my brother, but I'll kick your ass. I ain't scared of you shit." He sat down.

"I see your ass sat down though." She laughed.

"Right! Don't be talking to my friend like that. We'll jump your tall ass!" Jasmine said slapping hands with Cedes.

"You two short muthafuckas always fuck with me." He looked over at his brother and Kasim.

"Y'all are just going to sit there while y'all women plot on whooping my ass?" He asked them.

Kasim and Cree looked at each other and shrugged. "If we tried to help you we might get our ass whooped too. I don't know about Kasim, but I'm trying to get me some later on tonight. Shit I might help them whoop your ass." Cree said before taking the rest of his drink to the head.

"You ain't shit!" Cordell yelled.

"Whatever nigga."

Twenty minutes later they were all damn near drunk when Cortez came walking up to the V.I.P entrance. The security guard on the door must have thought he was trying to sneak in because he refused to let him through. That only caused a big scene because Cortez started acting a fool.

"Man if you don't get your big gorilla looking ass out my way, I will beat your ass!" Cortez yelled.

"Oh God, baby can you go tell them to let him in before they start fighting?" Cedes pushed at Cree to get up.

"Maaaan, get your damn fat fingers off of me. Looking like some fucking burnt sausage links. I'm telling you now if you touch me with those things again I'm going to knock your big ass the fuck out!"

"Cortez!" Cree yelled walking up to them.

"What? You see this animal trying to man handle me. Ugly beast looking muthafucka."

"It's alright Tommy. He's with us." Cree said patting the security guard on the back of his shoulder.

Tommy stepped out of the way and let Cortez and his guest pass. Both men mean mugged each other as he passed.

Jasmine and Mercedes glanced at each other after noticing the chick that was with Cortez. She looked like she was a few years older than him. The lime green dress she wore looked like it barely covered her breast and ass.

"She's busting out of that dress." Jasmine said with her face frowned up.

"Girl, can we even call it a dress?" Mercedes asked. They both laughed.

"What y'all big head asses over here laughing at?" Cortez said taking a seat at the table. He didn't even offer his date a seat first. She sat down next to him and crossed her legs causing her dress to raise up her ass a little.

"Boy, you really don't want to go round for round tonight." Jasmine laughed.

"Your little short, midget ass do not want these problems." He then looked at Kasim.

"You know she used to want me right? I told her she couldn't have me because she too damn violent. Did I tell y'all she tried to molest me one time?" He looked around the table.

"No this fool didn't!" She yelled out. She glanced over at Kasim and he seemed to think the shit was funny.

"What the hell you laughing at? He full of shit! Don't nobody want his little ass but her!" She shouted pointing to the chick next to him.

"Let me tell ya'll, she didn't take rejection very well. I had to threaten to tell my mama on her ass for her to stop. I felt so violated." He rubbed his hands over his chest.

"Cortez quit playing with me before I smack your ass. You ain't man enough for me to want your little ass. Your little peter whacker probably never even went for a swim in a PRIVATE owned pool that hasn't been overused already." Everyone at the table broke out laughing. Even his date laughed not knowing that her last statement was a shot thrown at her. She basically said that she was loose and probably fucked more niggas than he did chicks.

"I don't have a little dick. For your information I have a damn anaconda sitting between my legs. Why you think I have a limp when I walk? That muthafucka heavy. They call me the new Mandingo." He stood up and pounded on his chest. Everyone else that was seated in V.I.P area looked over at their section.

"Haaaaaaaa! Who the hell gave his little ass something to drink?" Cedes asked barely able to breathe from laughing so hard.

"Nigga sit your crazy ass down!" Cree shouted out to him.

"Psst, little dick? She got me messed up!" He mumbled.

Jasmine sat there laughing her ass off at him. "Aww poor little baby upset because now everyone knows he has a pinky in his pants."

"Jassy, stop making fun of him before you make him cry." Cedes teased.

"Maaaan, forget both of y'all. My women know I got a big dick. I put chicks in wheelchairs after they get some of this dick. Bitches have to go to rehab after I lay this dope dick on them." He said not caring that his date was sitting next to him.

"Women?" Jassy and Cedes both said at the same time.

Cortez smiled widely. "Yup, you heard right."

"Boy you ain't big pimping." Jassy smiled.

"Girl, please. I got different hoes in different area codes." He sang as he bounced his shoulders while still seated in his chair.

"Oooh get it baby!" The chick next to him encouraged.

Jassy and Cedes shook their heads. "These hoes nowadays get dumber and dumber by the year." She said grabbing her drink and finishing it off.

"Cedes used to want me too. I told her naw shorty you with my brother I can't do him like that." He continued on with his non sense.

"Nigga get the fuck out of here." Cree laughed.

"I'm serious. She wanted the kid. All the ladies want me but I'm selective of who I let get a taste of this caramel joy stick."

"Oh my goodness!" Cedes started cracking up laughing again.

"Cortez shut the hell up! Don't nobody want your ass." Cordell said trying to control his laughter.

"Cordell shut your hating ass up. You know, I think you and Cree jealous of me." He pointed his finger at them.

"Why the hell would we be jealous of you?" He asked.

"Because I'm handsome, all the women love me, and I have a big dick." Once again laughter broke out at the table. No one was able to hold it in any longer. They were all fucked up.

Kasim leaned over towards Jassy to whisper in her ear. "I think we might have to call a car for everybody. Nobody at this table needs to be driving."

She giggled. "You right. We all fucked up." Just then Trina song look back at it came on.

"Ooooh this is my shit!" She said struggling to stand up. When she did she started bouncing her ass in front of Kasim's face.

"Oooh get it get it get it!" Cedes cheered her on as she stood up and started dancing too.

"Y'all need to sit ya'll drunk asses down somewhere!" Cortez laughed as if he wasn't fucked up too.

His date stood up and started popping her ass to the beat. Everything was cool until she bent over and flashed everyone at the table her ass and pussy.

"Oh now that is just disrespectful as hell." Jassy said with her face scrunched up.

Cedes shook her head and sat back down in her seat. Only person that didn't see a problem with it was Cortez. He was cheesing hard as hell.

"Girl sit your ass down! I can't believe you walked out of your house with no panties on to the damn club. It gets too hot and sweaty up in here. Pussy probably musty and shit!" Cedes yelled just not giving a fuck anymore.

"I don't see how chicks walk around with no panties on and be sitting down on shit. Y'all going to catch something." Jassy said returning to her seat.

The chick rolled her eyes and pulled her dress down. "Y'all ain't the first jealous chicks I been around. Don't worry boo I don't want y'all man. I don't like wearing panties because it's easy for my men to get it any and everywhere they choose." She sat down in her seat and crossed her legs.

"Men?" Cedes and Jassy asked at the same time.

"Cortez, your little ass going to fuck around and catch something from these nasty chicks one day." Jassy said shaking her head.

"Bitch, who are you calling nasty?"

Jassy and Cedes hopped up out of their seats so fast Kasim and Cree had no time to stop them. Cortez stood in front of the chick blocking their way.

"Let her make it this one time. Y'all fucking up my buzz." He said trying to keep them from snatching her up.

"That's her last chance too. Next time she's feeling brave I'm going to leap over this table and beat her ass. I bet she'll think twice about saying some disrespectful shit." Jassy said as she returned to her seat.

"I don't know. I kind of still want to beat her ass for flashing us her ass and pussy. That was some real nasty shit."

"Cree get Cedes drunk ass!" Cortez yelled trying not to laugh.

"Whatever nigga! I'm a thug I can't be held down." She said causing them all to laugh.

"Come on baby don't beat his ass." Cree said grabbing her by the waist and guiding her to his lap.

"Right! Because you know I'm a thug and I'll beat his little ass, right baby?"

"Yeah baby. He not ready for those types of problems."

"Damn right he not! With his little punk ass. I'll beat her ass too if she jumps up to help him." She continued.

"Yeah, we know baby. They know you a muthafucking thug." Cree egged her on.

She turned in his lap sideways so that she could see his face. She grabbed his face with both hands. "When we get home I'm going to do all types of nasty shit to you." She said before tonguing him down.

"Nasty drunk muthafuckas." Cortez laughed.

Once the club was over everyone decided to make their exit. They all stood outside to get some fresh air while waiting for the cabs to arrive. As they talked amongst themselves Jassy made her way over to the chick that came with Cortez. Everyone figured she was going to talk to her to squash any problems they had when they were inside.

The chick thought the same thing. She smiled as Jassy stood in front of her. "Look, about that stuff that happened inside…"

"You don't have to apologize girl. It's okay." The chick said waving her off.

"Apologize?" Jassy looked confused for a second before she punched the chick in the mouth. Her lip split open on impact.

"Ohhh shiiiiit!" The guys all said at the same time.

"Why would I ever apologize for a bitch disrespecting me? You lost your damn mind."

"Damn Jass why you bust her lip? Now I ain't going to be able to get any head tonight." Cortez said with an attitude.

Cedes walked up to him and popped him in the mouth. "That's for bringing her ass to our club and allowing her to be disrespectful. I should beat your little ass." She said ready to pop him again. Cree walked over and snatched her up.

"Cree, you better get her little violent ass. I'm telling mama too. You little muthafuckas always putting y'all damn hands on somebody. It ain't our fault y'all short as hell and need help to reach shit. Jass, you're disrespectful as hell. You know I was going to be putting those lips to work tonight. I can't stand you muthafuckas when y'all drink." He complained.

"Cortez shut the hell up and help your date out."

"Naw don't tell me to shut up now. I'm calling mama." He said with his phone to his ear.

"That nigga ain't calling mama while he drunk. Especially at this time of night." Cree chuckled.

"Hello mama? Yeah… naw I'm not in jail. I was calling because Jass and Cedes putting their hands on people. Cree and Cordell just stood there too." There was a pause.

"Naw mama, I'm serious. I'm not drunk mama. They standing right here. You want to talk to them?" He turned to Cordell.

"Mama want to talk to you." He reached his hand out to him with the phone in it.

Cordell looked at him like he was crazy then pushed his hand away. Cortez shrugged his shoulders. "Mama he said he not talking to your ass right now." There was another pause. "Yup mama that's what he said and Cree said you need to take your ass back to sleep because he not getting on no phone." He glanced over at Cree with a sneaky smirk on his face.

"That fool talking to himself." Cordell said and everyone else agreed.

Cortez put his phone on speaker. "You tell them all that I want to see them over here tomorrow afternoon. I'm going to beat all y'all asses for waking me up with this bullshit! That's the problem now, y'all think because y'all grown I can't still whoop y'all ass. I can show you better than I can tell you. Whoever ain't here tomorrow afternoon, I'm beating they ass twice when I see them. Waking me up this damn early in the morning. Ooooh I'm going to tear y'all ass up!" She yelled before hanging up the phone.

Everyone stood around looking at each other. "This nigga really called his mama on us." Jassy said not believing what she just heard.

Cree and Cordell went to snatch him up, but he took off running across the street. "You heard what mama said nigga! Ya'll should have helped me."

Once the cabs got there everyone said goodbye and went on their way. Cree and Cedes laughed all the way home about Cortez telling on them. They thought that was some of the funniest shit they had ever seen. When they got home sleep was the farthest thing on their minds and apparently they weren't the only ones wide awake.

Chapter 8

Kasim and Jasmine had arrived at her house twenty minutes ago. They had sobered up a little on the ride to her place. When they got there she told him to make himself comfortable in her bedroom before she disappeared. He was about to go looking for her when the bedroom door slowly came open. In the doorway stood Jasmine wearing a pair of black lace panties, a red blazer that buttoned at the naval, and some red fuck me pumps. She wore a pair of eye glasses with a thick book in her hand. Her hair was pushed back into a messy bun.

"What are you doing?" Kasim asked licking his lips.

"You can call me Ms. Barber, the librarian." She said walking towards him.

"Oh yeah? Well Ms. Barber I would love to check a few books out. The problem is I don't know which ones to choose from. Can you help me out with that?"

Jasmine walked over and stood in front of him. "I think I have the perfect books for you. Follow me." She grabbed his hand and lead him out of the room.

She led him inside of her home library. She had it built a few months ago and loved it. It almost looked like a real library.

"So, here's how we going to do this. I have a few books scattered around the library with edible panties sticking out of them as bookmarks. Inside those books I chose certain sex scenes that we're going to try out. We're going to do it the exact way they do it in the book right there in that aisle that it's in. Do you have any questions?"

"Hell naw! I always wanted to fuck in a library." He grabbed her and pulled her to him. Before he could kiss her, she stopped him.

"Hold up Mr., rule number one in the library is no talking." She pulled out some duct tape.

"What are you going to do with that?" He asked confused.

She smirked at him. She pulled a piece of tape off and tried to place it over his mouth. He grabbed her hand before she brought it to his lips. "That ain't happening."

"Okay, but no talking in the library." She said again. He nodded before she led him to the first aisle.

Once they got to the bookshelf that held the book, she grabbed it. Smirking at him she opened the book on the page she put the panties on. She then handed him the book.

"Read, remember, and then repeat their actions." She said with a sneaky grin.

Kasim read it and licked his lips. He was finally about to live out one of his fantasies with the woman he had been dreaming about making love to for months. He placed the book back on the shelf before pulling Jasmine towards him. When their lips connected it seem as if a spark ignited between the two of them. As their kiss deepened their bodies seemed to move in sync with each other, slightly swaying from side to side. Kasim reached for the button on her blazer and undid it. When her blazer fell open he stood back and admired her melon sized breast.

Jasmine dropped her blazer to the floor as she stood and waited for his next move. She bit the corner of her bottom lip as he gripped her panties ripping them with ease. After tossing them to the side he picked her up throwing her legs over his shoulders. She kept her pumps on. She was so into the moment that the fear of him dropping her never entered her mind.

"Ooooh!" She moaned as she felt his tongue swipe across her pussy pearl.

Kasim threw her up against the bookshelf and ate her pussy like it was the best meal he ever had. When he felt her legs begin to shake he knew she was about to explode. She held on to the back of his head pushing his face farther into her pussy. He gripped her ass cheeks tighter as her cream started dripping on his tongue.

After lapping up every drop of her juices he placed her back down on her wobbly legs. He held on to her until she got her balance.

"I enjoyed that scene, but I think I did it better than the character in the book. What you think?" He asked wiping his mouth with his hand while eyeing her body lustfully.

Jasmine could barely talk. She was busy trying to catch her breath and control the sexual high she was on. It was just like the first time she let him taste her. It was as if his tongue controlled her body making her cum on its command. She had no complaints about it, but damn she wished it didn't leave her wanting to molest his mouth every time she saw him.

Kasim stood there grinning. He knew he put that work in with his tongue. He grabbed her around the waist as he pressed his hard dick into her ass. "I think it's time for the next book scene. For your sake it better be with me burying my dick deep inside you. If not I don't think I'll be following the rules you set for this library visit Ms. Barber." He whispered in her ear before licking her earlobe.

Jasmine's whole body felt like putty in his arms. She hurried up and led him to the next book. In this aisle there was a black chaise. When she reached for the book on the shelf Kasim smacked her on the ass. She got the book and removed the panties. She handed him the book with a smile on her face.

Kasim looked inside the book and found a large magnum condom on the page with the scene he's supposed to reenact. He smirked as he read the scene word for word. He knew she was watching his every move and anticipating when he would make his next move on her.

He dropped the book on the floor. "Undress me." He demanded.

Jasmine licked her lips and stepped in front of him. She removed his shirt, jeans, and boxers. Once the boxers hit the floor his dick sprang out pointing directly at her. His dick was long and fat. She could feel her pussy cream just looking at it. Jasmine stood there looking like a sexy naked librarian with just a pair of pumps and some eye glasses on.

"In the book it says that the female gives the dude head first. I prefer to feel the inside of your pussy walls. Your mouth can wait." He said as he ripped the condom wrapper open with his mouth. After placing it on his dick he laid her down on the chaise.

As he positioned himself between her legs with his dick poking the entrance of her pussy, he glanced at her face with a wide grin. "I'm going to enjoy this." He said before pushing his full length deep inside her.

"Oooooh shiiiiit Kasim!" She screamed out.

"I have been waiting for this moment Jasmine. You're going to take this entire dick like a big girl." He grunted as he thrusted in and out of her.

Kasim sat on his knees gripping her by the waist as he dug deeper inside her. Her moans got louder and louder with each thrust. He smiled as she started throwing the pussy back at him.

"Kasim!" She yelled out. She could feel herself about to cum.

"Damn you feel so good baby." He said leaning down and kissing her lips.

"I'm about to cum!" She moaned.

"I know baby, I can feel it."

"Shiiiiit this pussy tight!" He grunted.

"Ooooh baby! Fuck me harder!"

Kasim did just as she demanded. Four more hard thrusts later they both were cumming hard. Kasim felt like he had emptied a whole bucket a nut in the condom. When he pulled out of her and went to pull the condom off, he noticed that it was ripped. He made eye contact with Jasmine, who was staring at him with lust filled eyes. Then he remembered that she mentioned before that she was on birth control or that she was going to get on it soon. He wasn't sure at the moment and really didn't care either. He reached his hand out for her to grab on to.

Jasmine grabbed his hand and let him help her up. She smiled up at him as he lifted her chin up.

"What's next beautiful?" He asked.

"I think we can finish this in the shower. You're going to have to carry me though. I'm not going to make it if I have to walk." She giggled.

Kasim laughed as he picked her up and carried her out of the library. "After what we just did, I'm going to have to stamp my dick print on your pussy. You're mines now and I don't give up things that are mines. Ever." He said kissing her lips.

Jasmine just smiled as she enjoyed her sexual high.

Kasim and Jasmine wasn't the only ones still up having a little fun. Cree and Mercedes were having some role playing fun of their own. They were down in Cree's man cave with LL Cool J's 'doin it' song blaring through the speakers. They had already fucked once in the living room, bedroom, and shower. Still after all that they couldn't get enough of each other.

Cree sat on the couch butt ass naked eating a juicy peach as he watched Mercedes dance in front of him. She was wearing one of his white dress shirts with some black pumps. She didn't have shit else on underneath. Her hair sat at the top of her head in a messy bun.

They made eye contact as she started rapping along to the song while moving her hips. "All this time you been telling me that you were a don…"

Cree cut in and started rapping LL Cool J's part. "I tried to warn you girl, but you wouldn't listen now let's get it on." He finished off his peach and stood up.

Mercedes continued to dance and rap to the song. She watched as Cree walked up on her. He stared down at her for a moment before pulling her closer to him by squeezing her ass. He stuck his tongue in her mouth while picking her up. He carried her to the side of the couch and threw her over the arm of it. She could feel him lift the shirt over her ass. Before she had a chance to protest he rammed his big dick inside her.

"Shit Cree!" She half yelled and moaned at the same time.

"Shut up and take this dick!" He smacked her on the ass.

"Fuuuuck! If you going to give me the dick, give me all of it!" She yelled pushing her ass back against him.

Cree smirked as he grabbed her hips and thrust all the way inside her. She started screaming for him to fuck her harder. He did just as she asked. He pounded in and out of her. Cree reached under the shirt with his left hand as he held on to her hip with the other. He started squeezing and rubbing on her left breast. He knew she loved it when he did that while fucking her from the back.

Mercedes felt her orgasm coming. She tightened her pussy muscles around his dick. She knew that drove him crazy. She also knew that he would be cumming right along with her.

"Shiiiiit baby!" He grunted.

She threw her ass back at him as she started cumming all over his dick. She could feel him empty out his nut as he yelled out.

"Damn that was good!" He yelled falling on top of her.

She heard him yawning. "Cree get your big tall ass up off of me!" She yelled trying to get from underneath him. He was still buried deep inside her and didn't move.

"Cree, I'm not playing with you! Get your big ass up!" She could feel his body vibrating as if he was laughing at her.

"Oh you think this shit funny? Wait until I get up I'm going to shoot your ass in your big toe. Have you walking around all funny and shit. Get the hell up!"

Cree kissed her on the back of the neck before pulling out of her and getting up. He helped her up as well. When she turned around he tried to kiss her, but she kneed him in the nuts.

"Oh shit! What you do that for?" He asked holding his nuts.

"Because you play too damn much. I'm about to get in the shower and then go to bed. Don't bring your ass up there playing either or I will shoot your big toe off." She said then headed up the stairs.

Cree laughed even though he was in pain. He loved the hell out of that woman, but sometimes he felt no matter how much he showed her that, she would never understand. After turning the radio off he headed upstairs to join her in the shower.

Chapter 9

Car doors from three different cars could be heard being shut all at once. Cree, Mercedes, Jasmine, and Cordell all looked at each other as they made their way onto Cheryl's front porch. They all thought about not showing up but didn't want to have to deal with Cheryl's mouth later down the line.

"Come on let's just get this shit over with. I feel like a little ass kid about to be punished for some shit I didn't do." Cordell complained.

"I don't care what nobody says I'm whooping Cortez's ass when I see him." Jasmine said with a roll of her eyes.

Everyone laughed as the front door came open. Cheryl stood there with both hands on her hip shaking her head. "Un huh, bring y'all ass on up in here." She said stepping to the side.

"Where is Cortez at?" Cordell asked as they all made their way into the kitchen.

"He ain't here yet, but he better bring his ass on. I got something I need to tell all y'all." She said taking a seat at the table. Cree and Mercedes both looked at her with sad eyes. She smiled back at them.

"How he going to start some shit and don't show up on time?" Cordell went on to say.

"Cordell watch your damn mouth! I swear you and Cortez make me sick with all that disrespectful ass language y'all use." She snapped at him.

"We get it from you." He mumbled.

"What you say?" She glared at him.

"Nothing. I ain't said nothing mama. What you cooking today?" He changed the subject.

"I made a pot roast, mashed potatoes, string beans, dinner rolls, three layered chocolate cake, and a peach cobbler." She responded.

Cree and Cordell both rubbed their hands together with big smiles on their faces. "Ooh that sounds good as hell." He said taking a seat at the table.

"So, tell me why y'all drunk asses calling and waking me up early in the morning?" She asked looking at everyone that was seated at the table.

"That was Cortez retarded ass. We were all chilling on our way home." Cordell spoke up first.

"Why did y'all let his young ass drink anyway?"

"Honestly ma, he was already twisted when he joined us in V.I.P last night." Cree said speaking up for the first time.

"That boy is going to give me high blood pressure. He has been running around here with all those nasty hoes." She said looking as if she tasted something nasty.

Jasmine and Mercedes started laughing. That's when she placed her attention on them. "Look at y'all looking all cute in your business suits." She smiled at them.

"Thank you." They both replied.

Cheryl placed her elbows on the table. "So, what's this I hear about you two laying hands on folks last night? Who did you have to put the paws on?" She chuckled.

"I had to lay hands on the chick Cortez brought with him. She was getting fly at the mouth." Jasmine stated.

"I had to put the hands on Cortez ignorant behind." Mercedes said.

Cheryl broke out into a healthy laugh. "I'm not even going to ask what that fool did. It's probably a list longer than my arm."

They all turned when they heard the front door close. A few seconds later Cortez walked into the house all giddy.

"It's about time you brought your black ass home." Cheryl said glaring at him.

"I had to handle a few things. Did you start whooping their ass yet? I hope I didn't miss it. Start with Jasmine and Mercedes since they're always trying to beat on people. Especially Jasmine, she's an evil little midget."

"Cortez, please do not make me beat you in front of your mother. Stop calling me a midget nigga." Jasmine said glaring at him.

"Well, what would you like me to call you then? A little person?" He jumped back and ran around the table when she jumped out of her seat.

"You see, that's what I'm talking about. You are always trying to beat on people. As a matter of fact, all y'all need anger management. You too mama. They're going to take you to jail for child abuse. I'm not lying to the court either. Y'all need help." He said pointing at all of them.

Cheryl hopped up and popped him in the back of the head. "Ouch mama! This is what I'm talking about. Ouch... that hurt mama!"

"Stop playing with me then. Go wash your damn hands so we all can eat. Jasmine and Mercedes look like they need to get to work soon."

Cortez started walking out the kitchen. "They don't work mama. I think they're some female hustlers. They're probably some queen pins and we don't even know it. They probably put hits out on people for the fun of it." He joked.

"If that's true then why you keep testing us?" Mercedes yelled after him.

"Because I'm not scared of you two midgets. Plus, I know Cree ain't going to let you kill his baby brother!" He yelled from down the hall.

"What he doesn't know won't hurt him." She mumbled.

"I heard that." Cree said pinching her thigh.

"Ouch nigga! Stop pinching me." She elbowed him in the side. He laughed before leaning over and kissing her on the cheek.

After Cheryl made everyone plates, she made Cortez say grace. When he was finished they all dug in.

"So, Jasmine when am I going to meet Kasim? I hear so much about him but I need to put a face to it. I also need to threaten him about my baby. Just like I did Cree when he first brought Mercedes over here."

Jasmine smiled. "I will bring him over soon."

"Good. I'll make a nice dinner for us."

Cortez put his fork down and frowned. "Mama, why you don't ever invite any of the chicks I be seeing over for dinner?"

Everyone looked at him to see if he was being serious or just joking. From the expression on his face it looked as if he was serious as hell.

"Cortez, listen to what you just asked me. Why I don't invite any of the CHICKS you're seeing over for dinner? Why would I want all those nasty heifers in my damn house? When you find a girl that you truly like then I will invite her over for dinner. Until then, I'm going to pretend like you still think girls got cooties." Everyone laughed.

"Some of them nice though mama." He continued.

"Yeah, I bet they are nice when they let you do nasty things to them. You just better make sure you strapping up. I don't want to have to deal with no baby mama trouble."

"Yeah, I hear you mama. I ain't ready for no babies anyway. I'm just enjoying life at the moment. When I find what Cree found in Mercedes then I will be ready to settle down. Until then I'm just doing me." He said picking his fork back up and continued eating. A few seconds later he looked around the table and found that everyone was staring at him.

"What?" He asked.

"That's the first serious thing I ever heard you say." Mercedes said smiling.

"Yeah well, don't get used to it. People need to stop being serious all the time and just enjoy life. You never know when your time might be up here on earth." He said looking down at his plate.

Cheryl looked at her youngest baby with sad eyes. She knew now was the time to tell them about her being sick. She was just struggling with finding her voice at the moment.

"Mama, are you okay?" Cordell asked concerned.

Cheryl cleared her throat. "Um, I need to talk to you all about something important."

"What is it?" He asked with worried eyes.

Cheryl closed her eyes for a second then opened them back up. "I found out about a year or so ago that I have a bad heart. I set up an appointment with my doctors to have surgery done. When they find me a heart I will get a page on the pager. Even with the surgery there is still a chance that…"

"I don't want to hear this!" Cortez jumped up out of his seat with tears streaming down his face.

"Cortez baby…"

"Naw mama. You can't be sick. You the strongest person I know. You there for everyone when they need help or advice about something. Why would God try to take you away from us? Is it because I'm out here wilding?

I promise I'll do better mama, I promise I will. Please mama, you can't be sick." He cried.

Cordell and Cree jumped up and hugged him. Jasmine and Mercedes sat there with tears in their eyes as they watched on. Cheryl got up and walked over to her boys. She joined in on their hug.

"Everything is going to be okay. We're going to pray and get through this together. I just need you all to be there for one another no matter what. Families that stick together always prosper together."

After that everyone was basically silent as Cheryl explained to them everything that's going on with her. Once they were done eating and talking Mercedes and Jasmine headed off to work. They had a staff meeting that they needed to get to. Even as Jasmine drove to their main club, the car was silent. They couldn't stop thinking about what Cheryl may really be going through and how her boys were going to handle it if they had to live without the first woman they ever loved.

When Mercedes and Jasmine first arrived they had a meeting with the regular staff. Once that meeting was over the meeting with the staff of their secret club took place. Everyone was seated and waiting to see what the meeting was all about. The only time they really had meetings like this is when something was going on and all staff needed to be on alert. They haven't had a meeting like this in a while.

"First, we want to thank all of you for showing up today. We know last time we had to cancel due to an emergency. Now, let's get started on why we are here today." Mercedes said taking her seat next to Jasmine.

Jasmine was busy watching everyone's movements and facial expressions. She was good at spotting a phony person.

"Okay as you all know, we had a problem a while back about one of the client's husband coming to confront us about our business. He stated that his wife confessed to him about the club. When Jasmine and I caught up to her, she had no idea that he even knew about the club. That means someone else let our little secret out." Mercedes said looking around at everyone.

"The wife also let us in on some other important information." Jasmine said staring at one of the guys who refused to make eye contact with her or Mercedes.

"Got your ass." She thought as a smile spread across her face.

"Everyone may leave. This meeting is over." She said leaning back in her seat.

Everybody looked confused, but started making their way towards the door. When the guy got to the door she stopped him. "Mike let me talk to you for a minute." She requested.

He stopped and turned around nervously. He knew he was busted as he walked back to the table and sat down across from them. "What's up?" He asked once everyone else was out of the room.

"I think you know exactly what's up. You were one of Kelsey's main go to men if I'm not mistaken and I'm pretty sure that I'm not." Mercedes said glaring at him.

"So, what are you saying?" He had the nerve to ask with an attitude.

"Nigga don't play tough with us. You fell in love with a client and snitched her out to her husband. You thought once he found out that he would leave her and you could have her all to yourself. I bet you didn't tell him that you were the one fucking his wife. I'm here to let you know that shit not going to work out like that." Jasmine spat.

"Your contract has been expired. You can leave and never come back. Don't think about getting any ideas either. You know how my king gets when people play games with his queen." Mercedes stated.

He nodded his head and walked out of the door without saying a word. Jasmine and Mercedes looked at each other and shook their heads.

"Cree going to get some of his guys to follow him for a few weeks to make sure he doesn't try anything stupid. I doubt that he will though. Then again I never thought he would pull the shit he pulled." She said pissed.

"Yeah me either. Anyway, that shit that Cheryl told us got me in my feelings. I can't believe she needs a new heart. Seeing Cortez break down like that was hard to watch."

"Yeah it was. I never saw him like that before. That's why Cree is so stuck on us having a baby." She said sadly.

"It all makes sense now. That shit is just crazy. I have to take Kasim over there to meet her soon." Jasmine said checking her phone.

"Yeah, hopefully she doesn't scare his ass off. You know how Cheryl feels about us. We the daughters she never had." Mercedes said cracking a smile.

"You know she's going to put him through the test to see if he can handle it. I think he can though. Girl, I'm really falling for this nigga. I do shit with him that I never done with anyone before."

"Shit like what?" Mercedes asked.

Jasmine smiled. "That's another conversation for another time. We need to get some work done before we leave for the rest of the day."

"Yeah whatever heifer. You ain't slick we will be coming back to this conversation very soon."

Jasmine laughed as they both got up and walked out of the door. She was so busy texting Kasim on her phone that she wasn't watching where she was going. She bumped right into one of the guys named Kevin that worked for them.

"Oh my bad." She apologized.

"That's okay beautiful. I was actually coming to speak with you about something." He said with a pretty white smile.

She glanced up from her phone. "What's up?"

"Well, I was wondering if you would allow me to take you out sometime."

Jasmine looked at him with a shocked expression. She couldn't believe he was really standing in front of her asking her out on a date. She put her phone away in her pocket. "Look Kevin, that sounds really nice but I don't think my man would appreciate me going out with another guy." She said trying to let him down easy.

"Oh I didn't know you were seeing anyone." He said with a chuckle.

Jasmine smiled. "You weren't supposed to know because that's personal."

Kevin nodded. "I understand. Well, you have a nice day Jasmine."

"You too." She said before walking away.

When she got to her office she pulled out her phone. She laughed at a text Kasim sent her. Their relationship was really blossoming into something beautiful. She even told him about the situation with her ex. He wasn't too happy about him disrespecting her, but she told him that she took care of him. She loved his protective and possessive side.

Chapter 10

Kasim pulled up to the corner store where everyone seemed to be hanging out in front of. When he spotted the person he was looking for, he got out of the car. He said what's up to a few people he knew before approaching the dude.

"What's up, Spud? You got that for me?" He asked the dude.

"Yeah man, take a walk with me right quick." Spud said as he walked away from the group of dudes he was with.

Kasim started walking beside him. "Here's the information that you asked for. It wasn't hard to the find either. Muthafuckas nowadays are real predictable." Spud said handing Kasim a piece of paper.

"Good looking out Spud. I owe you one." He said slapping hands with him.

"Naw man, you don't owe me shit. When I got locked up a few months back you looked after my mom and baby mama for me. If you ever need anything nigga don't hesitant to ask."

"That's what's up man. I did that because it was the right thing to do. We had been boys since we were kids. I got your back."

"And I got yours." They slapped hands again before Kasim made his way to his car. He sat there for a minute and read what was on the paper. When he finished he started his car and pulled off.

Thirty minutes later Kasim found himself parked outside of a rundown house. If the lights wasn't on inside he would've thought it was vacant. He got out the house and made his way to the door. He knocked twice and waited for someone to answer. When no one came to the door he knocked again this time harder than before.

The door swung open and a funky stench hit his nose. He covered his nose and mouth with his hand and took a step back. "Damn what's that smell?" He asked.

The person at the door rolled their eyes. "Who are you and what the hell do you want? You're blowing my damn high." The woman snapped.

Kasim mean mugged her. "Tell Kasey to bring her ass up out of there now!" He demanded.

"She ain't here." The chick at the door said scratching her ass as if he wasn't standing right there in front of her.

"You one nasty muthafucka. I know she's in there. Either you tell her to bring her ass out here or I'm going to call CPS on your ass for having those kids living in them conditions." He spat at her.

She rolled her eyes and turned around. "Kasey, you have to get the hell out of here! This nigga is threatening to have my livelihood taken away!" She yelled out.

Kasim shook his head. He hated females that used their kids as a damn pay check. He took another step back as he watched as Kasey made her way to the door. She looked a damn mess. Her hair was nappy, clothes were dirty and ripped, and she looked as if she hasn't eaten anything in weeks.

"What do you want Kasim?" She asked with an attitude.

"Don't play with me Kasey. Bring your ass on so we can get the fuck out of here." He said grabbing her arm and pulling her along.

"Okay Kasim! You don't have to drag me. I know how to walk." She complained.

He opened the passenger door for her and she climbed in the car. He slammed the door and looked back up at the house. He shook his head as he walked around to the driver side and got in. This wasn't the first time he had to search for her and drag her out of a drug infested house. The places she seemed to hide out at were getting worse and worse. He hoped this would be the last time he had to do this.

They drove in silence for a good twenty minutes before he spoke to her. "Why you keep doing this Kasey?"

She looked at him and rolled her eyes. She folded her arms across her chest and sighed. "You didn't have to come and embarrass me in front of my friend Kasim."

He glanced over at her for a second before putting his attention back on the road. "You think that chick was your friend? She ain't a damn friend of yours. She used you just like she using those damn kids."

"Why do you care Kasim?" She asked.

"What kind of stupid ass question is that? You know what, don't say shit else until we get to the crib." He snapped turning the radio on to drown out some of his anger.

When they pulled up to his house he parked and got out the car. When he saw that she wasn't moving he walked to the passenger side door and opened it up.

"Either you get out willingly or I'll drag your ass out. The choice is yours because at this point I don't give a fuck. I think me babying you is what got you thinking you can keep pulling stupid shit like this. That's over with though. So, what's it going to be shorty? I don't have all day."

Kasey rolled her eyes again and got out the car. She stomped up to the front door and waited on him with her arms folded tightly across her chest.

Kasim opened the door and let her in. He headed straight for the bathroom in the hallway to run her a bath. When he walked back out she was in the kitchen eating a muffin like it was the last meal she would ever eat. When she finished he walked up to her.

"I ran you a bath. Go wash up and then come back out here so we can talk. I put some of your clothes in the bathroom on the rack." He said looking her in the eyes.

She nodded her head and walked away heading towards the bathroom. When he heard the door close he rubbed his hand down his face. He reached for his phone when he heard it ring in his pocket.

A small smile graced his face when he looked at the screen. "What's up, baby?" He answered.

"Hey, what are you doing?" Jasmine asked.

He looked back towards the hallway and closed his eyes. "I need you to come over to my crib."

"When?"

"Right now."

"This sounds important."

"It is. I really need your help right now. I will explain everything when you get here."

"Okay, say no more. I'm on my way." They disconnected their call.

Kasim looked in the fridge to see what he could whip up for them to eat.

Twenty minutes later Kasey was out of the bathroom and sitting on the couch watching TV. She glanced up at Kasim when she heard a knock at the front door. He walked out of the kitchen to answer the door.

She raised her head up when she heard a woman's voice. When the woman came into view she sat up on the couch.

"Jasmine this is my little sister Kasey. Kasey this is my woman Jasmine." He introduced.

"Why did you call her over here?"

"Maybe because he felt you could use a female to talk to since you seem to think he doesn't understand what you're going through." Jasmine said matching her attitude with one of her own. Kasim had told her all about his sister and the problems she was having.

"I don't even know you." Kasey said.

"That's okay because you're going to get to know me. Kasim wants nothing but the best for you. He might have babied you, but I won't. If I have to beat some sense into you then so be it. You need help Kasey and that's all we're trying to do is help you." She said taking a seat next to her on the couch.

Kasey looked over at Kasim and put her head down. She could feel the tears about to fall from her eyes.

"Kasim, why don't you go finish cooking and let me and Kasey talk." She suggested.

"Yeah okay." He walked out of the living room.

"He hates me." Kasey said sadly.

"That's not true. He may be a little disappointed, but he doesn't hate you. Do you really think someone that hates you would go through the trouble of looking for you?"

"I guess you right. I know I'm sick and I need help, but I won't be able to function without it." She cried.

Jasmine rubbed her back. "Kasey, I know you use drugs as a way to cope with losing your mother. There is a better way to do that. You don't have to kill yourself to try to fight the pain you feel inside."

"It hurts so bad! The drugs help me escape my reality of living without her. It started off as one pill every now and again. Next then I knew I was popping them every day sometimes twice a day. It got to the point that I just didn't care anymore."

"You forgot something very important though." Jasmine said turning her face towards hers.

"What?"

"You forgot that you still had someone here that loves you. Your brother is hurting just as much as you are but he's fighting to stay strong for you. I would rather you get better for yourself, but if you're struggling with doing that then do it for Kasim. Do you know what would happen to him if something happened to you while you're out on those streets?"

"No, I never thought about it like that." She glanced up towards the kitchen and found Kasim staring at them with sadness embedded in his eyes.

"Okay."

"Okay what?" Jasmine asked.

"I'm going to get better for the both of us. I'm going to make my brother and mother proud. It won't be easy though." She said looking at Jasmine.

"I know but you will have your brother and I here to help you." She smiled.

"Okay. It's crazy how I've never met you before but it was easy for me to talk to you. I see what my brother likes about you. You have a good aura."

"Dinner ready. Kasey are you hungry?"

"Yes, I'm starving." She said getting up and making her way to the kitchen table.

Kasim walked up to Jasmine and kissed her. "Thank you."

"You don't have to thank me. This isn't going to be a walk in the park Kasim. She's going to really have to fight this addiction."

"I know."

Jasmine grabbed his face with both hands pulling him down and kissing him again. "I will be here every step of the way. Now when she starts having withdrawals I might have to pop her ass a few times. They be getting fly at the mouth when they have the shakes. Going easy on her didn't work so we going to try some tough love."

"As long as the end result is me getting my sister back and healthy."

"Let's go eat. I can't believe you really know how to cook. I thought you were just trying to get in my panties when you first told me that."

"I was." He laughed when she punched him in the arm.

All three sat down at the table and had dinner together. Kasim admired the sight before him. He hoped it wouldn't be the last time.

Chapter 11

It had been three weeks since Jasmine and Kasim signed Kasey into a rehab treatment center. So far she was doing well there. Only time will truly tell if it works or not. As for their relationship it was turning into something amazing. They both expressed to each other how much they loved one another. When Jasmine told Mercedes how she really felt about him, she told her that it was about damn time she admitted it to herself. Everyone could tell that they had fallen in love. For some reason it took them a while to express how they felt to each other. Now that they did everything seemed to just fall into place for them. Jasmine and Kasey talked on the phone every other day. When she got time off from work she went to visit her at the rehab. Their talks meant a lot to Kasey and Kasim believed that it was helping her stay on the right track. Jasmine even took Mercedes with her a few times and that seemed to cheer Kasey up even more. She never really had any female friends that really cared about her. Jasmine and Mercedes became the big sisters she never had.

"Today after we check up on all of our clubs, Cedes and I are going to visit Kasey. What's on your agenda for the day?" Jasmine asked Kasim as he lay between her legs. They had just finished making love for the third time that morning.

"I have to go in to the office and make sure everything is straight. After that I'm supposed to meet up with Cree and a few of the guys to play some ball." Kasim said rolling off of her.

He owned a delivery company that was doing very well. Jasmine smiled at the fact that they were both young and successful business owners.

"Well, don't forget that we have to go over Cree's mother Cheryl's house for dinner tonight." She said getting up and following him to the bathroom.

"Okay cool. Do you want me to meet you there or what?"

Jasmine thought about it for a moment. "Yeah, you can just meet me there. That way we won't be late. Ms. Cheryl is not the type of person you want to piss off by being late." They shared a laugh.

"That's what I keep hearing. Are y'all trying to scare a nigga or something?" He asked as he turned the shower on for them.

"No, when you meet her, you will see that we are very serious when we tell you about her. She is the sweetest woman you will ever meet, but she doesn't take any bullshit either."

"Okay noted. Now get in here so I can wash you up." He said licking his lips.

She smiled before getting in the shower with him. They ended up fucking against the shower wall. After they finished and washed up, they got out the shower to get their day started.

Fully dressed Jasmine and Kasim headed out the door at the same time. They had been taking turns spending time at each other's house. So far it was working well for them.

Kasim opened her door for her. "Okay baby, I will see you later tonight."

"Okay." She stood on the tip of her shoes and kissed his soft juicy lips.

"Drive safe." He said as she got in the car and buckled up.

"You do the same and don't overdo it playing ball with your boys." She blew him a kiss before pulling off.

Kasim smirked then headed to his own car. He got in and pulled off heading to his office that was located downtown. As he drove he thought about if he should tell Jasmine about the other side of his business. He didn't want to mess up what they got going on. At the same time he didn't want their relationship to hold any secrets. He didn't know how he was going to tell her that some of those packages that his company delivers aren't quite legal. Kasim has no plans of losing her, but he won't let their relationship be built on secrets. He had some serious decisions to make.

About forty minutes later he pulled into his parking spot. Once he walked inside the building he nodded at the guard at the door. When he got to his office his assistant handed him the mail and messages that she had taken down for him.

"Thank you Diana. You can leave early since we'll be closing early today." He said heading to his office.

"Thank you, Mr. Davis." She said before walking back to her desk.

Kasim continued to his office closing the door behind him once he entered. He walked over to his desk and sat down. As soon as his butt hit the seat his office phone was ringing.

"Hello..." He answered.

"Sir there is a Mr. Martinez on line two." Diana said through the phone.

"Thanks Diana, send him through."

"Okay."

After a few seconds Martinez came on the line. "Kasim, how have you been?" He asked.

"I'm doing well. What about you?"

"I'm doing fine. I will be doing even better once the delivery is made for later today." He replied.

Kasim leaned back in his chair. "Everything will go as planned. Before the night is over you will have your packages."

"That's great! Kasim as always I love doing business with you."

"Like wise Martinez." They disconnected the call.

Kasim checked all of his messages and returned phone calls before calling it a day. He shut down his computer then headed out of the door. When he got out there Diana was putting on her jacket preparing to leave as well.

"See you tomorrow Mr. Davis. Have a great evening." She said while walking out the door.

"You do the same Diana." He said from behind her.

He nodded to the guard and headed to his car. He popped the trunk and grabbed his gym bag out of there. He decided to change clothes in his office. Kasim turned around and went back inside. Ten minutes later he walked back out with some basketball shorts, sneakers, and a sleeveless shirt on. After jumping in his car he pulled off and headed to the park where he supposed to meet the fellas at.

When he pulled up to Weequahic Park he noticed that the fellas were already there. He got out and gave everyone dap when he made it over to where they were standing.

"What's up Kasim?" Cortez shouted from over on the other side of the court.

"What's up?" He returned the greeting.

"Y'all ready to play some ball?" Cree said taking his shirt off.

"Yeah let's show these little niggas how the big niggas play ball." Spud said removing his shirt as well. They were getting ready to play ball against Cortez and some of his boys.

"Look at these fools over there stripping and shit! There ain't no damn females out here yet put y'all damn clothes back on!" He yelled out to them. A few of the dudes standing around started laughing.

"Shut up Cortez and get ready for this ass whooping!" Cordell yelled back.

"Whatever! Y'all just better have our money. We don't accept checks, but we might take some food stamps." He said walking over to them.

"Maaaan, get the fuck out of here with that!" One of his boys shouted.

"Man you tripping. You know how much shit I can get with food stamps? You don't have to pay tax on that shit." He explained.

The dude waved him off while everyone else just laughed. They decided to play four against four. Once they started playing more people started to show up. Men and women crowded around rooting for the team they wanted to win.

Cortez was talking mad shit even though they were losing. He was trying to distract them but it wasn't working.

"Y'all are playing like you waiting to get noticed by the NBA." He complained.

"You talked all that shit I thought you and your boys were going to show out." Kasim laughed.

"Naw see what had happened was... we didn't stretch first."

"We ain't trying to hear that shit!" Cordell laughed.

"We didn't stretch either so come up with another excuse." Cree said wiping his forehead off with a towel.

"Heyyy Cree!" A chick yelled out. They couldn't tell which one said it because it was a group of chicks standing together giggling.

"Damn Kasim is fine as hell!" another chick yelled out.

"Y'all must want to get y'all ass whooped out here or something." Cortez said looking over at the group of chicks.

"We are just being friendly. What's wrong with that?" A chick with some little shorts on that could probably double as underwear said.

"Being friendly with those two niggas will get your ass severely beat. Mercedes and Jasmine will drag your ass all over this park for being too friendly with what's theirs." He chuckled.

"They not trying to meet those hands Cortez!" Spud yelled out while laughing.

"Hell naw, they not ready! Those hands bad for your health! Shit, I should know they stay trying to whoop my ass!" He continued.

"Right! They muthafucking hands are deadly!" They slapped hands laughing.

"Jasmine ain't going to give a fuck if they speak to any of those niggas. That's all me so chill with that little nigga." They heard someone say from the crowd.

They all turned to see who made that statement. It was as if the crowd knew what was up and stepped away from the culprit. When Cortez saw who it was he scrunched his nose up at him.

"Davon, if you don't take your weak ass on somewhere with that shit. Jasmine doesn't want your ass. I heard a few weeks ago she made you shit on yourself." Cortez said loud enough for everyone to hear.

Davon acted as if he didn't hear that last part. "We going through a little situation right now, but that's all me." He said glaring at Kasim.

Kasim wiped his face off with a grin plastered on it. "I find that to be funny as hell." He said staring directly at Davon.

"Why is that?" Davon asked clueless.

"Well, during the four times we fucked this morning, not once did I hear your name. All I kept hearing seeping through those sexy ass lips were Kasim. So, what you are saying right now is funny to me. Your best bet is to take your ass home before you get your ass beat. I'm only going to let your bullshit slide once." He was now glaring at Davon as if he wanted to knock him the fuck out.

"Oh shit about to pop off now." Cortez said whipping his phone out preparing to record if anything jumps off.

Davon walked over to where Kasim stood angry as hell. He was letting his emotions get the best of him at the moment. If he took time to scope out the situation he would've known better than to walk up on Kasim.

"Nigga you got me fucked up! You ain't shit but a delivery boy. She didn't even upgrade. You keep talking shit about fucking my bitch and…" He didn't get to finish that sentence due to the fact Kasim's fist pounded into his mouth knocking out his front teeth.

"Oh shit did you see that?" Someone yelled out.

"He knocked that fool the fuck out with one hit!" Another person yelled out.

"I bet that dude think twice about fucking with that nigga again." Someone else said.

Davon hit the ground with a loud thud sound. Everyone in the park was shocked at what they just saw. Kasim went to punch him again, but Cree and Cordell held him back.

"It's not worth it man. He already knocked out." Cree said.

"Yeah man let's get the fuck out of here before someone calls the police." Cordell said pulling him towards the cars.

"Next time that nigga step out of line he not getting back up." Kasim said heading to his car and getting in.

Within just a few minutes the packed park was damn near empty. Davon was still laid out on the middle of the court unconscious. In the hood everyone was prepared to mind their own damn business. They weren't trying to bring any trouble to their doorstep.

Chapter 12

Jasmine and Mercedes decided to ride together over to Cheryl's house. They both jumped in Jasmine's car curious to see how the night turns out.

"So, how bad do you think she's going to threaten Kasim?" Mercedes asked with a giggle.

Jasmine glanced at her and chuckled. "I don't know, but I have faith that he will take it like a champ."

"Yeah, you probably right. I hope Cortez don't be on his shit tonight. You know Cheryl said that he barely shows up for dinner now? She said he been trying to pull away from the family."

"I think it's hard for him to sit there and know that he might lose his mother. I sort of get what he's trying to do even though I don't agree with it. He probably figured that it would be easier to push away now so if it happened he won't hurt as much. I doubt that it will work, but he feels that's the only way he will make it through." Jasmine tried explaining as best as she could.

"I really hope everything works out for the best. I can't imagine not having Cheryl here with us. I know Cortez is hurting, but so is everyone else. If he doesn't show up today I'm hunting his ass down and dragging him to the house with or without his consent. Cheryl needs all her family around her during a time like this."

She heard a ding on her phone signaling that she had a message. When she checked her phone she saw that it was a video message from Cortez. She pressed play and waited to see what it was. Her eyes got big as she watched Kasim knock Davon clean out with just one punch.

"Daaaaamn! I know that had to hurt." She said holding her hand over her mouth.

"What? What are you talking about?" Jasmine asked glancing from the road to her then back to the road.

"Cortez just sent me a video of Kasim knocking Davon out at the park." She said.

"Girl, you are lying?"

"Nope, he hit his ass one time and Davon was out for the count." She laughed.

"Damn Jassy I wish I was there to see that. I would've been just like Smokey off of Friday. I would've got right up on him and said you got knocked the fuck out!" They both busted out laughing at her silliness.

"You a damn fool. I wonder what made him do it." Jasmine said as they pulled up to Cheryl's house.

"Girl, knowing Davon punk ass, he was probably talking shit." Mercedes said with a shrug of her shoulders.

As soon as they got out of the car all the men started pulling up as well. Mercedes walked over to Cree and gave him a hug while he felt on her booty.

"Y'all are two nasty muthafuckas. It don't matter where y'all at, feeling up on each other always cross y'all minds." Cortez said frowning at them.

"Shut up fool! I'm glad you showed up now I don't have to hunt you down." Mercedes said.

Cortez smirked at her. "I only came to see Kasim sweat while mama threatens him to do right by Jass short evil ass." He said making his way in the house.

"Cortez, you going to make me smack you in the mouth!" Jasmine yelled after him.

"Whatever shorty!" He yelled over his shoulder.

"I'm going to hurt that boy." She mumbled as she walked over to Kasim. He had changed into a pair of black jeans, black and gold shirt, a black leather jacket, and a pair of black and gold sneakers. She could smell his cologne before she even made it over to him.

"Hey."

He grinned at her making her stomach flutter. "Hey beautiful."

"So, I saw your handy work you put in at the park."

"Oh yeah? Cortez really recorded that shit?" He asked.

"Yup and you got some hands on you. What made you do it?"

Kasim stared at her for a minute not saying anything. He wasn't sure if she was asking because she was concerned for him or Davon. He hoped it was the sooner and not the latter.

"He got out of line with his mouth and then violated even more by walking up on me. For his safety let's hope he learned his lesson."

She smiled at him and he gave her a smile in return. "For his safety let's hope so. Come on let me introduce you to the woman who I consider my second mom." She grabbed his hand and led him inside the house.

Cheryl was waiting at the door for them when they made it inside. She smiled at Jasmine as she pulled her into a big hug. She then turned her attention to Kasim.

"Ooh he is handsome." She winked at Jasmine.

"It's nice to meet you Ms...."

Cheryl stopped Kasim before he could continue. "Call me Cheryl."

"Okay."

"Come inside Kasim so that we can get to know each other and come to an understanding about my Jassy."

She led him into the living room. "Would you like something to drink?"

"Water would be fine." He replied.

"Okay. I'll be right back." She walked out of the living room leaving Jasmine and Kasim alone.

"Are you nervous?" She asked him.

He smirked. "No."

"Oh okay. That's good then. You don't want her to see fear in your eyes." She giggled.

"Cortez if you touch anything on my stove I'm going to beat your ass!" Cheryl yelled as she walked back into the living room. She handed Kasim a bottle of water.

"Thank you." He said grabbing the water.

Cortez walked into the living room with a frown on his face. He plopped down on the lazy boy and stared at them.

"What did you come in here for?" Cheryl asked.

"What do you mean?" Cortez asked looking at her confused.

"I meant exactly what I said. What do you want in here?"

"I'm here to be nosey. Since we have to wait for them I want to see what's going on." He said getting comfortable.

"You nosey as hell." She said before placing her attention back on Kasim.

"I know, I already said that. Kasim did she threaten to cut you if you hurt Jass? She should be threatening Jass since she's the violent one." He said staring at them.

"Would you shut up?" Jasmine mean mugged him.

"No. You better not get up and hit me either. I'm going to toss you in the pool if you do."

"Cortez shut up! How am I supposed to get to know Kasim if you over there doing all the talking?" His mother asked him with an attitude.

"Why we can't eat while y'all talk?" He asked knowing he was pissing her off, but didn't care.

Ignoring him she kept talking to Kasim. "Why did it take you so long to come and meet me?"

"I was going through some family issues and didn't have the time. Now that things are calmed down I told Jasmine that now would be a good time." He replied.

"I hope everything works out for you and your family." She said with a small smile.

"Thank you. I'm just going to come out and say it. I love Jasmine and I have no intentions of hurting her. She means a lot to me. When I need her as my woman, she's there. When I need her as my friend, she's there. Our relationship may not seem normal to others, but it works for us."

"I'm glad to know that you are taking the relationship just as serious as she is."

"I can see us creating a future together. When the time comes it will happen. Right now we are enjoying each other's company and friendship. I know she considers you a second mom. I can see how close everyone is. I would love to be a part of that if you would have me." Kasim said looking her straight in the eyes.

"I would love to have you as a part of our family." She stood up as he did the same. She hugged him and kissed his cheek.

"Now I'm warning you, I have a whole gun collection that I have stashed. Please don't make me pull them out and use them." She stated.

Kasim nodded as he tried to keep himself from laughing. "I got you."

"Good. Now come on so you can taste my good cooking." She said wrapping her arm around his and leading him into the kitchen where everyone else was seated at the table playing cards.

"Wait, that's it?" Cortez stood up with his hands stretched out.

"What are you talking about?" Jasmine asked staring at him.

"She barely said anything to him. I came here for nothing. I thought I was going to see Kasim bitch up, piss on himself, or something." He said with an attitude.

Jasmine shook her head. "You were supposed to come anyway. Today we're having family dinner."

"I know, but I didn't plan on coming at first." He said in a lower tone.

"Cortez why are you running from your family? During this time is when they need you the most. You supposed to stick together. Trying to separate yourself from them, especially your mother will only make you feel worse."

"I don't know how to handle the thought of losing her." He said putting his head down.

She walked over towards him and lifted his head up. "You haven't loss her and there is a chance that you might not lose her at all. You're giving up Cortez while everyone else is still fighting and hoping for the best."

"This is hard. Jass, she's my world. I don't want to see her in any kind of pain."

Jasmine thought about something. "Next week I want you to come somewhere with me."

"Where?"

"Just trust me. It will help you deal with this." She said.

"Okay."

"Good now let's go eat I am starving." She said walking towards the kitchen.

"You eat like me, but where does it all go? Oh wait I see… it goes to that big ass head of yours." He mushed her in the head then took off running.

"Cortez, you play too much! I promise before I leave here I'm going to punch you in the chest!" She shouted.

"You'll have to catch me first. Your little ass legs ain't running that far." He cracked up laughing.

"Ughhh! You make me sick."

"You know you love me so stop lying. Did Cedes show you the video of shitty boy getting knocked out?" He asked her as he took a seat at the table.

"Who is shitty boy?" Cheryl asked confused.

"Davon." He replied.

"Oh that punk ass nigga." She rolled her eyes.

"Mama!" Everyone but Kasim and Cortez shouted. They were too busy laughing their asses off at what she said.

"What? I couldn't stand his ass. He just always seemed sneaky to me. I didn't trust him." She explained.

Nobody disagreed with her because some of them had gotten the same feeling whenever he was around. They changed the subject as Cheryl got to know more about Kasim. She really liked him for her Jassy. They seemed to be the perfect couple, but she could sense that they were holding something back from each other. She hoped whatever it was that it didn't mess up what they were trying to build.

Chapter 13

At four in the morning the following day, Jasmine received a phone call from Mercedes. When she answered the phone her friend sounded pissed off. She was yelling and talking a mile a minute. Jasmine sat up in the bed and rubbed her eyes. Once she caught her bearings she tried to get Mercedes to slow down so that she could understand what she was trying to tell her.

"Cedes slow down I can't understand anything that you're saying." She said into the phone.

She took a moment to calm her nerves a little before speaking again. "I got a call from Stacy letting me know that someone had broken into Play Time and vandalized it."

"What?!" Jasmine yelled waking up Kasim, who was lying next to her.

"Yes girl! I'm on my way there now. She said that they had really trashed the place."

"I will meet you there." Jasmine said jumping out of bed.

"Okay, I will see you soon then." They ended their call and Jasmine went in her closet to find something to throw on.

"What's going on?" Kasim asked standing in the doorway of the closet.

"Cedes said someone had broken into one of our clubs and trashed the place."

"Damn. Well, I'm coming with you." He said walking to the dresser where he kept some of his things.

"I can't believe someone would pull some shit like this. They really must not know who they fucked with." She mumbled, but Kasim heard every word.

"Maybe it was some teenage kids thinking it would be fun to do something like this." He tried to think of a reason why someone would trash a night club.

"Have you guys ever had this problem before?" He asked tying his shoes.

"No. This is the first time we had this problem."

"Well, let's go and find out what's going on." He said grabbing his keys and walking out the door behind her.

With the way that Kasim drove it took them no time to arrive at the club. When they walked inside Mercedes and Cree were already there talking to the police. They looked around the place and shook their heads. Tables and chairs were thrown around. The bar was destroyed with glass everywhere from broken bottles. Someone had even sprayed painted the words 'EVIL BITCHES', 'SLUTS', and 'PAYBACKS A VENGEFUL BITCH' all over the walls.

Jasmine walked towards Mercedes and gave her a hug. After they finished talking to the police they sent Stacy home. The four of them stood around taking everything in.

"I don't believe this was the doing of kids." Mercedes said leaning with her back pressed against Cree's chest.

"I don't think so either." Jasmine agreed.

"I will have some of my people look into it." Cree said. He had a security company that handles legal and illegal things.

"Thanks babe." Mercedes said.

"Why would they put those words on the wall though?" Kasim asked with a confused expression as he studied the words on the wall.

Jasmine looked from him to Mercedes. They both didn't know what to say since she had yet to tell Kasim about her other business.

"Who knows, they were probably just writing anything that was offensive." Cree said grabbing everyone's attention.

"Yeah, you probably right. Let's close everything down and get out of here. After y'all get some rest then you can decide what you're going to do about the club." Kasim suggested.

Everyone agreed and walked around making sure everything was locked down. After they finished they said their goodbyes and went home.

While Kasim drove them back to her house, Jasmine stared out the window trying to figure out who could have trashed their club. She could think of a few names, but what would be their motives.

"Are you okay over there?" He asked catching her attention.

"I'm fine for now. I'm just thinking." She replied not sure if that was the truth or not.

"Everything will be okay." He said grabbing her hand and giving it a light squeeze.

Jasmine gave him a small smile hoping that he was right.

A week had passed and there was still no word on who vandalized the club. Mercedes and Jasmine decided to keep the club closed until they figured out who was behind the break in. Everything had been quiet at the moment, but they knew it was only a matter of time before someone let it slip who did it.

Jasmine sat outside of Cheryl's house blowing the horn. She had been waiting on Cortez for five minutes. He told her that he would be ready by the time she arrived, but once she got there he was just getting out the shower.

"This damn boy can't ever be on time." She looked at her watch and shook her head.

She was about to blow the horn again when the front door opened and Cortez stepped out onto the porch looking good. His hair was cut short with waves that would make you sea sick if you stared at them too long. He was dressed in all white from his shirt, jeans, and all the way down to his white Timbs. She watched him as he walked to the car and got inside.

"What's up Jass?" He greeted her as he got comfortable.

"It took you long enough. You take longer than a female getting dressed." She joked as she pulled off.

"You a damn lie. It didn't take me that long, but it does take time to look this good."

"Yeah, I guess it would take longer to cover up all that ugly." She laughed.

"That's a shame you have to lie to make yourself feel better. All my hoes tell me I'm sexy."

"Hoes will tell a nigga anything to get what they want. Remember that young nigga."

He glared at her. "You only a few years older than me. Stop acting like your ass got a lot of years on me. Why were you blowing the horn like that?"

"Because you were taking too damn long. I told you to be ready when I get here. You a hard headed little nigga."

"Kasim must not have given you any dick this morning. Your ass was just being impatient." He said smirking.

Jasmine reached over and mushed him in the head. "Shut up!"

"Stop abusing me dammit! I'm not going to keep taking this shit from y'all!" He yelled trying not to laugh.

"What you going to do about it?"

"You'll know when the police come and lock your short ass up. I'm sick of y'all abusive ass women."

Jasmine just laughed as she kept driving. "Where are we going anyway?" Cortez asked after a few minutes had passed.

"I'm not telling you. Just know that I'm doing this because I think it could help you."

"This better not be one of those scared straight missions. Bet not one nigga get in my damn face or I'm fucking them up."

"Shut up Cortez, your ass can't even fight." She joked.

Cortez looked at her and made a face. "Jass, you know damn well I got some mean hands on me. Remember that time I fought that big nigga that tried to punk me at the park?"

She chuckled. "Naw, what I remember was me and Cedes had to help you fight his big ass. You punched him and it didn't do shit to him. We all had to jump his ass. When Cree and Cordell showed up, I was on his back punching him while Cedes was hitting him with a big branch. You were punching him in the face but he wouldn't go down."

Cortez laughed. "That nigga was built like stone. Those punches were not fazing him. It took Cree and Cordell to knock him the fuck out."

"Right! We thought he was dead until we saw his big ass stomach move."

"Those were the days, man." Cortez smiled as he looked out the window.

Within a few more minutes they were pulling up in front of a small building. Cortez looked at the building then back at Jasmine as she turned the car off.

"Is this a rehab center? Who up in here?" He asked curiously.

"Kasim's little sister Kasey is up in here." She replied.

"She on drugs?" He asked looking from her then back to the building.

"She was. She's been clean for a little minute now. She was on those pills bad."

"How old is she?"

"She's eighteen."

"Damn. What made her start taking drugs that young?" He asked with his face frowned up.

"Maybe it would be better if you asked her that. I brought you here because Kasey went through something a little similar to you, but she went about it all wrong. She knows that now, but at first she was thinking the same way you are now."

Cortez didn't say anything he just stared at the building. "Come on let's go inside. She's expecting us." Jasmine said getting out the car and waiting for him to do the same.

Cortez looked around as one of the councilors led them to the yard where Kasey was seated at a table next to a pond. He let Jasmine walk a few feet ahead of him as he admired the chick. When she stood up and walked towards Jasmine he got a better view of her body. He had to stop walking and just stare at her. She didn't look like any drug addict he had ever seen. She was beautiful.

Cortez looked her over from head to toe. Her hair was braided into a neat bun that sat at the top of her head. Her light brown skin was smooth with no blemishes. Her eyes were chocolate brown and her lips were plump. She looked as if her body was starting to fill out in all the right places. The most impressive thing on her was her smile. When she smiled at Jasmine her eyes lit up as well. Cortez had been around a lot of females, most of them being a little older than him. He had never seen one as beautiful as Kasey that took his breath away.

"Ummm Cortez!" Jasmine yelled out trying to get his attention.

When he finally looked at her it was as if the trance he was in had been broken. "What?"

"Get over here so I can introduce you." She looked at him with a frown.

"What's up?" He greeted Kasey with a head nod.

"Hi." She responded shyly.

Jasmine looked between the two and shook her head. "How about we all have a seat and talk?" She waved towards the table.

They all sat down and Cortez stared at Kasey openly as she tried not to make eye contact with him.

Hustle*

"Kasey, this is Cortez and Cortez this is Kasey." She introduced them.

"What made you turn to drugs?" He asked right out the gate. He couldn't understand why a chick as beautiful and young as her would get addicted to drugs.

"Cortez!" Jasmine shouted while glaring at him.

Kasey smiled. "It's okay Jassy. I'm comfortable talking about it now thanks to you." She placed a hand on hers.

"I didn't mean to come off harsh, but I'm just curious." He said a little nicer.

"Well, I was about fifteen when we first found out my mother was sick. It had always just been her, my brother, and me. Our father left right after I was born. My mother had taken care of us on her own with no help. Not even from the state. When we found out she was sick it hit Kasim and me hard. I didn't know how to handle losing her so I started acting out." She looked down at her hands as she swirled them around.

"I wasted so much time trying to harden my heart so I wouldn't feel the pain of losing her. That was the time I could have been spending with her making new memories. I hate myself for giving her a hard time. It was as if I had punished her for being sick. The drugs seemed to help me with the pain and to forget." She paused and looked up to find Cortez staring at her.

Cortez wanted to snatch her up in his arms and hold her. He didn't know what was coming over him. He never wanted to wrap his arms around a female and just hold her before. He shook his head trying to stop the thoughts from roaming, but they wouldn't go away. He glanced back over at Kasey as she stared at him with sadness in her eyes.

"Jassy told me about your mom being sick. You shouldn't push her away Cortez. You will regret it if you do. After the surgery there is a chance she could live a long, healthy, and happy life. I used drugs as an escape, but I ended up locking myself in another prison. I was a prisoner to the drugs."

Cortez sighed. "I didn't think about it like that. It hurt to think that my mom could die from that shit."

"Have you talked to her about it?" Kasey asked.

"No. I haven't really sat down and really talked to my mom since she told us she was sick." He admitted. He felt horrible knowing that she's going through all that and he was too busy pushing her away.

"Maybe when you go home you should sit down and talk to her. She could probably explain to you exactly what's going on with her health."

"I tried telling him that. Maybe now he will listen." Jasmine said bumping him with her shoulder.

All three talked for a little while longer. Jasmine smiled inside at how well Cortez and Kasey were getting along. She wasn't trying to hook them up though because she knew Cortez was a man whore.

When they got back in the car she asked him what he thought about everything Kasey had said.

"She's right; I need to talk to my mom about everything. I can't believe she was a drug addict. She sure doesn't look like one." He said.

"That's because she's better now. It's a long journey, but it's one she's willing to take for a better life."

"Yeah, I guess you right." He paused for a moment.

"Thanks Jass for bringing me here. I needed this reality check."

"No problem. You like a little brother to me. I saw the path you were heading down and I couldn't let that happen." She smiled at him.

Cortez smirked. "That's because you really in love with me. I told you it would never work though. You better off with Kasim. He can deal with your violent ass."

Jasmine laughed. "I really can't stand you."

"Yeah that's what you keep telling yourself to hide your true feelings. I love you too Jass, but only like a big sister… well little big sister." She punched him in the arm.

"See that's why I can't be with you because you are abusive. I don't see how Cree and Kasim deal with you and

Cedes. Fucking with me y'all ass would be in jail. I don't give a fuck about what anybody has to say about it either. Men deal with domestic violence too."

"Boy I'm done talking to you for the rest of the ride. I can't deal with your ignorant ass." She said cracking up laughing. She turned the radio on before he could respond.

Chapter 14

$\mathcal{A}$ month had passed and still no word on who trashed the club. Mercedes and Jasmine had fixed it up and reopened it to the public. They decided not to keep it closed any longer. Cree had added extra security to the club just in case the person who trashed the place showed back up. They even set up new cameras everywhere inside and around the building. The old ones had been destroyed. Jasmine had continued her weekly visits to see Kasey. Every time she went up there Kasey would ask about Cortez. Since that day she took him up there he only asked about her a few times. It seemed like nothing major to him. She hoped that it wouldn't happen, but it seemed as if Kasey had developed a little crush on Cortez. When she told Mercedes about it she had thought it was cute.

The great thing about that visit was that Cortez had started back showing up for Sunday dinner. Cheryl had also mentioned that they had a long talk and came to an understanding. She was excited that he had even gone to some of her doctors' appointments with her. Everyone had taken turns making sure to mark days on their calendars so that could go with her as well. She and Jasmine also had a one-on-one talk about her and Kasim's relationship. Jasmine expressed to her that she loved him and how she saw their relationship moving forward. Cheryl then let her know that Kasim had mentioned the same thing when she talked to him one on one as well.

When Jasmine last talked to Kasim, he told her that he wanted to have lunch with her and talk. From the way he said it she knew it had to be about something important. He told her that he'll pick her up after his visit with his sister. It had been a week since he went to visit Kasey due to his busy work schedule. He planned on making it up to her by bringing her favorite snacks.

Kasim walked into the building and signed in. One of the staff led him to where they last saw Kasey. He knew it was probably at her favorite spot by the pond. When he walked out of the doors that led to the yard he glanced over by the pond. He saw her sitting at the table smiling, but she wasn't alone. Kasim made his way over to the table and stopped directly in front of it. The expression on his face was a mix between confused, curious, and anger.

Kasey noticed the look on her brother's face and immediately stood up. She went to stand by his side and try to explain.

"Kasim..."

He cut her off with a glare. "What are you doing here Cortez?" He asked after sitting the snacks on the table.

Cortez looked from him to Kasey. When he placed his attention back on Kasim, he could tell that he was pissed. "I came up here to visit Kasey." He replied with a shrug of his shoulders.

"How do you two know each other?" He asked trying to calm himself down. He had nothing against Cortez, but he saw firsthand how he treated females. He would hate to cause bad blood between himself, Cree, and Cordell because he whooped their little brother's ass for messing with his little sister.

"Jass had brought me up here a while ago to visit Kasey. She figured that we could help each other out with our problems. I wasn't so sure at first, but after really talking with Kasey it helped me a lot." He said honestly.

"Jasmine brought you up here? How come I haven't heard about this?" He asked with a confused expression covering his face. He looked over at Kasey who held her head down and shrugged her shoulders.

"I don't know. That's something Jass would probably answer better than us." Cortez said.

Kasim sighed and then took a seat at the table. "Have a seat Kasey." He demanded.

She walked back over to her seat and sat down. "So, the two of you have been talking, huh?"

"Yes, we are good friends now." Kasey said looking at her brother before she continued talking.

"Cortez visits and conversations help me get through all of this. You know I don't really have any friends. Never really did to begin with. It's nice to have someone around my age to talk to." She explained.

"What exactly do y'all talk about?" He asked with his attention now on Cortez.

"We talk about everything. Sports, food, television shows, and different stuff that we enjoy doing. We had even talked about school."

"School?" Kasim looked between the two of them. He was surprised because Kasey had never talked about going back to school after their mother died. She never finished high school, and he was very disappointed about that.

"Yeah. I got my high diploma, but that's it. Kasey said she never even finished high school. So, we were thinking when she got out of here that she could get her GED. After that we could both sign up at one of the Community Colleges."

Kasim sat there shocked for a moment. Maybe Cortez and Kasey hanging out as just friends wasn't a bad idea. He still planned to talk to him about his sister when they were alone.

"That sounds like a good idea. I'll support you both on that. I know that would make your mom proud too Cortez." He said grinning at him.

"Yeah, she'll probably start that crying shit and be jumping up and down praising like it's a miracle or something." Cortez chuckled.

"I can't wait to meet her." Kasey said excitedly.

Cortez stared at her for a moment not saying anything. "What?" She questioned. She was feeling a little nervous under his gaze.

"I never took a girl to meet my mom before." He said as he continued to stare at her.

"Well, I'm your friend so it's only right that I meet your mom. I bet your guy friends met her." She said placing her folded arms on the table.

"Yeah, but she doesn't really like too many of them."

"Well, that's their problem. I'm going to make her love me." She said as a matter of fact.

Cortez smiled at her. "I have no doubt that she would love you."

Kasim sat back and watched the exchange between the two. He shook his head because he knew that they had a crush on each other. ***"Yeah, I definitely have to talk to this little nigga."*** He thought to himself.

Once Kasim got over the initial shock of seeing Cortez with his sister, the three had a good flow of conversation. Afterwards, Kasim left to make his lunch date with Jasmine. They had a few things to discuss. The visit with his sister being one of them.

Kasim got out the car and made his way to the front doors of Jasmine and Mercedes other club Ambitious out in New York. When he got to the doors a security guard stood there with his arms folded across his chest.

"Jasmine is expecting me." Kasim said to the man.

After he spoke into his headset he stepped to the side and let Kasim into the club. Kasim headed straight for Jasmine's office. When he got to the door he knocked twice before letting himself in and locking the door behind him.

"If you was going to walk right in what was the point of knocking?" She asked staring at him from behind her desk.

He ignored her as he walked around the desk and stood next to her chair. He pushed the chair around so that she was facing him. He then grabbed her hands and pulled her up towards him. His hands then grabbed both her ass cheeks as he shoved his tongue down her throat. He lifted her up and sat her on the edge of the desk. He stood between her legs as the dress she wore rose up her thighs. The kiss was so intense that Jasmine got lost in it. She wrapped her arms around his neck deepening the kiss.

Kasim pulled away from her. "I needed that."

She bit down on her bottom lip. "I'm glad I could help you out with that."

"There is something else you could help me with as well."

"What's that?" She questioned as she stared in his brown eyes.

"You can tell me when you were going to mention to me that you took Cortez to see my sister?"

Jasmine hands dropped down to his waist. "I don't know why I didn't mention it. It wasn't on any sneaky shit though. I thought that maybe they could help each other get through their hard times. From the look of things I was right. Cortez is coming around more and spending time with his mother and Kasey seems to be in a better mood ever since the visit."

He sighed. "Did you know that he was still going up there to see her?" He asked making sure to look her directly in the eyes when she answered.

Jasmine looked shocked. "He's been up there to see her again?"

"Yeah, he was up there when I went. Apparently, after you took him up there, he started going up there on his own. They've become good friends. I know what you did was to help them and from talking to them both, together and separately, I noticed that it worked."

"So, you not mad at me for forgetting to tell you about it?" She asked nervously.

"I don't know. I'm still a little disappointed. Maybe you can help me forget all about it though."

She smirked. "How can I do that?" She asked.

Kasim leaned forward and whispered something in her ear. She hit him in the chest before throwing her head back and laughing. "You are so damn nasty."

"Does that mean you not going to do it?" He asked with a raised eyebrow.

"I didn't say all that." She pushed him back a little and reached for his belt buckle. After she undid it she unzipped his jeans and reached inside. When she pulled out his dick she gripped it tight in her hands.

"Mmmm." He moaned. Their eyes never left each other's.

"If I let you fuck me on my desk do I get to feed you lunch?" She asked slowly sliding her hand up and down his dick.

"As long as my lunch is that fat pussy between your legs then hell yeah."

Jasmine didn't say another word. She released his member and then leaned back using her hands to keep her balance. She then opened her legs so that he could remove her panties.

Kasim wasted no time sliding her dress above her waist and sliding her panties down. He positioned himself between her legs again. He saw that she was about to speak, probably asking if he had a condom, but Kasim ignored her and thrust deep inside her.

"Oooooh!" She moaned loudly as he started fucking her hard.

Jasmine leaned all the way back on the desk as Kasim pulled her waist closer to him. He was fucking her so good she forgot all about mentioning a condom.

He could feel her getting ready to explode, but he wasn't ready for her to cum yet. He pulled out of her slowly. He chuckled when she looked up at him with a mean mug on her face.

"Why the hell you stop?" She asked with an attitude.

"Because you were getting ready to cum."

She frowned up her face at him. "Ain't that the whole point of fucking?" She was pissed, and he knew it.

Kasim laughed. "I wasn't ready for you to cum yet."

She slid off of the desk with her dress still above her waist. "You think that shit is funny?"

"Yeah, a little." He chuckled.

Jasmine balled her fist up and swung at him. Kasim dodged her fist then grabbed her before he turned her around. Her back was now against his chest. She tried to get out of his hold, but his grip on her was too tight. He pushed her forward on the desk and spread her legs. Before she had a chance to protest He had his dick buried deep inside her again.

"Shiiiiiiiit Kasim!" She screamed out as he fucked her with no mercy.

"Shut up! Since you can swing on a nigga you can take this dick then." He grunted as he pounded away.

"Baby I wanna cum! Kasim make this pussy cum!" She moaned.

He smacked her on the ass. "Are you going to quit talking shit all the time?" He asked pumping in and out of her.

"Noooo!"

"Oh I don't think you want to cum then. Maybe I should stop."

"Baby NO! Please don't stop!"

"Answer my question then. Are you going to stop talking shit?"

"Yesssssss! Shit Kasim that's my spot!" She screamed out.

He smacked her on the ass again before they both came together. "Damn that's some good pussy."

He pulled her up off the desk. She turned around and punched him in the chest. "I should fuck you up for that stunt."

He laughed. "You enjoyed it too much to fuck me up."

"Whatever! Help me to the bathroom my legs feel like jello."

"That's what good dick does to you." He said then smacked her ass for good measure.

"I promise if you do that again I'm going to whoop your ass." She threatened as he helped her to the bathroom that was inside her office.

"I'm not Cortez so your threats don't work on me."

"You hard of hearing because I didn't make a threat, I made a promise."

Kasim chuckled as they walked into the bathroom. After they had both freshened up Jasmine walked back over to her desk.

"While you shut everything down, I'm going to go grab something to drink."

"Okay, don't forget that I get to feed you lunch either." She grinned.

"You're a little freaky muthafucka." He smirked.

"Call me what you want, but you going to get a mouthful."

Kasim shook his head as he walked out of the office. As he made his way to the bar he was stopped by an older white woman.

"Oooh I haven't had a chance to take you for a ride yet. You must be one of the new ones." She purred.

"What?"

"What's your name? I have to remember it so I could tell Jasmine or Mercedes that I want to take you for a ride on this pussy express." She giggled then rubbed her hand down his chest.

Kasim took a step back and stared at her like she was crazy. "What are you talking about lady?"

She looked at him confused. "Aren't you one of the men in their sex club?" She asked.

"Sex club?"

"Oh you really must be new. I want to be the first to fuck you. Let me go find Jasmine or Mercedes to let them know." She started to walk away, but then stopped to look over at him.

"You look young too. I bet you're packing a lot of inches in those jeans just by the way you walk. Listen, once

I get the chance I'm going to fuck your brains out. I'm going to turn you out so good that you wouldn't want to fuck anyone else." She snapped her teeth and growled at him before walking away.

Kasim stood there in shock. "What the fuck?"

Chapter 15

Kasim stormed back into Jasmine's office and slammed the door shut. She looked up at him with confusion written all over her face. She didn't know what his problem was and why he looked so angry. When he stomped over towards her, she stood up straight.

"What's wrong with you?" She asked when he got in her face.

"What the hell do you do at all these clubs?" He asked with a calm tone that didn't match his facial expression.

"What are you talking about? I run the clubs with Cedes."

"I know that, but what exactly do you do?"

She took a step back and placed her hands on her hips. "You want me to break down every detail that we do?"

"Yes."

"What the hell? I'm not about to sit here and do all that. What has gotten into you? You were just laughing and joking before you walked out of the door." She said with an attitude of her own.

"That was before I ran into one of your clients." He said folding his arms across his chest to keep from snatching her up.

"Clients?" She frowned.

"Yeah clients. She asked me if I was new to the sex club. She wanted to be the first to take me for a ride on her pussy express. Her words not mine."

If Jasmine was light Kasim would have seen all the color drain out of her face. She was stuck for words. She had no idea what to say when she heard the words sex club.

"Oh you don't have shit to say now? Usually you talk all shit now your ass on hush mode." He snapped.

"Kasim, I can explain everything."

"I can't believe this shit! Are you fucking other niggas too?"

Jasmine head snapped back as she glared at him. "No! I'm not a hoe."

"So, what the fuck is this sex club shit?"

"We run a club where women can live out their fantasies with the men of their dreams." She explained in one short sentence.

He glared at her not saying anything for a minute. "You and Cedes renting out niggas?"

Jasmine bit down on the corner of her lip. "Something like that."

Kasim couldn't even look at her any longer. He turned around and headed for the door.

"Kasim wait!" She yelled walking towards him.

He ignored her as he opened the door and found Cedes standing there getting ready to knock. She looked at him and couldn't find the words to speak to him.

"What's up pimp?" He nodded as he walked around her. He could hear Jasmine calling his name, but he kept walking out of the club's door and to his car. He jumped in and sped off not looking back.

Jasmine walked back to her office where Mercedes was still standing in the doorway. She walked inside and sat back down at her desk. She placed her face in her hands.

"I was just coming in here to tell you that one of the clients may have spilled some tea to Kasim. When she came to me about a new guy and described him, I knew she was talking about Kasim. I'm sorry Jassy."

"He looked more so hurt than pissed. I think he thinks that I'm lying about not sleeping with other guys."

"Maybe I can get Cree to explain it to him better. You know from a guy's point of view." Mercedes offered.

"Go ahead, but I doubt it would work. God Cedes I love that man and now…" Her voice trailed off.

"Now you will fix yourself up and go get your damn man! You will not let this stop you from being happy. You better make that nigga understand that business is business, but what y'all have is something totally different. Show him that your love for him is real, and you not given up on it."

Jasmine looked up at her surprised at what she just said. "I know that was some deep shit, huh? I think Cheryl is getting to me girl." Mercedes said as they shared a laugh.

Kasim surprised himself when he pulled into the parking lot of the gym he and Jasmine met at. He got out the car and headed inside. He wanted to work off some of the anger that was building inside him. Every time he thought about the words sex and club together he got pissed. He didn't want to believe that Jasmine was fucking around on him, but after finding out about the secret club he couldn't be too sure.

He walked to the men's locker room to change clothes. Once he was done he headed straight for the weights. As soon as he sat down, he felt his phone vibrate in his pocket. He put his phone on vibrate right after he left the club. He didn't want to talk to Jasmine at the moment because he was too mad. When he pulled his phone out his pocket he saw that it was a text from Cree.

Cree: What's up man?

Kasim: Nothing, just chilling.

Cree: I need to holla at you about something. Where you at?

Kasim: The gym about to work off some steam.

Kasim didn't know if Cree knew about what the women really do or not. He had a feeling that he did, but just in case he didn't he wasn't going to be the one to tell him. That was between him and Mercedes.

Cree: The regular spot?

Kasim: Yeah.

Cree: Okay cool. I'm not that far from there right now.

Kasim: Okay.

He placed his phone back in his pocket and started his work out. He was so into it that he didn't notice Cree walking towards him until he sat down on the bench next to him.

"What's up?" Cree greeted him.

Kasim sat up on the bench and wiped the sweat from his face. "What's up, Cree? What did you want to talk about?" He asked leaning down and grabbing the water bottle that he had brought with him.

"I heard about what happened with Jasmine at the club." He said catching Kasim's full attention.

"So, you know about what they do?"

He nodded. "Yeah."

"You okay with them renting niggas out? They're pimps." He said as if he was trying to get an understanding of everything.

"I should be okay with it since I helped them build it. Listen Kasim, I know the way you found out is probably what's really got you pissed off. You wanted Jasmine to be up front with you about what she does. In her defense though, with all the bullshit in her past relationships it's hard for her to completely give someone her trust not knowing what she might get in return."

He thought about what he was going to say before he spoke. "That's only part of it. I know I have to work on gaining her full trust and I'm willing to do that. My thing is you hear about pimps fucking their hoes to keep them in check or whatever. How can I be completely sure she's not fucking those niggas that work for her? I swear I love that woman Cree, but I'll kill her and all those niggas if I find out she's fucking them." He spat with his nostrils flared.

Cree couldn't help but laugh at what he said even though he knew he meant every word. "Man, you wild as hell. Jasmine not fucking any of those niggas. They keep that shit strictly business nothing more nothing less."

Kasim glared at him. "You know that to be sure?"

Cree glared back at him. "Hell yeah I know that to be sure and so do you. You know your woman Kasim. You know damn well Jasmine not fucking any of those niggas. You just pissed because you found out from an old hag who wanted to fuck you." He laughed.

Kasim tried not to, but he couldn't stop himself from laughing too. "Mannn, she straight told me that she wanted to take me on a ride on her pussy express." They cracked up laughing.

Cree looked at him and got serious. "Jasmine is like a little sister to me. I don't want to see her hurt because of a business move she made before you even came into the picture."

"I told you I love her little ass. I have no plans of hurting her."

Cree stood up and Kasim did the same. "This would be the perfect time to get everything out on the table. You have something important that she should know about too. Maybe today is the day for all secrets to be revealed so that y'all can move forward." He said while he patted him on the back.

"Yeah, you right. That was actually what I planned on doing before that bomb was dropped on me." Kasim admitted. Cree knew all about what his company does. He found out not too long after they had met. He kept it to himself because Kasim promised that he would tell Jasmine on his own time. Cree agreed because he knew that Jasmine was keeping the secret club from him as well. Now that it was out there he expected for Kasim to come clean.

"Well, let's get out of here so that you can get back to your woman and make things right."

"Once I tell her my shit, she probably tries to whoop a nigga's ass." Kasim chuckled.

"Oh no doubt she's going to curse your ass out."

Kasim grabbed his things from the locker and they headed out the doors. "So, tell me everything about this damn sex club." He said.

As they headed to their cars Cree broke everything damn to him. When he was done Kasim stood there in shock.

"Damn, I'm in love with a pimp."

Jasmine was at home pacing back and forth in her living room. She had called Kasim three times since he walked out of the club. On the third call he had finally answered her phone call. He didn't even let her speak. All he said was that he would be at her house in twenty minutes. She was about to curse his ass out for thinking he could talk to her like that, but he had hung up on her ass. She was mad, but at the same time glad that he was willing to talk things out. She prayed that he didn't come in talking that break up shit. If so he had another thing coming. She invested too much time and her heart into the relationship for him to break things off.

She glanced up towards the front door when she heard a knock at it. She stomped to the door and opened it without even checking to see who it was first.

Kasim scrolled right in and walked pass her to the living room. She closed the door and turned just in time to see his back before he turned the corner. She locked the door then walked back into the living room where Kasim was now pacing back and forth.

"Kasim…" She started but was stopped when he interrupted her.

"Naw, let me speak my peace first." He said.

"Okay." She stared at him.

Kasim sighed. "Look, I love you, Jasmine. If you don't know anything you should know that because not only do I tell you, but I also show you. I know that you need more time to fully give me your trust and I'm willing to work on that with you. That whole secret club shit caught me off guard. I'm man enough to admit that I was mad as hell and a little jealous that you may have been messing with some of the niggas in the club."

"I don't mess with any of them. I keep it hundred percent business only." She said taking a few steps towards him.

"Deep down I knew that, but I let my emotions get the best of me. You're not the only one who has been keeping a secret." He said staring into her eyes.

Jasmine glared at him. "If you are about to tell me that you got a baby mama or a wife, I will kill your ass." She snapped.

Kasim chuckled. "Naw, I don't have a wife or baby mama. Only kids I will be having will be birthed by you."

Jasmine let that last part slide before speaking again. "You better not say you have a boyfriend either."

He snarled at her. "Don't fucking play with me!"

She put her hands up in a surrendering motion. "Damn my bad I was just making sure shit."

"Jasmine Monique Baber, don't play with me about that bullshit!"

"I said my bad. You ain't got to say my whole damn government. You sounding like the police and shit. Let me check you for a wire." She grinned at him.

"Get your little freaky ass on somewhere. I'm trying to talk to you and your ass over here trying to feel up on me and shit." He chuckled.

She was now standing directly in front of him. "I'm just trying to be on the safe side."

"Whatever Jasmine. Like I was saying, I have something to tell you that's important. I was planning on telling you earlier before all that shit went down."

"Okay, what's up?"

"You know my delivery company that I own right?"

"Yessss."

"Well, my company deliver more than legal stuff."

Jasmine gave him the side eye. "What kind of other stuff do you deliver?"

"I deliver whatever my clients need delivered. From stolen merchandise to guns and drugs. As for the drugs I barely do that maybe once in a while on a favor. That's how my company got so big so fast. I dapple between legal and illegal. So, I guess you can say we both into some shit we shouldn't be doing." He said waiting for her to say something.

She stood there and just stared at him. "So, you're a dope boy?"

"No, but you're a pimp so let's not judge."

She gave him a frown. "You were pissed at me about some shit when you're doing something just as bad."

"Yeah, but what you doing had me about to body you and all those niggas that work for you."

Jasmine rolled her eyes. "You a punk ass nigga. Going to snap at me then walk out and not answer your phone. I should whoop your ass." She snapped at him.

Kasim laughed. "Jasmine, you can't beat my ass so shut the hell up. I'll admit I was wrong for getting mad when I was keeping something from you too. I'll make it up to you."

She raised her right eyebrow. "Oh yeah?"

"Yeah."

She stood there and thought about it for a moment. "Okay, I have an idea."

"What?"

"To make it up to me and to show me that you really love me, you have to let me rent you out to Mrs. Clarkson. She was very fond of you."

Kasim took a step back and glared at her. "What the fuck you just ask me? Have you lost your muthafucking mind? Why the fuck would you ask me to sleep with another damn woman? An old ass white woman at that! You real foul for that shit. I swear you about to make me slap the shit out of you!" He spat pissed off.

Jasmine folded her arms and stomped her feet like a little spoiled child. Next then Kasim knew she had tears streaming down her cheeks. He looked on shocked because he had never seen her cry before. Jasmine was a tough chick, and she had always held in her emotions well. So, to see her crying right now kind of weakened him.

"Come here baby." He tried pulling her to him, but she pulled away.

"No! You were so pissed at me because of what you found out. You walked out and ignored my phone calls. Then you come here and drop this big ass secret on me about being more than just an owner of a delivery company. I don't ask you for shit, but as soon as I ask you for one thing you get mad and say no. How am I supposed to know that you truly got my back if you won't do this one simple thing for me?" She sniffled as she buried her face in his chest.

"Simple? Fucking another woman is a simple thing for her?" He asked himself as he rubbed her back.

Kasim sighed deeply and said the only thing he felt would get her to stop crying. He wasn't going to do it, but she didn't need to know that right now.

"Okay baby, I'll do it." He said.

Jasmine pulled away from his chest and looked up at him. "Really?"

"Yeah man, I'll do it."

She stared at him for a minute before speaking. "So, all it takes is a few tears for you to sleep with another woman? It's that damn easy for you to fuck another chick? I should punch you in your damn face!" She pushed him up off of her.

"What the fuck?" He glared at her.

"Yeah nigga, what the fuck? A bitch shed a few tears and you all too happy to go fuck somebody else. Kasim let me find out you fucking another bitch. Watch they have us on a new episode of Snapped. As a matter fact your ass going to be on Unsolved Mysteries fucking with me. Give my shit away if you want to."

He just stood there and glared at her. He thought she was crazy as hell with how she just flipped out on him. "You're bipolar as hell. I'm calling your mama and asking her why the fuck she didn't get you any help as a kid."

Jasmine laughed at him. "I'm just playing with you baby. Why you got to be so sensitive?" She asked wrapping her arms around his waist.

"Naw, get your crazy ass away from me." He said, but didn't move a muscle to push her away.

"I love you, Kasim."

"I love you too, crazy."

"No more secrets?" She asked looking up at him.

"Yeah baby, no more secrets." They sealed the new phase of their relationship with a passionate kiss.

Chapter 16

Two weeks had passed and things were going smoothly for the couples. Business had been doing fine without any more problems, but everyone was still on alert. They refused to let their guard down while the person or peoples, who destroyed the club, was still at large.

Kasim was leaning against his car outside the rehab center with his arms folded across his chest. He waited nervously for Kasey to walk out of the double doors. Today was her first day outside of the place she had being calling home for a few months now. She had been working very hard with keeping herself clean and focus. As a reward she was allowed a twelve hour pass. He didn't want her to come out and have a relapse. She had begged him for this, promising that she wouldn't do anything to jeopardized letting him or anyone else that's been rooting for her down.

He looked up when he heard the doors open. Kasey came walking out with a huge smile on her face. He knew she was smiling for more than one reason. He fought hard not to frown at the thought of her smile having something to do with Cortez.

"Hey Kasim." She said walking up to him and giving him a hug.

"Hey baby girl. You excited to be out of there for a few hours?"

"Yesss! I mean, it's not a bad place, but there is nothing like being able to come and go as you please. Plus, you don't have to worry about people watching your every move." She said climbing into the passenger seat.

Kasim walked around to the driver side and got in before responding. "Yeah, but you only have a few more months then you're out of there."

"I know and I'll be able to have my life back. Of course I'll be doing things a lot different now, but still." She said with a shrug of her shoulders while still smiling.

"Yeah and before that time comes we'll be having a really important talk." He said pulling off the lot.

"Yeah, I know." She turned towards the window and stared out at the city view.

Kasim didn't say anything else letting her take everything in. He knew she was now looking at everything with new eyes.

When Kasey noticed that Kasim was starting to slow down she paid closer attention to her surroundings. After realizing where they were she glanced over at her brother with a panicked expression.

"Why… what are we doing here?" She questioned.

"I think it's time that you come here to say your peace, Kasey. You had been running from this for some time now. I think now that you're getting better you need to stop running." He said removing his seat belt and getting out the car.

He stood by her door and waited for her to get out. It took her a few minutes to get the courage to do so. She got out the car and grabbed his hand. She let Kasim lead her over to their mother's gravesite.

The closer they got the more nervous Kasey became. Once they stepped in front of her tombstone the tears immediately started to fall.

Kasim pulled her close and rubbed her back to soothe her. "It's okay. Let it all out. By the time we leave here I need you to forgive yourself Kasey. You can't continue to punish yourself for what happened." He kissed her on the side of the head.

They both turned around when they heard footsteps close by. "Jassy? What are you doing here?" Kasey asked looking between her and Kasim.

"Your brother told me where he was bringing you today and I wanted to be here for moral support." She replied.

Kasey smiled and gave her a tight hug. "Thank you."

"No thanks needed. I care about you just as much as I care about your brother."

"Except she loves me more. Don't be jealous it's just the way it is. I'm a lovable dude, I can't help it." Kasim joked.

"Whatever!" Kasey laughed before punching him in the arm.

"Damn I see Jasmine's violent ways are rubbing off on you." He said rubbing his arm.

Jasmine punched him in the other arm. "I'm not violent."

"Really Jasmine? You're going to just punch me in front of my mother? I can't believe you." He said with a straight face.

"She would have loved you." Kasey said to her before turning around to face the tombstone.

"Yeah, I agree." Kasim said smiling at Jasmine.

"Can I have a moment alone with her please?" Kasey asked with her back still facing them.

"Yeah, sure baby girl. We'll be over there by the car."

Jasmine patted her on the shoulder before placing her hand inside of Kasim's hand. They walked away leaving Kasey alone to talk to her mother.

Kasey closed her eyes and took a deep breath. She then opened them and stared at the tombstone before speaking.

"Hi mom, it's me Kasey. I want to first say how sorry I am for all the pain and trouble I caused you. I didn't know how to handle the fact that you were sick. I felt like if I acknowledged it then I would be making it seem like I was coming to terms with it. That would have been a lie. You were the only parent we had. Losing you hurt so bad mommy. I was young, and I needed my mother. I still do. Kasim tried to be there for me, but I ended up pushing him away." She wiped the tears that poured from her eyes. As soon as she wiped some away more would fall.

"You taught Kasim well mommy. He takes really good care of me. I went through a really hard time after your death, but I'm getting back on track. I have a great support team behind me. Kasim has this awesome girlfriend named Jasmine, who is really like a big sister to me now. She also has this friend named Mercedes that I consider a big sister as well. They are very nice and successful business women." She looked over her shoulder at Kasim and Jasmine standing by the car laughing with each other. They looked like a happy couple.

She turned back to her mother and continued talking. "I met this guy through Jasmine. He's become a good friend to me. His name is Cortez. He's Mercedes's boyfriend Cree youngest brother. I really like Cortez, mom. He makes me think about things that I wouldn't have considered before. Between you and me I think I am falling for my best friend. How cliché is that?" She giggled.

Then her face turned sad. "I don't think he looks at me that way though. Cortez is very experienced in areas that I am not. I might have been running around on the streets doing drugs, but I never lost my virtue. Yeah mommy, I'm still a virgin. Sometimes I think Kasim wants to ask me, but then he chickens out. It's quite funny if you ask me. Well, it's been good talking to you. I think I will make this a habit. I love you so much mommy." She kissed two of her fingers and then touched the tombstone with them.

Kasim released Jasmine out of his hold and walked up to Kasey as she approached the car. "How are you feeling baby girl?" He asked her.

Kasey looked around before making eye contact with him. "I feel a lot better. Thanks for bringing me here. I think now I can finally start the forgiving process."

He wrapped his arms around her in a tight hug. He then kissed her forehead before releasing her. "Come on let's go. I want to spend some time with you before you diss me for your 'best friend'." He chuckled.

"Shut up!" She giggled. She was excited to spend time with Cortez outside of the rehab. He told her that he had a whole day planned for them. She couldn't wait.

👄 👄 👄 👄 👄 👄 👄 👄

Cortez had picked up Kasey from Kasim's house twenty minutes ago. They were now on their way to the movies. Kasey didn't look at it as a date because she didn't want to fool herself like that. She knew they were just two friends going to see a movie together.

"So, what movie do you want to see?" He asked her as he glanced over at her out the corner of his eye.

Kasey shrugged. "I don't know. What's a good movie that's out?"

"We could go see Straight Outta Compton? I heard that movie was good, but I haven't had the time to go see it until now." He replied.

"Okay then let's go see that."

"Okay." There was complete silence for a few minutes. Both were lost in their own thoughts.

When they pulled up to the AMC Theater in Clifton, Cortez searched for a good parking spot. "Damn it looks packed." He mumbled.

Kasey heard him and looked over at him. "We don't have to go if you don't want to." She said softly.

Cortez looked at her and shook his head. "No, you want to see the movie, so we're going to see it. I see a spot up there close to the door."

Kasey smiled. "Okay."

After they parked and got out the car, they made their way inside. "I love the smell of popcorn." She said inhaling the scent.

"Why don't you go stand in line for the snacks while I grab the tickets?" He suggested.

"Okay." She walked towards the line that wasn't that long. When she made it to the register she remembered that she didn't ask him what he wanted. She turned around and bumped right into his hard chest.

"Damn, my bad." He chuckled.

"That's okay. I was about to come and ask what you wanted."

He looked over at all the candy. "Let me get, some skittles, sour patches, butter finger bites, nachos with extra cheese, large popcorn, two cherry slushes, and make sure you but extra butter on the popcorn." He then turned to Kasey.

"What you want?"

Kasey looked at him with a shock expression. "You're going to eat all that by yourself?"

"Oh you wanted to share with me?" He grinned.

"Not really, but I didn't think you would order all that." She giggled.

Cortez smirked. "I'm just fucking with you girl. We're going to share. Is there anything else you want though?"

"No, that's all fine." She replied.

Cortez pulled his wallet out and waited for the total. "Damn, thirty-five dollars just for that little shit? Y'all know damn well that shit not worth that much!" He yelled passing the dude who was behind the register his money. Some of the surrounding people agreed with him. Kasey was trying hard not to laugh because the dude looked like he was seconds away from pissing on himself.

"This is probably his first day on the job." She thought to herself.

They grabbed through snacks and headed to their theater. Once they were settled they had light conversation until the movie started. Throughout the movie they kept smiling at each other and talking about their favorite NWA songs. When the movie was over they threw away their trash and headed out the theater.

"I need to use the restroom before we go." Kasey said.

"Okay, I'll wait for you out here."

"Okay." Kasey walked into the restroom and handled her business. When she finished she walked to the sink and washed her hands. She kept looking at herself in the mirror and smiling. She was really having a great time with Cortez. She never done any of this before because she was too busy acting out. She was happy to have another chance.

After she dried her hands she walked out of the restroom smiling from ear to ear. Her smile was immediately wiped off of her face when she saw Cortez with a half dressed chick hugging all up on him. Kasey hurried up and got her composure together before he turned around and saw the sad look on her face. She held her head up as she walked passed him as if she didn't see him.

Cortez pushed Nika off him. She was the jump off that he took to the club with him that ended with Jasmine punching her in the mouth.

"What's up, Cortez? Why are you pushing me away?" She asked with her anger building up.

"Get the hell away from me. You know damn well I don't do that hugging all up on me shit." He snapped at her.

"You looked mighty cozy with that chick you came to the movies with. Who is she? Is that your flavor of the week? Is she the reason you haven't been answering my calls?"

Cortez wasn't paying her any attention. He had just noticed that the chick who walked passed them was Kasey. He left Nika standing there talking to herself. He rushed out of the doors and looked around the parking lot until he spotted her standing next to the car with her arms folded across her chest.

"Kasey, why did you leave out without me?" He asked walking up on her.

She took a step back. "I thought I would give you some time to talk to one of your girlfriends. I didn't want to intrude." She said with a shrug.

Cortez frowned at her. "She's not my girlfriend. She's just a chick I kicked it with a few times."

"By kick it, you mean fucked?" She gave him a raised eyebrow expression.

He laughed. "You sound so funny when you curse."

Kasey rolled her eyes. "Can you please open the car door so I can get in?" She faced the car with her hand on the door handle.

"Nope."

Kasey turned to looked at him. "What?"

"You heard me. I'm not opening anything if you mad at me. We're going to stand here until you're not."

"You can't be serious?"

"I most definitely am." He leaned against the car with his arms folded across his chest.

Kasey sighed. "I'm not mad at you."

"I don't believe you." He stared at her.

"Well, that's a personal problem that you have to deal with on your own. I'm really not mad at you. I mean why would I be? We're just friends. That's all we are to each other." She said feeling a sharp pain pierce her heart.

Cortez stared at her for a moment not saying a word. "That's how you truly feel?" He asked after a while.

She shrugged her shoulders. "Yeah, ain't that how you feel?"

He nodded his head not saying a word. The next thing she heard was the car door locks being unlocked. They got into the car not saying a word to each other. Cortez turned the radio on and let the music entertain them.

Kasey wanted to ask where they were going, but then she remembered him saying earlier that it was surprise. She wondered if he was still in the mood to hang out with her. She could sense that his mood had changed after she made that last statement.

"Does he have feelings for me?" She asked herself as she kept stealing glances of him.

Chapter 17

The whole car ride to their next destination was a quiet one. Kasey was afraid to say anything to him. Even if she wanted to she didn't know what to say. She never felt this way about a boy before. She made a mental note to talk with Jasmine and Mercedes about it.

Cortez kept his eyes trained on the road. He didn't want her to see how upset he was from her statement. Today he was planning on telling her that he wanted to be more than friends. He never had a girlfriend before, but he was willing to try something new with Kasey. When she said that she didn't see him that way, he felt a sharp pain in his chest. He stopped dealing with all the chicks he was messing with since they started getting to know each other. Now he wasn't sure how the night was going to end.

Kasey glanced out the window when she noticed they pulled up in front of a nice blue and white house. "Who lives here?" She asked as he turned the car off.

"This is my mother's house." He stated before getting out the car. He walked around to the passenger side and opened her door.

She got out the car looking surprised. He didn't mention anything about bringing her to meet his mother today. They walked up the steps and he used a key to open the door.

He led her inside then closed the door behind them. "Maaaa!" He yelled out.

Kasey looked at him like he was crazy. Then she heard a woman voice yell back at him. "Cortez, why the hell are you calling me like that?"

"So that you would know the king has arrived." He said when Cheryl came walking out of the kitchen with her apron on.

"Whatever boy! Get over here and give me some sugar."

"Naw woman! My kisses ain't free. Where the dollars at?" He joked.

"Boy, get your crazy ass over here!"

Cortez looked back at Kasey and grinned. "She loves the kid. She can't get enough of my sweet kisses." He then walked up to his mother and kissed her sweetly on the cheek.

"That'll be nineteen ninety nine, ma'am." He held his hand out.

Cheryl smiled at him and then smacked him upside the head. "That's on the house." She then walked away from him and stood in front of Kasey.

"You must be Kasey?" She smiled.

Kasey nodded. "Yes."

"Aw come here. I have heard so much about you. I am glad to finally meet you." She gave her a hug.

"Who told you about me?" Kasey asked nervously.

"Well, your brother, Jasmine, and Cortez. Mainly Cortez though. He can't seem to stop talking about you. I feel like I know you already." Cheryl chuckled.

"Oh really?" Kasey asked looking over at Cortez.

"Ma, why are you trying to blast me in front of my friend?" Cortez frowned at her.

Kasey felt sad at the mention of him calling her his friend. She didn't understand why because he calls her that all the time. After the talk in the movies parking lot something just feels different now.

"Whatever Cortez! Y'all are the first to arrive. Everyone else should be arriving shortly. I guess that would give me and Kasey time to talk." Cheryl said grabbing her hand and leading her to the same spot where she first talked to her brother.

"Well, while y'all do that I'm about to go see what you cooking." Cortez said walking towards the kitchen.

"You better not touch a damn thing in my kitchen either! I swear that boy going to make me hurt him."

Kasey laughed. "You know, this is the first time that Cortez has ever brought a female to my house. I told him that if the chick doesn't mean anything to him other than sex he better not ever bring her to my house. I guess he finally found someone that means a lot to him."

"Yeah, he's a really good friend to me."

Cheryl gave her a knowing look. "I'm glad you two are building up a great friendship. I'm not crazy though Kasey. I just saw the way you two looked at each other. I also know my son. The way his eyes light up when he talks about you, I know it's more than just a friendship brewing there."

She put her head down. "I didn't think he looked at me that way. We went to the movies and when we were leaving he ran into one of the chicks he messes with."

"Girl those hoes don't mean anything to him. I haven't even heard about him messing with anyone since he started talking to you. You shouldn't let those chicks get to you." She said and then waved her off.

When Kasey didn't respond she decided to change the subject. "So, Cortez told me about what happened to your mom and the path you was on. I'm glad to see you doing better. You're a beautiful young lady and have a full life a head of you."

"Thank you."

"If you ever need to talk about anything I am always here. We're a big family around these parts. I look at Mercedes and Jasmine as my daughters. There's always room for one more." She smiled at her.

Kasey looked up at her with a huge smile on her face. "Really?"

"Of course. I know you lost your mother during a time when a girl really needed that motherly guidance. I don't mind being that woman for you."

Tears filled the brim of her eyes. "Thank you so much."

Cheryl got up and sat next to her on the couch. She then gave her a tight hug. "No thanks needed baby."

"What happened?" Cortez walked into the living room eating a piece of cornbread.

"Cortez, I just know your black ass did not cut into my cornbread?" Cheryl asked getting up off the couch and walking towards him.

He backed away from her. "Mama, you remember what I told you about abuse. You don't want to go to jail do you?" He ate the rest of the cornbread and ran around her when she tried to hit him.

"You get on my damn nerves! Touch something else in my kitchen again and watch Kasey see you get your ass whooped." She stormed out of the living room.

"That woman violent as hell. She lucky I love her or she'll be doing time in the penitentiary by now." He said taking a seat next to Kasey on the couch.

She laughed and hit him on the arm. "You so silly."

"No, I'm so serious." He laughed.

Kasey shook her head at him. "So, what's with the tears?" He asked wiping her cheeks with his thumb.

"Your mother is a great woman. You and your brothers are very lucky to still have her." She said softly.

"Yeah, I know." He said staring at her.

"Cortez, I'm sorry about what I said at the movies. I was a little mad that you had another chick all over you. I cherish our friendship, but I will admit that I started growing feelings for you."

Cortez smirked. "So, you want the kid, huh?" He asked.

"Shut up, Cortez. I'm trying to be serious and you making jokes. You know what, never mind." She went to get up, but he stopped her.

"Kasey, life is short for most people. I don't want to be serious all the time. I want to take my time to enjoy life. I know you're serious and I was too. I really like you. I never felt this way about a chick before. We're young so let's not act like old ass people who think you have to be serious all the time."

"Okay."

"Now, since we both admitted that we have feelings for each other, I think we should try that relationship thing that people be talking about."

Kasey giggled. "So, you saying you want the kid, huh?" She asked.

Cortez chuckled. "Yeah, I want the kid."

"I think we should continue to build our friendship as well."

He nodded. "I agree."

"I also think that we should wait for sex."

He raised an eyebrow. "What made you say that?"

"Well, I know that you are used to having sex. I'm not because I'm still a virgin."

"Kasey, I'm not going to rush you to do anything that you're not ready for. Sex barely crosses my mind when I'm with you."

She gave him a look. "So, you don't think about sex when you're around me?"

"Naw, I didn't say all that. I said it BARELY does. You're beautiful to me. I'm very attracted to you."

"Okay. I also think that if at any time you feel like you want to cheat, you should break up with me. If you cheat on me, I'll be forced to kick your ass." She said as if she didn't just threaten him.

Cortez chuckled again. "You don't ever have to worry about me cheating on you. I would never want to hurt you like that."

"Good. Well, I guess now we go together." She giggled.

Che grabbed her chin and brought her face towards his. When their lips touched they felt a shock go through their entire bodies.

"What was that?" Kasey asked looking at him.

"I don't know." He shrugged just as confused as she was.

"Let's try that again." He said leaning towards her. He kissed her softly on the lips.

"Ma your favorite son has arrived!" They heard someone yell out.

"Cordell thank you for announcing my arrival. That was nice of you. Her favorite son has arrived. That would be me!" Cree yelled out.

Cortez pulled away from Kasey and rolled his eyes. "Both of you niggas late. Her favorite son arrived about an hour ago." He said standing to his feet and giving his brothers a smirk.

"Whatever!" They both said at once.

Cree, Mercedes, Cordell, Jasmine, and Kasim walked into the living room where they were. Jasmine and Mercedes walked over to Kasey and gave her a hug. They then introduced her to Cree and Cordell. They heard a lot about each other, but this was the first time they laid eyes on each other.

"It's nice to finally meet you Kasey." Cree said giving her a hug.

Cordell gave her one too. She stood there smiling at them. ***Damn! All three of them are fine!*** She thought to herself.

"Y'all came just in time the food is ready." Cheryl said walking into the living room.

"Finally! I'm hungry." Cortez said.

"Boy you always hungry." Mercedes said popping him in the back of the head as she walked passed.

"Right! He greedy." Jasmine co-signed.

"I'm not even going to respond. For now on, you have to be at least five feet four inches for me to respond."

"Ooooh I can't stand him." Jasmine chuckled.

"Did y'all hear something? It sounded like it came from down on the floor." He joked.

"Cortez, don't make me punch you."

"Whatever midget." He ran when she tried to grab him.

Kasim walked over to Kasey and wrapped his arm around her. "Did you enjoy yourself today?" He asked.

She looked up at him. "Yes, we went to the movies and saw Straight Outta Compton. It was a good movie."

"Good. I'm glad you enjoyed yourself."

"Would it be okay if Cortez took me back to the rehab center tonight?" She asked nervously.

He stared at her for a second before responding. "Sure."

"Thanks, Kasim." She stood on the tip of her shoes and gave him a kiss on the cheek.

"Come on let's go eat. Cheryl can cook her ass off. You're going to love her food." He said leading her into the kitchen where everyone else was already seated.

Kasey sat next to her brother on one side and Cortez on the other side of her. Everyone held hands as Cheryl said grace. When she finished everyone started passing dishes around and filling up their plates. Kasey was so happy that she had tears in her eyes. She missed being a part of a family. She smiled over at her brother, who was whispering in Jasmine's ear. She felt a nudge in the shoulder and turned to Cortez. He was smiling at her with that perfect smile that she found herself falling in love with.

"This is where I'm meant to be, not in the streets." She thought before she started eating her food.

Chapter 18

As the weeks went by Cree started planning for Mercedes surprised birthday party. Jasmine did most of the planning. She really had a nick for event planning. He told her that price wasn't an issue and to go all out for his baby. The only problem they were having was keeping Mercedes from finding out.

"What you doing?" Mercedes asked Jasmine when she walked into her office at club Ambitious.

Jasmine closed her laptop. "I'm not doing anything at the moment." She smiled at her from behind her desk.

She gave her the side eye before rolling her eyes. "You and Cree have been acting real funny lately. Do I need to find a new best friend and man?" She asked taking a seat in one of the chairs in front of the desk.

"Girl, please! You can't replace us. We're irreplaceable."

"Yeah okay, keep thinking that. Anyway, Zanni said she's coming in town around the same time as my birthday. We should all do something." She said.

Jasmine looked at her for a moment without saying anything. "Uh hello! Did you hear me?" She asked with a frown.

"Yeah, I was just thinking about something. Anyway, let me call Zanni. I haven't heard from her in about a week." Jasmine said grabbing her phone off the desk. She scrolled through her contacts until she found what she was looking for.

"She probably got her some new dick." Mercedes said with a chuckled.

Jasmine laughed while she listened to the phone ring. She put the call on speaker.

"Helloooo from the other side!" They heard her sing when she answered the phone.

"Zaniela muthafucking Wise, you better not dare quit your day job and pursue singing. It ain't going to work out baby." Mercedes said, and they all laughed.

"Fuck youuuu!" Zanni yelled.

"Nope, I prefer Cree's d…"

"You better not finish that damn sentence heifer!" She shouted.

"Whatever! What are you doing?" Mercedes asked laughing.

"Girl I was supposed to be going on a date." She replied.

"What happened?" Jasmine asked.

"Okay, so this nigga comes to pick me up from the park…"

"Why the park?" Jasmine and Mercedes both asked.

"Because I don't know that nigga like that for him to know where I live. Shit he could've been a serial killer or something."

Mercedes laughed. "But you was about to get in the car with him though."

"Shut the hell up Cedes and let me tell my fucked up story!"

They laughed again. "Okay, go ahead."

"Anyway, I was standing there looking all cute in my thigh length purple dress. I thought I was the shit too. I was getting compliments from men and women. So he texted me and said that he was pulling up. I look around for the car. He said his car was red. He didn't mention what kind it was. So, I'm getting ready to call him up and ask him. Tell me why a damn red beetle pulls up in front of me."

"Wait! Wait… hold up! You talking about one of those little ass cars?" Mercedes asked while cracking up laughing.

"Girl yes! You know me, I'm thinking it's somebody else because I just know this nigga didn't come and pick me up in that shit."

"Was it him?" Jasmine asked.

"Yes! This fool gets out the car smiling and shit. You know what I did?" Zanni asked.

"You cursed his ass out." They said at the same time.

"No, I didn't say shit." She replied.

"You didn't say shit?" Jasmine asked confused.

"Nope. I walked away without saying a damn word. He started calling my name and following behind me and shit. I ignored his ass. I walked to my car, got in, and pulled the fuck off." They all laughed.

"Y'all I was so damn mad I got all cute for nothing." She said with an attitude.

"I probably would've cursed his ass out." Mercedes said.

"When I come out there in a few weeks, I'm going to need the friend discount on a man." She joked.

"Naw ain't no damn friend discount."

"Cedes, you an evil heifer. Cree must be acting stingy with the dick or something. Tell him don't do my friend like that. Share the meat." Jasmine was drinking some water out of a bottle and spit it out when she heard that.

"I can't stand your ass!" Mercedes said laughing.

"The lies you tell yourself. Anyway, how is my future baby daddy doing?" Zanni asked changing the subject.

"Who Cordell?" Jasmine asked.

"Yes, girl! I'm going to have his babies one day. First, he has to stop being a hoe."

"He ain't as bad as Cortez used to be." Mercedes said.

"Oh I heard he done calmed his little ass down. That's good because he was going to catch something if he kept fucking with all those nasty ass females." Zanni said.

"Right, but now that he and Kasim's little sister is dating he calmed all the way down." Jasmine said.

"I can't wait to meet the both of them. My friend done went and fell in love."

Jasmine giggled. "Shut up, Zanni!"

"Tell Cheryl I want a home cooked meal when I get there. That's my homie. I can't believe she didn't tell me she was sick. I cried like a baby on the phone when I called to check on her and she revealed that she was sick." Zanni said sadly.

"I will be glad when they find her a heart." Mercedes said.

"Me too." Jasmine and Zanni agreed.

"Okay ladies I need to get back to work. I'll call y'all later. Tell Cree and Kasim that I said don't forget to share the meat. It keeps you two heifers in a good mood. Tell Cordell that I said stop being a hoe so I can have his damn babies!"

"Byeee Zanni! Get your crazy ass off my line!" Jasmine said hanging up on her.

"She so damn silly." Mercedes said getting up.

"You about to head out?"

"Yes, I'm tired as hell." Jasmine said getting up after shutting everything down.

They walked out together before saying goodbye and going their separate ways to their cars. Jasmine was searching for her keys in her purse. She found them then she continued to her car. When she got there she was about to press the unlock button when her keys fell out her hand. She bent down and picked them up. As she stood back up she felt a little dizzy. Her head started spinning and before she knew what was happening darkness surrounded her.

Jasmine woke up in a hospital bed with a familiar face staring back at her. She sat up in the bed and glanced around the room. "What am I doing here?" She asked confused. The last thing she remembered was leaving out of the club with Mercedes and heading to her car.

"You had passed out by your car. I saw you and rushed you to the hospital." Kevin said standing next to the bed.

"Oh, where is Mercedes?" She asked him.

"I don't know I didn't see her. She must have had left already."

She looked at him funny. "You didn't call her and tell her that I was in the hospital?"

Kevin shook his head. "It slipped my mind. I was in a rush to get you to the hospital. I'm sorry, but if you want me to call her right now, I can."

"No, that's okay. I'll call her right now."

"Okay."

"Did the doctor happen to say what was wrong with me?" She asked him.

"No, she hasn't come back in here since she took some blood from you." He replied.

"Oh okay. Thanks for bringing me here Kevin."

"No problem, boss." He smiled at her.

Jasmine grabbed her phone and decided to call Kasim first. She listened as the phone rang three times before he picked up.

"What's up, baby?" He greeted making her smile.

"Hey babe. I'm just calling to let you know that I had to be rushed to the hospital. I don't know why yet, but I passed out, outside of the club. One of our employees brought me to the hospital."

"What? Which hospital did they take you to? I'm walking out of the office right now." He said. She could hear things being moved in the background and then the sound of a car alarm.

"Baby, you don't have to do that I can just have Cedes come and get me."

"Jasmine, I asked what hospital they took you to. I'm not trying to hear all that other shit you talking right now."

She rolled her eyes and then told him the hospital she was at. They ended the call with him telling her that he was on his way. She was about to dial Cedes number when they heard a knock at the door and a woman doctor walking inside the room.

"Hello, I'm Dr. Andrews. Is it okay to speak freely?" She asked looking from her to Kevin.

Jasmine looked over at Kevin. "Would you excuse us for a moment?"

"Sure." He nodded then walked out of the room.

"Okay, we got your blood work back, and it gives us a little clue to why you may have passed out."

"I know I haven't been getting much sleep because I'm always tired." She said.

The doctor nodded. "It also seems that you haven't been getting many fluids either. That and the fact that you're pregnant. Those factors combined were the cause of you passing out today." She said as she looked over her chart.

Jasmine stared at her. "What did you say?"

Dr. Andrews glanced over at her. "I said that you're pregnant Ms. Baber. We won't know how far along you are until we do an ultra sound."

"No, no that can't be." She said shaking her head.

"I'm sorry to tell you that it is."

"But how?" She asked herself, but the doctor still responded.

"Well, when a man and woman…"

Jasmine glared at her and the doctor closed her mouth. "Can I have some time to process all of this?"

"Sure I will start getting your prescription for parental vitamins ready." The doctor walked out the room at the same time Kasim was walking in.

"Baby, are you okay? What did the doctor say?" He asked walking up to the bed.

Jasmine glared at him. "You trapped me!" She yelled at him.

Kasim frowned. "What?"

"You heard me nigga. You trapped me. The doctor just said that I passed out because I haven't been getting any fluids and I'm pregnant. So, yeah you trapped me." She snapped.

He smirked while rubbing his chin. "It must have happened when the condom broke or when we fucked without wrapping it up."

She leaned back a little and stared at him. "When the fuck was you going to tell me the damn condom broke... fucking trap king!"

"I thought you saw it when I threw it away. Plus, the times we forgot to strap up you knew damn well I wasn't pulling out. So, here we are with the end results. You going to be a mama and I'm going to be a papi. Let's celebrate with a quickie." He grinned.

"Kasim if you don't get the hell away from me I will punch you. You make me sick!" She said rolling her eyes.

He laughed before leaning forward to kiss her. She tried to push him away, but he grabbed her cheeks and pulled her towards him. He gave her a big juicy kiss on the lips.

"I'm happy just so you know." He said looking her in the eyes.

"I bet you are happy. Going around trapping people and shit." He laughed again.

"Is everything okay Jasmine?" Kasim turned around at the sound of a man's voice.

"Who the fuck are you?" He asked with his face scrunched up.

"I'm Kevin, I work for Jasmine." He said with his hand held out.

Kasim looked at his hand then over at Jasmine. "What kind of work you do for her?"

Kevin put his hand down to his side and looked at Jasmine. He then put his attention back on Kasim. "I work at the club."

"I didn't ask you where you worked. I asked what you do there."

"Kasim stop it." Jasmine glared at him.

"Whatever. Thanks for bringing her to the hospital, but I can take it from here." He told Kevin.

"Are you sure?" Kevin asked looking at Jasmine.

"Yeah WE sure. What the hell you asking her that for?" Kasim didn't like dude at all. He was tempted to bust him in his shit.

"You can go Kevin. Thanks for everything." Jasmine said smiling at him.

"Okay. I hope you feel better. I'll see you when you get back to work." He said giving Kasim a smirk before walking out of the room.

Kasim went to follow him, but Jasmine stopped him. "Where are you going?" She asked confused.

"I'm about to go whoop his ass. You see that nigga try to smirk at me like he knows something that I don't. He got me fucked up!" He went for the door again, but she stopped him once more.

"Boy, get your ass over here. You always trying to fight somebody, but you call me violent." She laughed.

Kasim walked back over to the bed. "That's because you rubbing off on me. I already know our baby going to be bad as hell."

"You really excited about this baby, huh?" She asked softly.

"Yeah, I really am. What about you?"

She sighed. "I don't know how I really feel about it yet. I just know that I never really gave being a mother any thought. I don't even think I'll be any good at it."

He grabbed her hands in his. "You'll be a great mother Jasmine."

"How do you know that?"

"Because you're a great person period. You care about the people that are in your life. Even though you don't take any shit, you also give to anyone who needs it. All a baby ever truly wants is to be loved. You one of the most loving people I know. Look what you did for Cortez and Kasey without a second thought to what anyone else would think about it. I love you and I already love our baby too." He kissed her lips.

"I guess you right. I'm still going to tell people you trapped me though. I have to keep my street cred." She smiled at him.

He laughed and kissed her again. When the doctor came back inside to do an ultra sound, they found out that she was about eight weeks pregnant. Kasim grinned knowing it had to be one of the times they didn't strap up. Jasmine was shocked that she wasn't showing any signs of pregnancy. She hasn't experienced any of morning sickness people talked about either.

They left the hospital wondering how they were going to tell their family and friends. Especially Cree since he has been begging Mercedes about having a baby. They hope it doesn't cause any drama within their circle.

Chapter 19

Two weeks had passed by within a flash. Mercedes' birthday was a day away, and she was not happy. She had just gotten off the phone with Zanni. She had told her that she wouldn't be able to make it for her birthday tomorrow. They were supposed to go out and bring her twenty-seventh birthday in partying and drinking. Now she didn't know what she was going to do for her birthday. Jasmine told her that she was going to be out of town with her mother tomorrow, so she wouldn't be able to make it either. She couldn't wait until those heifers' birthdays came so that she could ditch they ass too.

She plopped down on chair at the kitchen table right when Cree came strolling into the kitchen. "What's up, baby?" He kissed her on the cheek before heading to the fridge.

"I need new friends, babe. Those heifers ditched me for my birthday." She pouted.

He grabbed a water bottle and closed the fridge. "Good." He said before taking a sip.

"Good? What the hell you mean good?" She asked with a frown on her face.

"That's good they ditched you. Now I can take my woman out on a romantic date just the two of us. We haven't done that in a minute."

She grinned at him. "Oooh babe, I can't wait. Let me go get my hair, nails, and feet done." She hopped up out the chair. She walked up to him and kissed his lips.

"Yeah make sure you get those bunions taken care of. You can't have my brother choking on those critters." Cortez said walking into the kitchen followed by Cordell.

"Shut up little punk! Baby why you didn't tell me we had company?" She turned back around to face Cree. He just shrugged his shoulders.

"What's up, Cedes?" Cordell greeted her.

"Hey Cordell. Oh I forgot to tell you a few weeks ago that Zanni said stop being a hoe."

He laughed. "Tell her that I said I'll stop being a hoe when she ready to take this dick. It's a lot for one woman to handle, but I think she can do it. I have faith in her." He half joked.

"Annnnnd on that note, I'm out of here. Bye baby." She gave Cree another kiss then headed out. On her way out the kitchen she smacked Cortez upside the head.

"Cedes, I'm going to kick your ass. Quit beating on me and shit. I can't wait for the day you muthafuckas go to jail. I'm getting on the stand with tears in my eyes and all that good shit." He said walking over to the fridge. He could hear her laughing all the way out the door.

"What's the plan for tomorrow?" Cordell whispered after making sure she was out of earshot.

"I'm going to take her on a romantic dinner and then I'm going to suggest we go to one of the clubs. When we get there she's going to be clueless to what's going on. When we walk through the doors I want the DJ to play Stevie Wonder version of happy birthday. I want all you muthafuckas to be singing along for my baby." Cree said breaking it down for them.

"I'm not singing shit unless I'm getting paid." Cortez said taking a bite out of his apple.

"Then your punk ass ain't getting in the club." Cree glared at him.

"Nigga, you and your woman going to stop calling me a punk. I'll beat both of y'all asses... but I'm not because I don't want to hear mama's mouth." He said.

Cree and Cordell shook their heads at him and continued discussing Cedes' birthday party.

The following night Mercedes was in her bedroom getting ready for her night out with Cree. She had been getting phone calls, messages, and posts on social media with birthday wishes from family and friends. When

Jasmine and Zaniela called she made sure to curse them out before telling them thanks for the birthday wishes.

"You almost ready baby?" Cree asked walking into the room. One look at her and he was ready to snatch her clothes off and fuck the shit out of her.

"I'm almost ready baby let me put on my lipstick." She said turning towards the mirror.

"Damn you looking good." He said licking his lips.

She didn't say anything just smiled. She did agree with him one hundred percent. She looked good as hell tonight. Her hair was done in black and honey blond curls that stop at her shoulders. She wore a black and see through long sleeve shirt with a knee length skin tight leather skirt. She matched it with a pair of sliver and diamond encrusted heels. She kept it simple with the jewelry by wearing the diamond heart pendant that Cree gave her for Christmas last year and some silver bracelets.

Mercedes turned around to find Cree still staring at her. "What?"

"You're beautiful. I feel like the luckiest man in the world."

She walked up to him and wrapped her arms around his waist. "You trying to get you some tonight huh?" She asked with a little giggle.

"Oh I'm must definitely getting me some tonight. You don't have to worry about that." He slapped her on the ass.

"Come on let's get going." He took her hand and led her out the door after she grabbed her clutch and phone off the dresser.

It was going on nine o'clock when Cree and Mercedes arrived at the restaurant. He took her to The View Restaurant and Lounge on Broadway in New York. It was a revolving rooftop cocktail lounge on the eighth floor of the Marriott Marquis with the view of Times Square.

"Oh my goodness, baby this place is amazing." Mercedes said looking around as they were escorted to their table.

Cree pulled her chair out for her before taking his own seat. "Did I tell you how beautiful you look tonight?" He asked her.

She grinned. "Yes, but I won't complain if you tell me again." They laughed.

They looked through the menu before their waiter came over and took their orders. They had small talk until their food had arrived. Mercedes was very happy to be spending this night with him. Cree was always making sure she was good no matter what. If she needed something, and it was out of his way he would still get it for her. He rubbed her feet after she had been working all day. At least three days out of the week he makes dinner for the both of them. So, she finds herself asking, why won't she give him the one thing that he want most in the world... a baby? She knew that marriage was one of the answers, but it was something more lingering in the back of her mind. She was scared. She was afraid of being responsible for another person.

"Baby did you hear what I said?" Cree asked grabbing her attention.

"Uh no, I'm sorry baby what did you say?"

"I said after dinner I want to go for a walk in Central Park. You cool with that Birthday girl?" He smirked at her.

"That sounds romantic. I would love that."

"Good. After dessert we'll head out."

"Okay."

They talked a little more while they ate their food. Mercedes was still amazed at the breathtaking view of the skyline. When dessert had arrived Cree wanted to feed her the chocolate lava cake with vanilla ice cream and caramel drizzled on top.

"Mmmm, this is so good." She said licking the ice cream off her lips.

"Damn do that again." Cree demanded.

Mercedes giggled. "Do what again?"

"Lick your lips real slow." He ordered.

She did as he asked and watched as he bit down on his lip. "When we get home I'm tearing that ass up. You won't be able to walk tomorrow."

"Baby don't tease me." She flirted.

"Check please!" He yelled out.

Mercedes started cracking up laughing. The waiter came over to the table with the check. After Cree paid the bill he stood up and walked over to her side of the table. He held his hand out for her. She placed hers inside of it. They made their way out of the restaurant with Cree whispering all the things he planned to do to her tonight.

When they got to Central Park they held each other's hands as they walked. Cree asked her how she was enjoying her birthday so far. She told him that she was having one of the best nights of her life. She thanked him for giving her the perfect birthday memory.

"The night is still young baby." He said.

She looked confused and was about to ask him what he meant when two people popped out in front of her and started rapping. She looked closer at their faces and saw that it was Papoose and Remy Ma rapping their song **Black Love.** She glanced at Cree smiling from ear to ear. When

they finished rapping Tamia walked over singing her song
So Into You.

"With every passing moment.

Thoughts of you run through my head.

Every time that I'm near you.

I realize that your heaven sent.

I think you're truly something special.

Just what my dreams are really made of.

Let's stay together you and me boy.

There's no one like you around.

Oh Baby!

I really like what you've done to me.

I can't really explain it, I'm so into you."

"Oh my God, babe! It's Tamia!" She yelled,
jumping up and down. When she looked over at Cree she
noticed he was down on one knee.

"Oh… oh… oh my goodness! What are you
doing?" She asked before placing her hands over her
mouth.

"I'm trying to propose over here." He chuckled.

"Baby are you serious right now?"

He pulled a small red box out his pocket and opened it. "Does this look like I'm playing?"

Mercedes stared at the 10 carat round diamond ring. It was a beautiful ring. It had one large diamond in the center with smaller ones surrounding it. She looked into Cree's eyes as he started talking again.

"Mercedes since the first day I laid eyes on you, I knew that you would be mine. You didn't make it easy for me and that's what I loved about you. You made me work for your attention and when I got it you made sure I continued to work just as hard to keep you. When it came to women it was nothing for me to have a different one for every day of the week. Then you walked into my life and showed me that there was more to life than the fast paced lifestyle I was living. The best part of my day is coming home to you and holding you in my arms. I love you, baby. I want to spend the rest of my life with you as my wife. Mercedes, will you do me the honor by making me the happiest man in the world… will you marry me?"

She stood there with tears running down her cheeks as she stared him in the eyes. She was trying to find her voice. She took deep breath. Tamia was still singing.

"Oh I really like,

What I feel when I'm with you.

You're a dream come true.

Don't you ever leave my side.

Cuz it feels so right.

I really like what you've done to me.

I can't really explain it, I'm so into you."

"Yes, I will marry you!" She answered excitedly.

Cree placed the ring on her finger then stood to his feet. He pulled her closer to him by the waist and kissed her passionately.

"Now that's black love at its finest." Someone walking pass said.

Mercedes giggled when she pulled her lips away from his. "I'm so happy baby."

"That means I did something right. I want to continue seeing a smile on your face." He then turned to the three artists.

"Thank you for doing this for me." They smiled and shook his hand. After they congratulated them they left.

"So, what's next? Should we go home and celebrate?" Mercedes asked.

Cree shook his head. "No let's go to one of the clubs and celebrate."

"Okay." She let him led her back to their car. She couldn't stop herself from smiling even if she wanted to. She couldn't wait to call Jasmine and Zaniela and tell them about her engagement.

Chapter 20

Cree and Mercedes pulled up in front of Club Ambitious forty minutes later. He turned the car off and got out. She watched him walk around to her side and stood by the passenger door. She glanced up at him to see what he was doing. He had his phone out and typed on it for a few seconds. When he put the phone away he opened her door and helped her out of the car.

"Who was that?" She asked him.

"Who was who?" He played dumb.

She placed her hands on her hip and stared him down. "Who were you texting?"

Cree smirked. "Damn you nosey as hell. That was Cortez, I was texting. He didn't want shit though."

"Oh okay. I want to announce our engagement to everyone together. We should call them over to your mom's house tomorrow and share the news." She said hyped up.

"Yeah that sounds like a good plan baby. Now let's go celebrate your birthday and our engagement together."

"Okay." She smiled as he took her hand in his.

They walked to the doors of the club and nodded to the security guard that was at the door. Before he opened the door Mercedes noticed that it was a little too quiet inside tonight.

"It must be a slow night tonight." She thought to herself.

The security guard opened the doors for them and as soon as she stepped foot inside the music changed to Stevie Wonder's happy birthday song. Everyone started singing along to the song. Mercedes was so surprised and shocked that happy tears started sliding down her cheeks. She wiped them away and looked over at Cree, who was grinning at her.

"You're going to pay for making me cry all damn night." She said loud enough for him to hear her over the music.

"I just know damn well the thug ain't crying?" Cortez said walking over to them.

Mercedes smirk. "I told you before that I'm a thug, but I get one day to cry every few months." She joked.

He laughed and then gave her a hug. "Happy birthday, Cedes."

"Thanks Cortez."

She looked around and noticed all her friends and family were in attendance.

"Ahhhhhhhhhh, it's my friend's birthday bitches!" Zanni yelled running over to her and giving her a hug.

"You lied to me heifer!" She said playfully pushing her off of her.

"Ooh, don't be like that." Zanni laughed.

"Happy birthday, bestie!" Jassy yelled as she gave her a hug too.

"Both of you heifers were about to be fired. I had plans to start the interviewing process for new friends and everything." She told them.

"Girl, please! You can't replace us. How many times do we have to tell you that?" Jassy asked with a roll of her eyes.

"Right! If you want a new friend, bitch you better get a pet." Zanni snapped.

"Whatever!" They all stared each other down before breaking out into a loud laugh.

"Oh shit! Who let these three get together?" Cordell asked with a smirk. He walked up to Cedes and gave her a kiss on the cheek and a hug.

He then looked over at Zanni and smiled. "What's up, Zaniela?"

"Are you still running around here being a hoe?" She asked him causing Jassy and Cedes to laugh.

"You ready for me to settle down?" He asked in return.

She rolled her eyes. "I take that as a no. In that case, ain't shit up."

Cordell laughed and walked away. "You and Cordell need to quit playing and fuck already." Cedes said.

"Nope. I'm waiting on him to change his nasty ways. I want him to want to do it on his own because he wants me. I don't want to get involved with him and he's still being a hoe."

"Where did you get that he was a hoe from anyway?" Jassy asked.

"Yeah, I want to know too because I never really heard anything about Cordell being a hoe until you started calling him that a few years ago." Cedes said.

"Remember that Christmas Eve party Cheryl threw that year and everybody got fucked up?"

"Yeah." They both replied.

"Well, I had gone in one of the rooms to lie down because my damn head was spinning. I didn't know the room I was in was Cordell's old room. That nigga came in there and laid out on the bed next to me. Next thing I knew we were making out. Now, I was drunk, but I won't ever forget the way his lips felt on mines. Anyway, kissing was as far as we took it that night. The next day when I got up and walked into the bathroom, there he was sitting on the toilet with a bitch on her knees between his legs giving him head. He a hoe. He was just kissing me and telling me how he always wanted me a few hours before he's getting head on the toilet and shit. Fuck him."

"Damn why you never told us about this?" Cedes asked.

"I guess I was too embarrassed. I fell for his bullshit. I'm so glad I didn't sleep with him. Cheryl would have hated me."

"Why?" They asked at the same time again.

"Because I would have killed her damn son. Don't play with my heart and think shit going to be okay." Zanni said seriously.

They all laughed and went on to enjoy Mercedes birthday with her. It wasn't until they were all seated at the table after the women had come from the dance floor that Jasmine noticed the ring on her finger.

"Oh my goodness! What is that?" She reached over and grabbed Mercedes left hand and looked closely at the ring. Zaniela was on the other side of Mercedes. She leaned over to get a look at her ring.

Mercedes looked at Cree then back to her friends when he nodded his head. "Well, I got engaged tonight." She said excitedly.

"Ahhhhhhhhhh!" They wrapped their arms around her for a group hug. She went on to tell them all about her romantic night with her man and how he proposed. When she was done everyone congratulated them.

Jasmine looked over at Kasim and smiled. She pulled her phone out and started texting him.

Jassy: I know the plan was to break the news about the baby tonight, but I think we should wait.

Kasim: I agree. This is Cree and Cedes moment. We should let them have that.

Jassy: Yes. I love you.

Kasim: I love you and our baby more.

She glanced over at him and grinned. She never thought she would luck up and find a man like Kasim. He was so demanding, but understanding at the same time. When he tells her that he loves her not only can she see it in his eyes, she could feel it in her soul. The saying must be true when people say that there's someone out there for everyone.

Jasmine, Mercedes, Zaniela, Kasey, and Cheryl were all sitting around in Cheryl's living room planning Mercedes and Cree's engagement party. Kasey was out on another day pass and excited to be included in the planning.

"Where are you thinking about having it at?" Cheryl asked as she flipped through different magazines.

"I was thinking we have it at Play Time during the day. Decorate it really nice with the colors I'm going to choose." Mercedes replied.

"That sounds like a good idea."

"Where are the guys?" Kasey asked.

"They went to play basketball, but they should be back soon." Jasmine answered.

"Oh okay. So, Cedes are you excited to be getting married?"

"Yessss. I can't believe that I'm about to marry the love of my life. The only thing I hate is the stupid argument we keep having." She frowned.

"What does it be about?" Jasmine asked her.

"The same thing it's always about... having kids."

"Well, once you get married you're going to give him some babies, right?" Zaniela asked.

"I told him that once we get married and have been married for about a year I will give him a baby. I want to get used to being a wife first."

No one said anything they just continued working. The front door opened up, and the guys came walking into the living room.

"Hey baby." Kasim said walking over to Jasmine and giving her a kiss.

"Did you miss daddy?" Cree asked Mercedes before kissing her on the lips.

She giggled. "Boy, you better gone on with that." She blushed.

"Yeah you missed me, but don't worry baby. Daddy missed you too." He chuckled.

"Dang I want a kiss too. Come here Zanni." Cordell said walking towards her.

"Boy, don't play with me. You better go over there and kiss your mama. I don't know where your lips been." She said with an attitude.

He laughed and then leaned in closer to her ear. "I know a place nice and wet where they could be if you stop playing around." He then kissed her ear.

She squeezed her legs tight and glared at him. "Get away from me, Cordell. Cheryl please come and get your son before I hurt him."

"Ohhh, if you want it rough all you had to do was ask." He smirked.

"Ughhh! You make me sick." She rolled her eyes.

"I can make you feel good too." He licked his lips.

"Cordell, leave that damn girl alone! If she cut your ass I don't want to hear shit. You know Zanni keeps a blade on her at all times." Cheryl said with a chuckle.

Zaniela smirked at him then placed her attention back on what she was doing before he started messing with her. Jasmine and Kasim was off in a corner whispering to each other. Mercedes curiously glanced over at them.

"What y'all over there talking about?" She asked causing everyone to stare over at them.

"Nothing." They both said at the same time. That only made her more curious to what they were discussing.

"It didn't look like nothing. Y'all over there smiling and giggling at each other." She said.

"Damn Cedes, you nosey as hell. Cree get your woman." Cortez said laughing at her.

"Shut up little punk before I punch you." She responded.

"There you go with that violent shit again. You and Cree going to be getting married in the jail if you keep it up." He said sitting next to Kasey on the couch.

"Whatever! Anyway, back to you two over there. I want to know what got y'all so happy." She said with her arms folded across her chest.

"Let's just tell them." Kasim whispered to Jasmine.

"I don't know if now the right time." She whispered back.

"What's not the right time?" Mercedes asked now standing next to them.

"Damn Cedes, Cortez is right you nosey as hell." Jasmine joked.

"Girl, please! We're a team, you and me. I need to know what got you all happy. I got years invested in this relationship dammit." She joked.

Jasmine and Kasim started cracking up laughing at her. "Yeah, you right. We have been rocking for a long time now."

"Right! So, you need to tell my nosey ass what's going on."

"Her little midget ass probably pregnant. They worse than you and Cree freaky asses." Cortez joked.

Kasim and Jasmine looked at each other. Mercedes caught on to their facial expressions and started jumping up and down.

"Oh my God! You're pregnant for real?" She asked.

"Yes!" They both answered at the same time.

"Aw my bestie about to have our baby!" Mercedes shouted before wrapping her arms around Jasmine.

"Our?" Kasim asked with a chuckle.

"Yes nigga I said our baby. This is a three way relationship. We share everything, but men." She said as a matter of fact.

Zanni walked over and gave them both a hug. "I'm so happy for my friends. You two heifers got me about to cry, knowing damn well I'm a gangsta and I have a reputation to uphold."

"Girl shut up." Mercedes laughed.

"Damn Kasim, you got her little ass pregnant. You know your baby going to be a little mean muthafucka right?" Cortez chuckled.

Kasey smacked him upside the back of his head. "Do not talk about our niece or nephew like that." She then gave Jasmine and her brother a hug.

"You need to stop hanging with Jass. You're like a miniature version of her and she already short as hell." He said, catching another smack upside the back of his head, this time from his mother.

While everyone was congratulating the couple, no one noticed Cree slip away. He walked out of the living room and headed for the back porch. He sat down on the bench and stared out into space. He was happy for Jasmine and Kasim. He couldn't wait to be an uncle so that he could spoil the baby. That didn't mean he wasn't feeling some type of way about the situation. He really wanted a baby of his own. Someone that's apart of him and Mercedes. To him it seemed as if she didn't feel that way. That's what's fucking him up the most.

"Here." He looked up to find Cordell handing him a shot glass with some brown liquor in it. He looked behind him and saw that Kasim and Cortez had followed him outside with shot glasses of their own. He stood to his feet as they all stood in a circle.

"Congratulations man." He said to Kasim.

"Same to you." Kasim replied back.

Cordell held his drink up. "This is to Cree for finally asking Mercedes to be his wife. It's been a long time coming." He then looked over at Kasim.

"This is also to Kasim to celebrate him getting ready to become a father. We love Jasmine like a sister and we're going to love that baby just as much."

"I'll drink to those two things." Cortez said as they all took the shot to the head.

"Our family is growing." Cree said.

"Yeah it is. All we need to do now is pray that mama gets that heart she needs and makes a full recovery." Cortez said with everyone agreeing with him.

They all chilled on the back porch until Cordell and Cortez went back inside. When Kasim and Cree were alone he asked him about how he really felt about the whole baby situation with Cedes. After he explained everything Kasim gave him a little advice.

"Hide her birth control." He said as if it was that simple.

Cree laughed. "What?"

"When you go home tonight, find her birth control pills and hide those muthafuckas. I think Mercedes real problem with the baby situation is that she's scared. She's afraid of being a mother. I noticed that she's more close to your mother than her own. That could be one reason why she's afraid."

"Damn I never thought about it like that." Cree said.

"That woman loves you and she probably would love to start a family with you. But if she's scared then that could be holding her back." He said.

"I don't know why I didn't think about that. You wild as fuck though. Talking about hiding the birth control." Cree laughed at him.

Kasim laughed too. "Shit I was trying to help you out nigga."

"Now I'm wondering if Jasmine was right about you trapping her."

"Maaaaan, she need to stop saying that shit. She fell in love with the dick and we forgot all about strapping up." They both fell out laughing.

By the time they went back inside Cheryl had finished making dinner. Everyone sat down at the table as one big happy family. If only their lives could stay happy and drama free. That would only be wishful thinking though.

Chapter 21

Kasim and Jasmine had just come from the doctors' office. Everything was going well with the baby. They were both thankful for that. Jasmine was driving him back to his car that was parked at his office. They were a few minutes away when he got a call from his assistant.

"Hello…" He answered the phone, but didn't get the chance to let another word out before being interrupted.

"Mr. Davis, we have a huge problem!" Diana yelled into the phone. He could hear the distress in her voice. He leaned forward in his seat.

"What kind of problem?" He asked, catching Jasmine's attention.

"Someone had slashed the tires on all the trucks. We have three large deliveries that needed to be on the road five minutes ago." She explained.

"What the hell? Did the cameras catch who did it?"

"I honestly haven't checked the cameras. I called you as soon as it was brought to my attention."

"Damn!" Kasim shouted banging his fist on the dashboard."

"Baby, what's wrong?" Jasmine asked, but Diana's next words caught his attention.

"Mr. Davis, the tires weren't the only thing that was destroyed." She said.

"What else was destroyed?" He asked trying to keep calm.

"Your car was vandalized. The windows were busted out, tires slashed, and they spray painted some nasty words on there." She revealed.

"You got to be fucking kidding me?"

"What would you like me to do?"

He sighed. "Go back inside. I'll be pulling up in about two minutes."

"Okay." They disconnected the call and Kasim closed his eyes trying to control his temper.

"Kasim, baby what happened?" Jasmine asked again.

He told her everything that Diana told him. They didn't have to wait long to see for themselves. Jasmine pulled into the parking lot next to where his car was parked. They got out the car and checked the damage.

The thing that really caught Jasmine's attention was the words spray painted on his car. On the hood of the car in bright red paint were the words, **'LYING CHEATING**

BASTARD!!!' On both sides of the car were the words, **'FUCK YOU, BITCH'**. When she looked at the back of the car she saw that they even spray painted the trunk. She had chuckled a little at the words, **'YOUR REAL WOMAN WAS HERE'**.

Kasim stormed into the building heading straight for his office. Jasmine followed behind him.

"Why would someone write that on your car?" She asked with her arms folded across her chest.

He glared at her. "How am I supposed to know? I wasn't here when they did that shit." He snapped.

"Don't snap at me!" She shouted at him.

"Don't ask me stupid ass questions then."

"I'm going to let that shit slide because you pissed off, but don't try me Kasim." She glared at him.

"Jasmine just shut the fuck up!" He yelled. He turned on the screens that showed all the angles the cameras were located at.

"You shut the fuck up." She muttered.

"What?" He turned around facing her.

"I said where the security guard that was supposed to be out there?" She asked.

Kasim thought about it for a moment. "He was supposed to be guarding the building."

"Yeah, you might want to check into that."

"I'm about to check the cameras first."

"Oh yeah and I said you needed to shut the fuck up." She said as if she forgot to mention it the first time.

He glared at her again. "What? You asked what I had said. I'm just letting you know." She shrugged.

"Aye Jasmine, take your ass out there and ask any of the employees if they'd seen anything. You're going to make me fuck you up." He spat.

"Whatever Kasim! I'm only going to do it because I want to help. You ain't running shit, but your mouth."

"I'm about to put something long and hard in your mouth." He mumbled.

"What you say?" She asked halfway out the door.

"I said, thanks baby I love you." He replied.

"Yeah that's what you better had said." She said walking out the door.

Kasim shook his head and placed his attention back on the screens. He had rewind the tapes to around the time he had left out with Jasmine to go to the doctors' office. Only a few minutes had passed before he saw someone sneaking around his property. He was disappointed when they didn't show their face while slashing his trucks' tires. He was about to throw the remote when he saw the person head over to his car. He watched quietly as they busted out each of his windows. When they started spraying the words on his car, the person face showed up clearly on the screen.

"What the fuck?" He mumbled angrily.

He turned the screens off and grabbed his phone. He made some phone calls to get the tires changed so that the deliveries get to their destinations. When he finished he headed out of the door.

"Baby, no one saw shit. The guard that was supposed to be working had received a phone call that his wife was in a car accident. He said when he got to the hospital his wife wasn't there. He went home to look for her and when he got there she was there chilling. Her phone had been stolen earlier in the day and that's why she wasn't responding to his calls." Jasmine explained to him as they walked to the car.

"Damn so they went all out just to destroy my shit." He stated more to himself than her.

"So what did the cameras sh…" She was interrupted by the sound of her phone ringing. She pulled it out of her pocket and looked at the screen. It was her and Cedes' assistant Stacy.

"What's up, Stacy?" She answered.

"I couldn't get in touch with Ms. Taylor. I know you were busy at your doctors' appointment and I didn't want to interrupt, but this is very important." She got out all in one breath.

"Okay, slow down and tell me what's going on."

"Someone set club Play Time on fire." She stated.

"What?!" Jasmine yelled through the phone.

"Whoever it was started the fire from inside of the club. One in the men's restroom and another one near the back of the club."

"I can't believe this shit. I'm on my way, but keep trying to get in touch with Mercedes."

"Okay, I'm on it."

"Thanks Stacy." She hung up the phone. She felt like crying. They worked their asses off to get where they are today and someone was trying to destroy all of that.

"What happened baby?" Kasim asked walking up to her.

She explained to him everything that happened and he became enraged. "Give me your car keys. I'm going to drive you to the club so that you can see for yourself what's going on. Then I need to take care of a few things concerning my business." He said.

Jasmine handed him her keys and got in the car on the passenger side. They drove in complete silence. That was the only way they were able to control the rage that was building up inside of them.

Mercedes walked over to Jasmine when she and Kasim pulled up to the club. It felt like déjà vu all over again. All emotions were removed from their faces as they stared at each other for a minute before speaking.

"Somebody is really trying to force us to shut down." Mercedes said.

"Yes, but the question is which club they're trying to really shut down?" Jasmine looked at what was left of the club. It was burned badly on one side, but it looked like they could have it remodeled and back up and running within a few months.

"What do you want to do?" Mercedes asked.

"This time we should keep it closed until the person who did it is found and brought to justice."

"I agree."

They looked over at Cree and Kasim talking in a whisper. Jasmine turned back to Mercedes and told her what happened with Kasim's business.

"Damn, who did it?" She asked while shaking her head.

"I don't know, but what they wrote on the car got me giving his ass the side eye."

"Girl, please! You can't really believe he was creeping on you?"

Jasmine sighed. "I don't want to believe it."

"Then you shouldn't. When he ain't working, he with you or his sister. That nigga ain't got any time to cheat even if he wanted to."

"You right."

"I know. I think we should let the employees from the secret club know that we're shutting down until farther notice." She said staring at the burnt building.

"That's fine with me." Jasmine replied. Her phone started ringing in her pocket. She didn't even check the screen before sliding her finger across and answering the call.

"Hello…"

"So, I heard your nigga going around town creeping on you. I guess that's what you get for thinking the grass was greener on the other side." The caller laughed.

Jasmine looked at her phone and saw that the call was from a private number. She already knew who it was from their annoying voice.

"Davon, how did your stupid ass get my number?" She asked pissed off.

"I have my ways. You know you might as well come on back to daddy. Even though you've been acting up, I'm willing to forgive you."

"What?" She frowned.

"I heard he got a bitch pregnant too. So, you willing to pass up a good thing with me, but stay with a nigga that's about to have a baby on you?" He asked sounding disgusted.

Jasmine laughed. "I know all about the baby he's about to have."

"You know he's cheating on you and about to have a baby? Damn, I didn't know you were that damn stupid Jasmine."

"Not as stupid as you though. I am the chick he's having a baby with. Not that it's any of your damn business. Speaking of business why are you all in my dude's business? Does he inspire you to be a real man?"

Davon didn't hear shit she said after the part about pregnant with Kasim's baby. "You about to have that nigga baby?" He asked angrily.

"Bye Davon! Stop calling my phone before I have my nigga beat your ass again." She hung the phone up in his face.

Mercedes shook her head. "That nigga asking for more than just an ass whooping."

"Right! Let's get this shit in order so that we can go home. I'm hungry."

"Your pregnant ass always hungry. It feels funny saying that, but I can't wait until the baby come."

Jasmine rolled her eyes. "All I know is, you better hurry up and have the wedding. I'm not going if I'm big as a damn house."

"Stop lying. If you big as a damn whale you're going to walk your ass down the aisle as my maid of honor." Mercedes smiled.

"Naw, I feel like I should be the one to walk you down the aisle. Shit I raised you to be the woman you are today." She joked.

"I'm done talking to your ass for the day." Mercedes said walking away.

Jasmine followed closely behind her. "Soooo, is that a yes or a no?" She laughed.

They walked over to where the guys stood discussing what they assumed were business. No matter what they go through Jasmine and Mercedes always seem to overcome any obstacle. The club burning down was just a minor setback in their eyes. They hoped the world would be ready when they make their comeback, because when they do, they're coming back hundred times harder than before.

Chapter 22

"This is the house right here." Spud said pointing out the window from the back seat of Kasim's car.

"So, how you want to do this?" Cree asked from the passenger seat.

Kasim leaned on the door and stared at the house. He could see the lights on in what he assumed were the living room and upstairs bedroom. "We're going to wait until he come outside and then snatch him." He replied.

Cree nodded while rubbing his chin. They sat in the car staring at the house for an hour before the door came open. "There that nigga go right there." Spud said sitting up.

"Wait until he starts walking, and then Spud I want you to follow him. Cree and I will pull up after you get at him and snatch his ass up." Kasim said, watching as his prey started making his way down the street. The night was a good cover for what they had planned.

Spud got out the car and crossed the street. He started following the dude at a safe distance until they hit the corner. He jogged up behind the dude while pulling his gun out the back of his waist. Before the dude knew what happened he was knocked over the back of the head. He was unconscious before he hit the ground.

Kasim pulled up at the corner and got out the car. He helped Spud pick the dude up and threw him in the trunk. They were back in the car and pulling off before anyone saw them. Once they hit the highway no one said a word. It took them an hour to get to where they were going. Kasim pulled up to some train tracks. There was no one in sight for miles.

All three got out of the car then walked to the trunk. They looked at each other before opening it up. The dude was still knocked out cold. Kasim grabbed the rope that was next to him and tied his feet together with it. Cree then helped him pulled the dude out the trunk and dragged him over to the train tracks.

"Spud, you want to do the honors of waking this nigga up?" Cree asked.

Spud walked over to the dude and stood over his head. Kasim and Cree turned their heads as he unzipped his pants and pulled his dick out. He started pissing all over the dude's face. The dude woke up coughing and spitting. Spud stepped back and zipped his pants up.

"He's up." He said folding his arms across his chest.

Cree and Kasim turned their heads and glared at the dude. "What the fuck is going on?" He asked looking around at the three of them.

"Davon, you had been a busy nigga. I always knew you had bitch tendencies, but to vandalize my car? That was some fuck boy shit." Kasim sneered.

"I never liked you, but I at least thought you had enough sense not to fuck with my family." Cree spat.

"I... I... I never fucked with your family." Davon stuttered.

"When you call and harass Jasmine, that's fucking with my family. When you bust out my boy's car windows and fuck with his business, that's fucking with my family. You of all people should know I don't take too kindly to that shit." Cree kicked him in the face with his timberland boot.

Davon's lips and nose busted on impact. He held his hands to his face to try to stop the bleeding, but it was no use. The blood was pouring out at rapid speed.

"When I knocked you the fuck out, I thought you would know to leave what's mines alone." Kasim said stepping closer to him.

"I didn't fuck with your business." He lied.

Spud took his gun and hit him in the back of the head. This time it didn't knock him out. "Stop lying!"

"I saw your dumb ass on the cameras I have set up on my property. I didn't tell Jasmine it was you yet because I didn't want her to stop what I have planned for you."

Davon looked around at his surroundings and finally realized where he was at. He looked up at Kasim, who was now sporting an evil grin. He swallowed hard and ignored the pain that shot through his mouth.

"Wh… wha… what are yo… you going to do… do… do to me?" He asked barely getting it out.

Kasim smirked. "I'm going to kill you." He answered nonchalantly.

"Help! Somebody please help me! Help me please!" He screamed out. Tears started to pour out of his eyes.

"There ain't any point in doing all that yelling man. No one can hear you way out here." Cree said pulling a blunt out the back of his pocket and lighting it.

"Damn nigga let me hit that." Spud said as he walked over towards Cree.

Cree took three hits then passed it to him. They stood back and watched Kasim walk back and forth from the car. When he came back over to where they stood he had a jug in his hands.

"What the hell is that?" Spud asked hitting the blunt then passing it back to Cree.

"Acid." He replied, and then headed over to Davon, who was crying so hard he had snot running down his face.

"No… no… no… please I'll do anything man! Please man, I got two kids to take care." He cried.

"Two kids?" They all said at the same time.

"Nigga since when do you have any kids?" Cree asked mean mugging him.

Davon started hiccupping. "I have a two and one year old at home." He said.

"That nigga stay fucking lying!" Spud spat.

"I'm not I swear I'm not. You can call my baby mama Lisa and ask her."

"This fool must think we're stupid or something." Cree said shaking his head.

"I'm not lying. I didn't tell Jasmine about my first son because she made it clear that she didn't date dudes with his. My second son came while we were together." He admitted.

"So, you cheated on my sister?" Cree asked taking a step towards him.

He put his head down and nodded. Kasim started laughing. "So, let me get this shit straight. You lied about having a kid, cheated on Jasmine, and had another baby on her, and you running around pulling stupid shit to try to get her back?" There was a short pause.

"You the dumbest nigga I have ever met." He stated.

"Man, let's do this so I can get home to my woman." Cree said finishing off the blunt.

"Wait... wait... wait... please don't do this, please!" Davon screamed as Kasim walked over towards him with the jug in his hand.

"See you in hell!" Kasim yelled before pouring the liquid all over him.

"Noooooo!" Davon screamed. He was so scared to die that he pissed and shitted on himself.

Cree, Spud, and Kasim all stood there laughing at him. "This nigga doing all that over some water being poured on him." Kasim laughed even harder.

Davon looked over at them and then down at his body. The only pain he felt was from his face and the back of his head.

"This is just a warning. Next time it really will be acid. Stay the fuck away from my woman and my business." Kasim spat before walking to the car and getting in.

"If I was you, I would take heed to his warning." Cree said as he and Spud walked to the car and got in.

Davon watched as the car sped off leaving him in an unknown place. He didn't complain though. He was just happy to still be alive. He vowed to never contact Jasmine ever again. If he saw her in public he would run the other way. That was the last time they ever had any problems out of him.

Kasim walked inside of his house exhausted. He threw his keys on the table as he walked passed. He headed straight for his bedroom. When he entered the room he smiled at what he saw. Jasmine was laid out across the bed in a pair of booty shorts and sports bra. She was knocked out with her face in a frown. He chuckled as he stripped down completely naked. He went to the bathroom to take a quick shower. When he came back out he had a towel wrapped around his waist.

He stood there for a moment and just stared at Jasmine. She was beautiful, and he was blessed to call her his woman. He knew when he first laid eyes on her at the gym that she was the one. He didn't know how, but he just knew. If he had to he would move heaven and earth for her and their child. He removed his towel and walked towards the bed. He slid her legs to the edge of the bed towards him. When he reached the top of her booty shorts to pull them off, he felt her lift her ass to help him out. He chuckled at her freaky ass trying to play sleep. He continued to pull her shorts and panties down at the same time. Once he removed them, he threw them across the room.

"I know your ass not sleep. Open those legs so I can taste my pussy." He demanded.

Jasmine spread her legs eagle style giving him a perfect few of the pussy. She still kept her eyes closed. Kasim got down on the floor on his knees. He hungrily licked his lips before swiping his tongue across her pussy lips. He used his tongue to spread the lips. Before Jasmine knew what hit her he was attacking her pussy with his tongue.

"Oooooooh." She moaned loudly. She squeezed her eyelids tightly.

"Hmmm huh." Kasim mumbled as he twirled his tongue around her pearl. She tried to close her legs, but he stopped her by gripping them tight.

"I'm about to cum!" She yelled out.

When she arched her back, Kasim knew she was about to explode. He still didn't let up his assault on her pussy. About five more strokes of the tongue and her entire body was shaking.

Kasim pulled away licking around his mouth. "Damn that was good." He grinned before standing to his feet.

Jasmine was trying to control her breathing. "I bet your ass awake now, huh?" He chuckled.

"Shut up!" She giggled.

"Okay." He replied before grabbing her legs and wrapping them around his waist.

"Hold on baby wait!" She tried to stop him, but it fell on deaf ears.

Kasim slid all the way inside her with one thrust. He closed his eyes as he pumped in and out of her. Her pussy felt so tight and warm around his dick he thought he was going to explode within a minute flat. He tried hard to fight the urge to cum, but when Jasmin tighten her pussy muscles and threw the pussy back at him he lost the battle.

"Shiiiiiiiit!" He grunted as he empty his seeds in her. If she wasn't already pregnant he knew after that she would've been.

"You just don't know how bad I needed that." He said leaning forward and kissing her softly on the lips.

"Yes, I do. I'm your woman so I know when my man needs a good release. Now help me up so that we can shower and then go to bed." She raised her arms up.

Kasim helped her up off the bed and removed her sports bra. He kissed her again before they walked into the bathroom. Kasim knew he had to tell her about what Davon did. If he didn't he knew her mind would be filled with questions on whether it was a woman he was creeping with that vandalized his car. He figured that he would tell her tomorrow after they both got some much needed rest.

After a quick shower they both climbed in bed completely naked. She buried her face in his chest and he wrapped his arms around her. It didn't take long for them both to fall asleep in each other's arms. Unbeknownst to them, they both shared the same dream. A dream of what they would be like as a family. Some dreams are known to come true.

Chapter 23

Two months had gone by without any trouble. Everyone was happy for that. Mercedes and the rest of the women were almost finished planning her and Cree's engagement party. She got excited every time they discussed it. Lately though, Cree had been really getting on her last nerves. If she asked him a simple question he would get an attitude. She didn't know what his problem was now. They talked about the baby situation and she thought they had an understanding now. So, now she was confused to what brought on his new attitude.

"Cree!" She called out to him as she stomped out of their master bathroom. She didn't see him in the bedroom so she walked out the room and down the stairs.

"Cree, I know you hear me calling you!" She yelled out again. She looked in the living room, kitchen, and the den. He wasn't in either of those rooms. She back tracked her steps and headed straight for his man cave. Without knocking, she opened the door and walked down the stairs.

Cree was sitting on the couch with his eyes closed as he puffed on a blunt. He nodded his head to the sounds on Tupac playing on the stereo.

She rolled her eyes and walked over to the radio and turned it off. She then stood in front of him with her arms folded across her chest. When he opened his eyes the first thing he saw was her glaring down at him.

"What you come down here bothering me for?" He asked taking another pull from his blunt.

"I had been calling your name for at least five minutes straight." She replied with an attitude.

Cree sat up on the couch and looked up at her. "If you came down here to argue, I'm not in the mood. Take your fucked up attitude somewhere else because I'm not trying to deal with it right now."

Mercedes took a little step back and stared at him. "Who the hell are you talking to like that?"

Cree looked around the room. He then lifted up pillows off the couch and looked under them. He moved her to the side and looked behind her. When he looked back up at her, he sighed. "I don't see anyone else up in this muthafucka, but me and you." He then pointed to his chest.

"I know that I'm not talking to myself. So that leaves your little mean looking ass."

"You know what?" She tried to calm herself down.

"Naw, I don't know anything." He responded then finished off his blunt.

"I'm not even about to arguing with you. I came down here to ask you if you had seen my birth control pills. They're usually in the medicine cabinet, but I don't see them."

"Maybe you misplaced them somewhere else. I haven't seen them." He said with a shrug.

She stared him in the eyes and knew that he was lying. "I don't believe I misplaced them. I always put them in the same spot and now they're not there." She looked around them.

"It's only you and me up in this muthafucka. I know I didn't touch them. That only leaves your big mean looking ass." She said using some of his words against him.

Cree chuckled. "I don't know where they at. Now can you turn my music back on?"

"You get on my damn nerves, Cree. I know you took my damn pills. Ole big head ass nigga. Let me find out you got them, we're going to square up." She mushed him in the forehead and then walked back up the stairs.

"Mercedes, you better quit playing with your punk ass." He smirked.

"Cree, I'll smack the shit out of you in your sleep nigga, don't play with me!" She yelled down the stairs before slamming the door.

Cree started cracking up laughing. He loved the hell out of her little tough acting ass. "I bet you don't find those pills." He had hid the pills in a pair of his old sneakers. He knew she would never look there. Usually he wouldn't have pulled anything like that, but desperate times called for desperate measures.

Jasmine was laughing so hard on the other end of the phone that her chest was starting to hurt.

"That shit is not funny Jassy!" Mercedes snapped. She was in the car on her way to the doctors' office. She was going to get more birth control pills.

"Wait, so you really think he took your birth control pills and hid them?" Jasmine asked again.

"Yes, I know that nigga did. He was just too calm about the situation."

"Damn these niggas are really out here trapping chicks. We're dealing with some damn trap kings, Cedes." She laughed again at her joke.

"That's a damn shame girl. Cree going to make me whoop his ass while he sleep." Mercedes said turning onto the clinic's parking lot.

"Why are you going to wait until he's sleep?" Jasmine asked with a chuckle.

"Girl, you see how big that nigga is? I'm not crazy enough to take his big tall ass on while he's awake. Then I'll have to shoot my baby and I don't want to do that because I love him." She smiled.

"Y'all some crazy ass people."

"I know. Let me call you back later when I get home." She said grabbing her phone off the dash board and getting out of the car.

"Okay." They ended the call and Mercedes made her way inside of the clinic.

After she got settled in a room she waited for the doctor to come in. It took her five minutes to walk into the room. Mercedes was just about to go out there and look for her ass. All she needed was another prescription for birth control.

"Here I need you to pee in this cup for me." The doctor handed her the small cup.

"What for? All I need is a prescription." She said staring at her.

"Ms. Taylor, you know I have to check to make sure everything is okay before I give you a prescription of anything."

"Fine." Mercedes got up and went to the bathroom. When she was done she gave the doctor the cup and waited for her to come back with her prescription.

A little while later the doctor came back into the room. "Here is your prescription Ms. Taylor. You can get them filled at any pharmacy." She handed Mercedes the paper.

"Thank you." Mercedes read the paper and looked at her.

"Hold on, I think you made a mistake. This prescription isn't for birth control, it's for parental vitamins." She said trying to hand the doctor the paper back.

The doctor just smiled at her. "That is the correct prescription Ms. Taylor. You're going to be a mommy!" The doctor giggled excitedly.

Mercedes thought about her options. *"If I hit this bitch I'm going to jail. Do I really have time to be sitting down in a dirty cold ass jail cell right now? I mean, I have a lot of shit to do. I still haven't picked out the menu for the engagement party yet. Damn! I can't put my hands on her giddy ass."* She came out of her thoughts putting her attention back on the doctor.

"When I ran the test, and it showed that you were pregnant, I thought about how I was going to share the news with you. Before you go, I need to do an exam to see how far along you are."

Once the doctor finished the exam, Mercedes rushed out of the clinic. After the doctor had told her that she was about four weeks pregnant she knew something wasn't right. She had been taking her pills faithfully until recently when she couldn't find them. She was in a complete daze. She was surprised that she even made it back home safely without getting into an accident.

When she walked in through door she could hear noise coming from the kitchen. She slowly made her way to the kitchen. Cree was in there making dinner. He turned around smiling, but quickly replaced it with a frown when he saw her face.

"Baby, what's wrong?" He asked concerned. He walked up to her and cupped her face.

"What's the matter? Are you hurt?" He asked rubbing over her body to see if she was hurt anywhere.

"No." She said softly.

Cree sighed. He was relieved that she wasn't physically hurt, but something was still wrong with her.

"Please talk to me baby." He begged.

"I went to the doctor to get more birth control." She said in a low voice, but he still heard her.

"Okay and what happened?"

"The doctor said she couldn't give me any more birth control."

"Why?"

"She said that she can't give a pregnant woman birth control pills." She revealed then looked up into his eyes.

Cree didn't say anything for a minute. He just looked her in the eyes as he rubbed her back. "How do you feel about being pregnant?" He finally asked.

"I'm scared." She admitted.

It was the first time she actually said it out loud. For a long time she had been claiming that she just wasn't ready for that yet. The truth was she was scared to be a mother. She and her mother weren't as close as she would like for them to be. Her father was a non-factor in her life. She didn't want to bring a child in the world and screw them up. She spilled all of that to Cree.

"Baby, you're not going to screw our child up. For starters, our baby will know how to be a hustler. I'm not talking about the illegal way either. You have so much ambition that I know it will rub off on our child. I get that this is new territory for us, but if we stick together we can get through this."

"You think so?" She asked.

"I know so. Can we be happy about the fact that we're going to be parents?" He asked.

Mercedes smiled. "Yes."

Cree lifted her up in his arms and swung her around. "We're having a fucking baby!" He shouted before kissing her.

"Yes, we're having a fucking baby!" She shouted before laughing with him.

Cree kissed her again and then returned to cooking dinner for the two of them. He was so happy that he smiled the entire time. Now that he and Mercedes had an understanding, he prayed things go smoothly from that day forth.

Jasmine and Kasim had picked Kasey up from the rehab center about an hour ago. She was finally home for good and everyone was excited. Now that she was on the right track everyone agreed to help her stay that way. Her first night home she decided to spend with her brother and Jasmine. Kasim had prepared dinner for them all to enjoy. As they sat down at the table Kasey offered to say grace. When she was done they dug into the lemon butter chicken, mashed potatoes, French string beans, and buttery dinner rolls that he made.

"This is so good." Kasey said as she took another bite of her chicken.

"Well, you know I'm great at a lot of things. Cooking just happens to be one of them." He bragged.

"He's so conceited." Jasmine laughed.

"Right!" Kasey joined her.

"Y'all just hating because nobody wants to eat y'all burnt food." He joked.

"My food doesn't be burnt." Jasmine resorted.

"Whatever you say to make yourself feel better about it baby."

Kasey placed her fork down and looked at her brother. "What's wrong?" He asked her.

"I have something to tell you."

"Okay, let me hear it." He said placing his fork down. Jasmine kept eating as she looked between the two of them.

"Well... umm... I..." She was stuttering and Kasim tried hard not to laugh.

"Just spit it out Kasey." He encouraged.

"Cortez and I have been going out for a few months now. I was going to tell you, but I was afraid that you would make us stop seeing each other. Cortez wanted to tell you because he didn't like keeping things from anybody. I asked him not to. I'm sorry for keeping it from you, Kasim. I'm not sorry for being with Cortez though. He makes me happy. I'm able to be myself around him without being judged. I really hope you're not mad at me, but if you are I would understand." She spit out in one breath. She put her head down afraid to look over at her brother.

Kasim didn't say anything. He just stared at her with an emotionless facial expression. Jasmine looked over at him and frowned. When he continued to just stare at Kasey, she kicked his leg underneath the table.

"Ouch! What the hell you kick me for?" He asked glaring at her.

She glared back at him. "What the hell you just staring at her for? Say something, fool." She snapped back at him.

"Your nosey ass just wants to see how it all plays out." He smirked.

She chuckled. "I will walk around this table and punch you. Stop staring at her and tell her how you feel."

"Ugh! Y'all females always want to get all emotional and shit."

Jasmine held her fork up like she was thinking about stabbing him. Kasim laughed and shook his head. He then looked over at Kasey, who was pushing the food around on plate with her fork. She still kept her head down.

"Kasey, look at me." When she did he continued.

"I love you, baby girl. I would do anything for you that I know would make you happy. I already knew about the relationship you and Cortez started. I actually noticed it the same day y'all made it official. I pulled Cortez to the side and asked him about you two. He admitted that y'all were exploring a real relationship. He and I had a long talk about it and I gave him my blessing."

"Really?" She smiled at him.

"Yes. I told him if he hurt you that I was going to whoop his ass. He told me that he would rather hurt himself than hurt you. I guess the little nigga okay with me." He chuckled.

Kasey jumped out of her seat and rushed over to him. She wrapped her arms around his neck and gave him a kiss on the cheek. "I love you, Kasim."

"I love you too. Now eat your food before it gets cold."

They heard sniffles coming from across the table. Jasmine was wiping at her eyes. "Baby, I know you not over there crying?" He asked her.

"Nigga you know me better than that. I got some stuff in my eyes, but that was some beautiful shit." She said causing them all to laugh.

"Aww, my pretty little thug over there shedding tears and shit." He teased.

"Kasey can you help me out?" She asked her.

Kasey nodded and smacked Kasim upside the back of the head. "Thank you, K bear." She said calling her the nickname she gave her.

"You're welcome." She smiled and sat back down in her seat.

Kasim glared at them causing them both to laugh. They continued eating their dinner and talking about the future. Kasey had finished her GED a month ago during her day passes. She now had plans to sign up for college classes with Cortez. All of their futures were looking bright at the moment.

Chapter 24

Congratulations Cree and Mercedes were written across the big screen in the back of the room. It showed different pictures of the couple from when they first met to now. The women had done an amazing job putting together the engagement party for them. Club Ambitious looked so elegant that you couldn't tell that it was actually a night club.

Almost everyone in attendance were enjoying themselves. Everyone except Cordell, who was already three drinks in. Mercedes now had second thoughts on making the event an open bar affair.

"What the hell is wrong with your brother?" She leaned over and whispered in Cree's ear.

"Which one?"

"Cordell. He's on his third drink and his facial expression says if you say something to him, he might curse you the hell out." She replied.

Cree looked over at him and smirked. He then looked at her. "Do you really want to know what's bothering him?" He asked with a grin.

"Yes." She said as if that was a dumb question to ask her.

"Over on the dance floor, three feet from where Jasmine and Kasim are dancing. That is the reason he's in a sour mood."

She followed his directions and smiled at what she saw. Her friend Zaniela was on the dance floor laughing and dancing with her date. He was a handsome man, but Mercedes could see that the chemistry was a little off.

"Maybe if he would stop playing games and go after what he wants then he wouldn't be sitting over there looking all miserable." She said to Cree.

"I agree. We're not going to interfere with that though. They need to figure that out on their own."

"What if they never figure it out?" She asked watching Cordell as he watched Zanni like a hawk.

"Then maybe it's not meant for them to be together."

Mercedes didn't agree, but she didn't speak anymore on it. She got up and grabbed Cree's hand. "Dance with me baby." She said leading him to the dance floor.

"What do I get out of it?" He asked.

"I won't tell you, but I can show you when we get home." She flirted.

"Oh shit, you know I love when you surprise me."

"I bet your freaky ass do." She laughed. They hit the dance floor right when the DJ started playing **black love**.

Zaniela got tired and decided to grab a drink with her date Jason. She thought he was a sweet guy. He had been asking her out for a while now. She finally caved in and invited him to the engagement party. Even though they came together, they didn't share a hotel room. As a matter of fact he stayed at a hotel, but Zanni stayed with Cheryl in her guest bedroom. He was cool with that and so was she.

When they got to the bar she told him to order her a drink while she went to the restroom. After using it and freshening up she headed back out. When she walked out the door she was stopped by a hand gripping her arm. She was about to turn around and punch the person in the face for touching her without her permission when she saw that it was Cordell.

"What the hell is your problem?" She asked pissed off.

He didn't answer her question. He pulled her closer to him and crushed her lips into his. She tried to fight it at first, but after a while she had finally given in. The kissed lasted less than a minute. Zaniela pulled away from him. She glared at him before slapping him hard across the face.

"I'm sick and tired of playing this game with you! You should do us both a favor and stay the hell away from me!" She stormed away leaving him to stare at her back.

Zaniela was tired of going back and forth with Cordell. She finally came to the conclusion that he didn't really want her the way that she wanted him. She had to move on and that was exactly what she was going to do. She joined her date at the table they were seated at before they got up to dance. She put on a smile as if nothing happened.

"Can I have everyone's attention please?" Cortez stood up and looked around.

"Oh my goodness! Who gave that nigga the mic?" Someone in the crowd yelled out.

"Shit I asked your gorilla looking mama who gave her ugly ass some nut to produce you. I'm still waiting on my answer." He snapped back. Everyone started laughing.

"Cortez, you better stop." Cheryl mumbled to him trying not to laugh.

"They started it mama. You didn't hear me asking how they mama was able to keep they ugly monkey looking asses in a house and not at the zoo. You don't see too many people walking around the hood carrying a monkey."

"Baby don't pay them any attention. Say what you got to say to your brother." Kasey said smiling.

"You right! They not even worth my attention. They daddy didn't think they was worth his attention either. That's why he's been gone for twenty years to go get some milk. That nigga still haven't come back with that milk for they cereal." People was falling out all over themselves laughing.

"Come on Cortez either pass the mic or say what you gotta say." Cheryl said.

"Okay. I just wanted to congratulate my big brother and his beautiful fiancé. Cree and Mercedes, I'm truly happy for the both of you. I hope that you guys have a fulfilled life together. I appreciate the advice y'all give me when I need it. I'm glad that y'all are finally taking the big step to marriage. I hope this doesn't change anything. I still plan on coming to y'all house and eating up all y'all food. If you change the locks on me, I promise that I will climb through a window and break in y'all shit." They all laughed at the last part.

"I love y'all." He said walking over and giving them both a hug.

He walked back over to his mother to give her the mic. She was just about to reach for it when she heard a beeping noise coming from her purse. She opened it up and searched through it. When she pulled the hospital pager out and saw the red light flashing as the beeping sound got clearer.

"Mama what's that?" Cortez asked confused.

She looked up at him in shock. "It's the hospital pager." She answered.

"What does the beeping sound and red flashing light mean?"

"It means that they found me a heart." She said anxiously.

"Whaaat?" Multiply voices shouted.

"We need to get to the hospital now!" Jasmine yelled out.

"This is really happening." Cheryl said as they all headed for the doors.

"Yeah mama, this is really happening." Cree said looking as if he was on the verge of tears.

Cordell got in the car with them as they all headed to the hospital. The time for her to have heart surgery has finally arrived. Everyone was nervous, anxious, scared, and excited all at the same time.

They had been at the hospital for three hours so far. The doctors had just taken Cheryl in for surgery about an hour ago. The family had waited in the waiting area for any updates on how she was doing. They had prayed three times already. Cree sat with Mercedes on his lap while they watched whatever that was playing on the television screen. Cordell sat next to them stealing glances of Zanni who was off in the corner with Jason. Jasmine was sitting on Kasim's lap nodding off. She jumped up off his lap and stretched.

"Baby, I'm going to go for a walk and get something to drink. Do you want anything?" She asked him.

"No, I'm good." He replied.

"Okay. Do anybody want anything to drink?" She asked everyone else.

"No." They all said at once.

"Okay, I'll be right back then." She walked out of the waiting area. She got on the elevator and made a detour to the nursery. At first she wasn't so sure about having a baby. Now that her baby was growing and moving around inside her, she couldn't wait for him or her to come into the world.

She looked through the glass at all the babies. A smile immediately graced her face. She rubbed her baby bump while staring at the babies. Jasmine stood there for another ten minutes before she decided to head back down to the waiting area. She stopped at a vending machine and grabbed an apple juice.

"Jasmine!" She heard someone call out her name before she could open the door to the waiting area.

She turned around with a shocked expression covering her face. "Kevin? What are you doing here?" She asked.

"I was here with a friend of mine when I saw you walking pass. Is everything okay with you?" He asked seeming concerned.

"Oh yes, I'm fine. I'm here with family because someone close to us is having surgery done."

"Oh okay. I hope they make a full recovery."

"Thank you."

"If you ever…"

"Baby are you okay?" Kasim asked interrupting him.

Jasmine turned around and smiled at him. "Yeah, I'm good babe." She then turned back around to face Kevin.

"I hope whatever reason your friend is here for that they are okay. See you around." She waved at him and then turned to walk inside.

"Or not." Kasim finished off her statement with two words of his own. Jasmine elbowed him as she walked passed. She grabbed his hand and led him back inside.

"I don't like that nigga." He snarled.

"You don't like no damn body." She giggled.

"I like you. As a matter of fact I looooove you." He said wrapping his arms around her waist.

"Your ass better love me. You already trapped me."

He pinched her booty with his left hand. "Keep telling people that shit."

"I plan to." She laughed when he started nibbling on her neck.

"I'm about to go use the restroom. I'll be right back." He said kissing her cheek.

Jasmine turned around and looked at him. "You better not be trying to go do something crazy." She warned him.

"I'm going to be on my best behavior. If you don't believe me you can come and hold it while I piss." He joked. She punched him in the arm before returning to their seat.

Kasim chuckled as he made his way to the restroom. He really did have to take a piss. When he was finished he washed and dried his hands. He pulled his cell phone out his pocket and called Spud, who was also sitting in the waiting area.

"What's up?" Spud answered on the first ring. He got up out his seat and walked out the door.

"Did you see the dude that Jasmine was out there talking to?" Kasim asked into the phone. He looked around to make sure he was still alone.

"Yea I saw him."

"I need you to follow him. I need to know what his every move is. Something doesn't seem right with him."

Spud laughed. "Nigga, we already know what's wrong with him."

"What?" Kasim asked confused.

"He wants your woman. That nigga got the hots for her."

"Just follow that nigga and see what he up to. If it's nothing then I'll let it go. He can want her all he wants as long as he keeps his hands to himself." He said seriously.

"Okay, I got you man."

"Thanks Spud."

"No problem."

Kasim walked back out where everyone was still sitting around waiting for some good news.

Chapter 25

Many hours later the family was finally able to relax. The doctors said that the surgery was a huge success. With a lot of prayers and healing she should be just fine. Everyone crowded in her hospital room and watched her sleep. It wasn't until the next day that she woke up to find her babies all spread around the room knocked out. Kasey was the first to see her. She got up and stood beside the bed.

"How are you feeling?" She asked.

"Painful." She responded with a smile.

"It will get better. I'm happy that your body is responding to the heart well."

"Yeah me too. You all had been here the whole time?" She asked looking at the same clothes they had on at the party.

"Yes. No one wanted to leave until we made sure you were okay."

"Mama, you're finally up." Cortez walked over and kissed her forehead.

"I'm going to be just fine baby." She said already knowing what his next words were going to be.

Soon they all started waking up one by one. She talked a little while before falling back to sleep. When she woke back up everyone was still there, but they were all in different clothes. They had taken turns going home to shower and change clothes. Only person that wasn't in the room was Zanni's date Jason and Spud.

"Now that everyone is here, Mercedes and I have some news." Cree said holding her hand.

All eyes were on them. "We're having a baby!" He shouted. There was so much cheering and shouting that a nurse had to come in and shut the door.

"Dang, so you got trapped too huh?" Jasmine joked.

"Yeah, but you won't believe by who." Mercedes said shaking her head.

"What does that mean?" They all looked at her confused.

"The company that I got my birth control pills from misplaced the wrong pills in the package. Instead of taking birth control I was taking placebos." She explained.

"I'll sue the hell out of them if I was you." Cortez said what everyone else was thinking.

"Oh please believe I am."

Jasmine and Zaniela gave her a group hug. "Now I get to spoil two babies!" Zanni squealed.

"Our babies are going to be best friends just like their mommies." Jasmine said.

"I'm telling y'all now so that y'all can be prepared. I'm going to be their favorite uncle and all around favorite person in the whole world." Cortez said seriously.

Cree and Kasim laughed. Mercedes and Jasmine shook their heads at him. Zaniela glared at him. "I hope when the babies come you will stop lying like that. Their auntie Zanni is going to be their favorite."

"No you're not. I'm going to be the one spoiling them and teaching them stuff. They're going to learn how to be some ambitious hustlers from their uncle Cortez."

"The lies that just keep spilling off your tongue. You should be ashamed of yourself." The entire room erupted in laughter.

"Zanni, shut up! If you try to steal the title as the favorite, I'll call the cops and tell them you be trying to molest my big brother." He said nodding towards Cordell.

"Not even in his dreams will that happen. That ain't even a possibility anymore." She said walking over to Cheryl and kissing her cheek. Mercedes and Jasmine gave each other a worried look.

"I will call to check up on you." She said before walking out the door not saying another word to anyone else.

Everyone turned to glare at Cortez. "What? I was just joking. I didn't know that she would take it serious. Cordell must have done something to her."

"Shut up Cortez!" He snarled at him.

"Cortez, baby come here." Cheryl called out to him.

He walked closer to the bed. She waved for him to lean in closer. When he did she smacked him upside the head. "Sometimes it's best not to say anything." She told him.

He rubbed the back of his head glaring around at everyone who laughed at him. "Forget all of y'all." He glanced over at Kasey and smiled.

"Except you, baby." Kasim rolled his eyes.

They all talked and joked with each other until it got late. Cortez and Kasey decided to spend the night with Cheryl while everyone else went home to get some sleep. Cheryl went off into a peaceful sleep knowing that her family was growing and their bond was getting stronger by the day.

A week went by in a flash. Jasmine and Mercedes had just come from visiting Cheryl. She was doing very well and would soon be able to go home. They decided to head over to check up on the club. When they arrived they found Stacy outside speaking with two detectives. They got out the car and headed over to see what was going on. When they did they received another blow to their business.

"Stacy, what's going on?" Mercedes asked her.

Before she could answer one of the detectives started speaking to them. "Hello Ms. Taylor, Ms. Barber. I'm detective Stevens and this is my partner detective Jacobs. We received word that you are running an illegal business inside of your clubs."

Jasmine and Mercedes glanced at each other before laughing. "I'm sorry we didn't catch the joke. Would you mind letting us in on it?" Detective Jacobs asked.

"The joke is what your partner just stated. We run a good business. We worked our asses off to get to this point. You're standing here telling us that someone told you we're running an illegal business. I know you don't have proof of those claims because if you did you would have a warrant to search our property." Jasmine said staring at them with a stone facial expression.

"You're right we don't have any evidence yet. When we do we'll be back."

"Well, until then we would appreciate it if you didn't step foot on our property." Mercedes said.

The detectives chuckled. "Have a nice day ladies." Detective Stevens said as they walked away to their car. The three women watched as they pulled out of the lot.

"This shit is getting crazier every damn day." Mercedes spat as she stormed inside the club.

Jasmine and Stacy followed behind her with the same thoughts. "Somebody is feeding information to the police. Whoever it is has to be an inside person. I think it's someone that knows what's really going on." Jasmine stated as they sat down at the bar.

"I agree. The police don't make any moves unless they got a feeling that the person is telling the truth." Mercedes said grabbing a bottle of water.

"Yeah, you're right. So, what are we going to do?"

Mercedes thought on it for a minute before speaking. "I'll call Cree and see if he can get any information on who could be talking to the police about our business."

"Okay, let me know what he says. I'm about to go to my office and see if I can get some work done." Jasmine said getting up of the stool she was occupying.

"Is there anything that you need me to do?" Stacy asked her.

Jasmine nodded. "Yes, you can help me with a few things."

"Okay." She followed her to her office.

Mercedes took a few sips of her water before picking her phone up and calling Cree.

"Is everything good baby?" He asked as soon as he picked up the phone.

"No babe. The police was just here. I need you to come down to the club so we can talk. I don't want to talk over the phone." She replied.

"I'm on my way. I should be there no more than thirty minutes."

"Okay, I'll be waiting." She ended their call and took another sip of her water.

"Damn I wish I could have a drink." She mumbled eyeing the alcohol that was behind her.

Cree arrived ten minutes sooner than he stated. He turned the music on just in case someone was listening in on their conversation. Mercedes explained to him everything the detectives said when she and Jasmine had arrived. They thought about who could be spilling their business. Two names came to mind. Cree told her not to worry about anything and he would take care of it. He kissed her on the lips and headed out the door.

Cree waited until night hit before he and one of his best men from his security team arrived at the first suspect's house. They crept up to the side of the house. There was a door there that led to the kitchen. They knew this from the blueprint they had of the house. Cree picked the lock and granted them entrance inside. The place was quiet, but they knew the person they were looking for was inside. They saw him come in an hour ago. He never left back out.

"You check down here and I'm going to check upstairs." Cree instructed as he made his way to the stairs. He didn't wait for a reply. He wanted to find the dude, do what he came to do, and get home to his baby.

He looked in all the rooms upstairs and didn't see him anywhere. He went back down stairs and followed the sounds of two voices. They were coming from the basement. He walked down the stairs and saw his security guy holding Mike up be the collar of his shirt.

When Mike saw Cree his eyes got big. "Man, what is this about?" He asked him nervously.

"This is about you trying to first fuck up my woman's business. You've been talking to the police Mike?" Cree asked walking towards him.

"Wh… what? I haven't been talking to anyone! I swear I haven't. After they fired me, I went and got a job as a porn star. I make a little less than what I'm used to, but it's a nice gig." He said.

Cree stared him in the eyes. He felt like he was telling the truth. He still left him with some parting words.

"If I find out that you're lying to me, not even the police would be able to help you from my wrath." He watched as Mike was pushed back on his ass. They left out the same way they came in.

After they got in the car the guy looked over at Cree. "What now?" He asked.

Cree started the car and pulled off. "We have one more person to question." Nothing else was said as they made their way to their next destination.

It took them thirty minutes to get there, but they wasted no time finding a way inside the house. All the lights were off except one coming from an upstairs bedroom. They quietly crept up the stairs as noises of the bed squeaking got louder and louder. They stood on either side of the door. Cree put his finger to his lips signaling for silence.

"Ooooh yessss! Yesss John, fuck me harder!" They heard a woman scream out.

Cree smirked as he twisted the door knob and gently push the door open. They stood and watched as John lay between a woman's legs while fucking the shit out of her.

"I'm cumming baby!" He grunted.

"John, baby I'm about to cum again! Fuck me harder! Ooh... Oooh... Oooooh! Yesssssss!" The woman shouted out.

"Shit that was good, Kelsey." John barely got out. He was trying to catch his breath.

"I'm glad we worked everything out baby. The sex is amazing now." She said kissing him.

John rolled off of her on to his back. That's when he noticed that they weren't alone. "What the hell?" He asked pulling the sheet over his wife.

"Hey there Johnny boy." Cree said walking farther into the bedroom.

"Who are you? What are you doing in my house?" He asked sitting up in the bed.

Kelsey stared at Cree. She had saw him around the clubs a few times. She was afraid to speak thinking he was there to hurt them.

"John, I got word that you were talking to the police about the club you heard your wife was visiting." Cree said trying to see if he would catch him in a lie or not.

"What?" Kelsey looked over at her husband.

"Please tell me you didn't John? Those are not the kind of people you want to cross." She stated on the verge of tears.

"I didn't do anything!" He shouted.

"I don't like liars John." Cree said taking another step closer to the bed.

"I'm not lying. Yes, I was pissed about my wife cheating on me. Yes, I got drunk one night and went to the club to confront those two women. I swear to you though, I didn't go to the police about any of the things I was told. I actually took those ladies' advice. My wife and I are working on our marriage. Things are going well for us. I swear I'm telling you the truth. If someone is talking to the cops, it's not me." He admitted.

Cree glared at him. He felt that John was being honest with him. He still left him with the same message as Mike. After they left out the house they got back in the car not saying a word. He was out of ideas on who could be snitching to the police. Mike and John were the only two that would've had motives to destroy Mercedes and Jasmine's businesses. He would've added Davon to the list, but he figured after what Kasim had done to him, he wouldn't dare try anything else stupid. Not to mention the fact that he didn't know anything about the secret club.

He dropped the guy that rode with him off at home before heading home himself. As he pulled up in his driveway, he wondered if there was anyone that he could be overlooking. When no one came to mind, he knew that Mercedes and Jasmine were going to have to go through not only their staff list, but their clients as well. He sighed as he made his way inside the house. He didn't like the thought of an unknown snake slithering around in their backyard. They needed to find the culprit before the police got the evidence they needed to indict Jasmine and Mercedes.

Chapter 26

Another month gone by and no word on who was talking to the police. Jasmine and Mercedes were glad that they stopped all activity with the secret club until farther notice. On the bright side of things Cortez and Kasey were doing well with their classes. They both decided on a business major. Union County College was their school of choice. So far, they didn't have any complaints. Cheryl expressed to them every other day how proud of them she was. The rest of the family was still shocked that they were actually going forward with furthering their education. They were also very proud of them.

Cortez stood beside his car as he waited for Kasey to come out of the building from her Business Management class. He had just walked out of his Speech class three minutes prior. He scrolled through his facebook page on his phone. Since his eyes were focused on his phone he didn't see when she approached him.

"Hey Cortez, I missed you boo." She said wrapping her arms around his neck.

He looked up and frowned. He pushed her up off of him. "Gone somewhere with that bullshit." He snapped.

She placed her hands on her wide hips. "Why are you acting like that towards me?"

"Kim, since when have I ever let you hug all up on me?" Kim was one of the old flames that he used to mess with on and off. The day Jasmine took him to visit Kasey for the first time he erased all their numbers out of his phone. That was the day he set eyes on his future and her name was Kasey.

"You didn't used to complain when you were fucking me." She said with an attitude.

"Key word, were. It's been a minute since I saw you. I'm chilling with my lady now. I don't be tripping off none of you chicks no more." He said calmly. He could see the anger building up in her eyes.

"Hey babe, what's going on?" Kasey asked walking up to him.

Cortez grinned. He wrapped his arms around her waist and kissed her lips. "How was class baby?" He asked ignoring the hole Kim was burning through the side of his head with her eyes.

"It was okay. I might need your help with some of the homework." She glanced over at Kim, who was still standing there.

"Babe, who is that?" She nodded in her direction.

"Bitch, don't worry about who I am!" Kim snapped at her.

Kasey was about to step to her, but Cortez pushed her back. He then got up in Kim's face. "You know I don't hit females, but call her a bitch again and I'm going to let her whoop your ass." He stepped back over by Kasey.

"She's not going to touch me."

"Kim, what's going on?" One of her friends asked. A group of four girls walked over to where they stood.

"Girl nothing. Cortez is over here acting funny because his new flavor of the week is right there." Kim and her friends laughed.

Cortez turned to Kasey and kissed her so deeply that she almost forgot that they were standing in front of a group of people. He then walked her over to the passenger side door and opened it.

Before Kasey could get into the car she heard someone yell out, "Oh I think I seen her before. She used to be with Stephanie crackhead ass. You know she used to be on that shit just like her too." They all laughed.

"Damn Cortez, you messing with dope fiends now?" Kim laughed.

Kasey glanced over at him then put her head down. She got in the car and closed the door without saying a word. Cortez got pissed. He knew that she was embarrassed from the harsh words, but she shouldn't be. She's not the person she was in her past. He wasn't about to let her shut down because some chicks was jealous of what she got.

He walked over to the group of girls while Kasey watched from the car. She was curious to see what he was about to do. She hoped that he didn't touch any of them because she didn't want him to get locked up over chicks being petty. "Let me tell you basic bitches something. While you're worried about who the fuck she is, you should be worried about finding out who your baby daddies are. Worry about why your ass got an eviction notice taped to your front door, but your rent only twelve dollars a month. You worried about my girl because you can't have her nigga. You should be worried about why the fuck niggas don't have any respect y'all because y'all don't have any respect for yourselves. At the end of the day, don't worry about what the fuck my girl did or doing. Just know that whatever it is she's doing, she's shitting on you basic, tired, loose pussy bitches!" He spat and then jumped in the driver seat. He pulled off leaving them all standing there with their mouths gaped open in shock.

They rode in silence for ten minutes before Cortez spoke. "You better not let a word those chicks said get to you. You've come a long way from the person you used to be. I'm proud of you, ma." He said looking between her and the road.

"A lot of people are going to say things like that to you about me." She mumbled.

"They going to get their asses beat too. You think I care about what another muthafucka got to say about you? You my woman, so anything an outsider has to say don't mean shit to me."

"I don't want you to start feeling like people coming at you sideways because of me. My past is probably going to be brought up a lot."

He sighed. "I don't care about that Kasey. I love you for the person you are right now. You're a fighter. I better not hear about you taking any shit from no one. If you got a problem let me know and we will figure out how to handle it." He didn't want her to have a relapse because of messy ass people.

"Yo… you lo… love me?" She asked looking over at him.

Cortez smirked. "Yeah, I love you, Kasey. You my baby."

Kasey blushed. She got a warm feeling in her chest at his words. "I love you too, Cortez."

He grabbed her hand and held it all the way until they arrived at his mom's house. They walked in the house and headed straight for the den. They wasted no time starting on their homework. Throughout the two hours they were working they kept stealing glances of each other. Cortez even helped Kasey with some of the homework she was having problems with. When they finished they went in the living room to watch television with Cheryl. She called in to one of their favorite spots for dinner. Cortez had gone to pick it up. After they ate and had dessert, he took Kasey home. He knew with them expressing their love for one another was a huge step forward in their relationship.

Two days later Kasey was walking out of her accounting class. Cortez didn't have class that day, so he was going to pick her up after she got out of her creative writing class. She was walking through the cafeteria area when she was bumped in the shoulder hard. The impact sent her crashing to the floor landing on her butt. Her books and papers went flying into the air landing only a few feet away from her. She looked up to see who had bumped into her and noticed it was one of the chicks Cortez had gone off on a few days ago.

"You need to watch where the hell you're going." The chick said mean mugging her.

"Kim did that crackhead just bump into like she didn't see you walking right there?" One of her friends asked walking over to her.

"Girl, yeah. She was probably in a hurry to get that next high." Kim laughed.

Kasey jumped up off the floor and shoved Kim. "Bitch, you don't know me, so don't get knocked out in front of your friends!" She snapped at her.

"Oh shit, Kim you better be careful. You know those crackheads got super strength." Another one of her friends said causing everyone around them to laugh.

Kim reached out to hit Kasey, but missed. Kasey in turned punch Kim in the face, splitting her lip. The two started fighting going blow for blow. Kasey was giving Kim the business until four of her friends jumped in the fight. Kasey was giving them as much as they was giving her. Somehow she ended up losing her balance. When she hit the floor she started receiving punches and kicks from all directions. She balled up in a fatal position to try to block out some of the blows to her stomach and face.

A minute later and the punches and kicks had stopped. She felt a hand touch her arm. "Are you okay young lady?" She looked up and found a female security guard trying to help her up.

"Would you like for me to call an ambulance for you?" The guard asked.

"No, no thank you. I will be fine. I'm going to call my sisters to come and get me." Kasey responded as she stood to her feet. She was in so much pain. One of her eyes felt like it was swollen. The guard handed over her books and papers that had fallen to the floor.

She thanked the guard and pulled her phone out as she headed to the nearest restroom. She entered slowly and checked to see if she was alone. Once she saw that she was, she sat her books down on the sink's counter. After scrolling through her contacts, she pushed the call button on the number she was looking for.

"What's up, K bear? I thought you didn't get out of class for another hour or so?" Jasmine asked when she answered the phone.

"I wasn't supposed to." She sniffled.

"What's wrong? Are you crying?" Jasmine asked alerted by the tone of her voice.

"Some girls had jumped me on my way to my next class. I can hardly see out my left eye." She cried into the phone.

"Oh hell naw! I'm on my way. Stand in front of the building. It should take me no more than ten minutes to get to you."

"What happened?" Kasey heard Mercedes ask in the background. Jasmine explained to her the situation.

"Where my vaseline at? These little bitches these days quick to jump a muthafucka!" She shouted.

"Kasey we're on our way." Jasmine said again.

"Okay." She replied and then hung the phone up. She looked in the mirror and shook her head. After doing her best to clean her face up she left out the restroom. It didn't even take Jasmine and Mercedes ten minutes to make it to her. They were there in less than six minutes.

"Where those bitches at?" Jasmine asked as she got out the car and saw Kasey's face.

She shrugged. "I don't know. I think they left when they thought the guard was going to call the police." Kasey said walking towards the back seat of the car.

"We're going to find them today. They not getting away with that shit." Mercedes said pissed off.

"Guys don't trip off of it. The two of you can't fight anyway, you're pregnant remember?" She said getting in the car.

Jasmine got back in and slammed the door. She was pissed that somebody had put their hands on Kasey. She was also pissed because Kasey was right, she's pregnant and shouldn't be fighting. Her damn baby bump was big as hell.

As she pulled off she started asking Kasey questions. "Do you know who the chicks were that jumped you?"

"I don't know them personally. I know the ring leader was one of the chicks Cortez used to mess with named Kim. A few days ago he had gone off on her and her friends for coming at me wrong. I guess when she saw me by myself she thought it would be a good time to attack me."

Mercedes and Jasmine gave each other a look. "So, Cortez knows who the chick Kim is?" Mercedes asked making sure she understood her right.

"Yes."

"Did you call him?" She asked.

"No, Jasmine was the only person I called. I knew if I called him or Kasim they would flip out." She admitted.

"You didn't think I would?" Jasmine asked her.

Kasey sighed. "I mean, I knew you would flip out a little. I just figured since you're pregnant I would have had a better chance of you not going on a rampage."

Jasmine chuckled at that statement. When she first got the call her first thought was to come and beat somebody's ass. Being pregnant had completely slipped her mind for that split second.

"I'm calling Cortez. He's going to tell us where that bitch stay at. You going to get your round with that hoe." Mercedes said pulling her phone out.

"I was giving her the business before her friends jumped in." Kasey defended herself.

"I know you probably were. That's why they jumped in because she was getting her ass whooped. Don't worry though; you're going to get your rounds with those bitches too." She said listening to the phone ring in her ear.

"What's up, Cedes?" Cortez answered the phone on the fourth ring.

"Where you at Cortez?" She asked.

"I'm at my boy's house playing the game. When I leave here I have to pick Kasey up from class. You need something?" He asked.

"Yeah, I need the address for that bitch Kim that you used to mess with." She said getting to the point of her call.

"Kim? What you need her address for?" He asked confused.

"She and a few of her friends jumped Kasey today when she was heading to class. We just want to talk to her that's all." She lied.

"What? Who jumped Kasey?" He jumped up off the couch and headed for the front door without saying a word to his boy.

"Nigga are you deaf? I just told you who jumped her. Now give me the bitch's address so she can have a talk with my fist... I mean with me."

Cortez ignored her smart ass comment. "Where Kasey at?" He asked jumping in his car.

"She in the car with me and Jasmine. Are you going to give me the address or not?" She asked getting irritated.

"Cedes, you and Jass pregnant asses are not about to fight. Meet me at mama's house." He said hanging up the face in her face.

"Cortez rude ass going to make me fuck him up." She mumbled.

A minute later they heard a phone ring. Everyone looked at their phones at the same time. "It's mines." Kasey said answering the phone.

"Hello."

"Baby, are you okay?" Cortez asked as soon as she answered.

"No, not really." She said in a low tone.

"I'm so sorry that this happened to you. I'm going to make it right though, baby. I promise."

"Okay."

"I love you."

"I love you, too." She replied without hesitation. Jasmine and Mercedes both grinned.

"We're going to talk later about why I didn't get a phone call from you first." He said. Kasey sighed knowing that it was coming sooner or later.

"Okay, Cortez." They ended the call.

"Go over to Cheryl's house. Cortez is going to meet us there." Mercedes instructed Jasmine.

Chapter 27

As soon as they pulled up in front of the house, Cortez was at the back door of the car. He opened the door and helped Kasey out the car. The minute he saw her face he became angry all over again.

"I'm going to kill that bitch!" He spat gently touching her eye.

"No you are not Cortez. You're not getting in trouble because of me." She told him.

"This shit is only happening because she mad I don't want her ass no more." He said in a frustrated tone.

He stood there examining every bruise on her face. When he pulled her close for a hug, she flinched. "What's wrong?" He asked concerned.

"My ribs hurt." That sent him over the edge. He grabbed her hand and led her to his car. Once she was in the passenger seat he walked over to the driver side.

"Uh no! You are not leaving without us. The fuck you thought?" Mercedes jumped in the backseat while Jasmine jumped in the car on the other side.

They drove not saying a word to each other. The moment they pulled up to a familiar house Mercedes shook her head. They watched as Cortez got out the car and knocked on the front door.

"Shit is about to get mad real." Mercedes said.

"Why you say that?" Kasey asked looking back at her.

"You about to see." She chuckled.

They all watched as Cortez came back out the house with a chick wearing a tee shirt, sweat pants, and some sneakers. She was putting her hair into a ponytail as they headed for the car.

"Who is that?" Kasey asked confused.

"That's their cousin Brittany. She's crazy as hell and just don't give a fuck. She cool with me though I never had any problems out of her." Mercedes said.

She got out letting Brittany in the car. She was around the same age as Cortez and just as wild as him too. Some people say she was the female version of him. Minus the part about sleeping around.

"What's up, Cedes and Jassy?" She greeted them.

"Hey." They both replied.

Brittany leaned forward so that she could get a good view of Kasey. "Hi Kasey, my name is Brittany, but people call me Britt. I'm Cortez's cousin. I heard so much about you so it's nice to finally meet you in person. I hate that it's under these circumstances."

"It's nice to meet you too." Kasey said softly.

Britt leaned back in her seat. "Cortez had told me what happened today. I can't believe they pulled some shit like that." She shook her head.

They drove for ten more minutes before Cortez pulled up to the park where people were standing around kicking it. He jumped out the car and so did everybody else except Kasey. When he saw that she didn't get out he turned back around heading for the car. He opened her door and stared at her.

"Get out the car Kasey." He demanded.

"I don't want all those people to see my face." She mumbled with her arms folded across her chest.

"Kasey, I don't give a fuck about none of these people and neither should you!"

She huffed, but didn't make an attempt to get out the car. "Okay, cool stay in the car." He said before slamming the door shut.

He walked up to his cousin and then they walked towards the group of people standing near a bench.

"What's up, Cortez?" One of the dudes greeted.

"Where's Kim and her little crew? I heard they was over here." He wasn't there to be friendly, he was on a mission.

"There they go over there. Kim over there looking like somebody beat her ass." Another dude said pointing to where a group of girls and dudes stood talking.

Cortez walked over there with Brittany, Mercedes, Jasmine, and surprisingly Kasey following behind him. She had got out of the car right after he shut the door and walked away.

Kim saw Cortez coming and damn near pissed on herself. She tried to play it off. He walked over to them and just glared at her. He then turned to his cousin.

"Drag that bitch!" He ordered.

Brittany didn't even have to be told who he was referring to. She knew it was Kim from her fucked up face. Kasey did a number on her, but Brittany was about to add to those bruises on her face. She ran up on Kim and upper cut her in the chin. Kim went falling on her back holding on to her mouth that was now pouring out blood. She then proceeded to kicking her in the face, stomach, and chest.

One of Kim's friends tried to run up on Brittany, but caught a two piece from Mercedes. Cortez walked over and grabbed Mercedes and held her back. Brittany then started putting work in on the chick's face by stomping her in it.

"You're pregnant Cedes! Stand your little ass back. You run up again I'm calling Cree on your ass." He threatened.

"Boy…" She got started, but he stopped her.

"What? Say something else and I'm dialing." He held his phone up.

She walked away and went to stand next to Kasey. "Ole punk ass little nigga." She mumbled and rolled her eyes.

While Brittany was working on the one chick Cedes hit, another one tried to run up. Jasmine walked over and slammed her pistol in the chick's face. "Next bitch run up getting shot! Now try me if you think your life not in danger!" She glanced around at the rest of the people standing around. No one made a sound or a move.

Cortez walked over, grabbed her arm, and led her over to where Mercedes and Kasey were standing. "You two pregnant muthafuckas going to give me high blood pressure." He complained.

When Brittany finished whooping all the girls' asses that jumped Kasey, she stood back and admired her handy work. "Not bad, right cousin?" She asked Cortez.

He grinned. "Naw, not bad at all." He walked over to Kim, who was laying on the ground looking a bloody mess. He kneeled down beside her.

"This is just a warning. Next time you even think about looking at my girl I'm going to get my cousin to bash you. If I get word that you or your funky ass friends got my girl's name in your mouth, I'm going to get my cousin to give you a repeat of today. Oh and you better believe that when my girl is back to hundred percent all you bitches are going to give her the one-on-one round you owe her." He spat before standing up straight and walking away with the women following behind him.

They got back in the car and Cortez sat there messing around on his phone for a few minutes. When he was done he pulled off into traffic. Again, they all rode in silence. Jasmine was pissed that she didn't get to whoop nobody's ass. Mercedes was mad that she only got off two hits. Brittany sat back in the back seat with a smile on her face. She was a fighter, and she loved the rush of bashing someone's face in. Cortez dropped her back off at home before heading back to his mom's house so that Jasmine could get her car.

The instant they pulled up to the house and saw Cree and Kasim standing there Mercedes and Jasmine knew Cortez had rat them out. Jasmine reached over the seat and popped in the back of the head.

"Snitch!" She yelled before getting out the car.

"I don't care what you call me. I told y'all hard headed asses not to do anything. Now deal with the consequences." He said laughing at them.

"You ain't shit Cortez. Now I got to hear this nigga's mouth. If I have to shoot his ass his blood will be on your hands." Mercedes said getting out the car.

Cortez raised his window down and yelled out. "You better not shoot my brother! Your ass going to jail too. Pregnant and all!" She flicked him the middle finger over her shoulder.

Kasey got out the car and walked over to her brother. When Kasim saw her face he got pissed. "What the fuck happen to your face?" He asked but then turned to Cortez, who was walking towards them.

"Some girls jumped me on my way to class today. Everything is fine now." She said trying to ease the tension a little.

"Everything is fine? Look at your fucking face, Kasey! You barely even know females your age, so who is the bitches that jumped you?" He glared at Cortez.

"This shit better not have anything to do with you." He spat at him.

Cortez scrunched his face up. "On some real shit Kasim; don't come at me like that. I told you from the beginning that I would never hurt Kasey. I can't control other people's actions, but I did take care of the situation."

"Kasim it's not Cortez's fault. Those girls are jealous and this was the result of it. I'm tired, sore, and hungry. I just want to go eat something and lay down." She said sounding exhausted.

"I'll take you home." He said.

"No, that's okay. Cheryl said she was making my favorite meal today. I'll just have Cortez take me home when I'm done eating." She said standing on the tip of her shoes and kissing his cheek. She then walked around him and headed inside the house. Cortez followed close behind her. He needed to prepare himself for when his mother sees Kasey's bruises. She's going to flip the hell out.

Cree and Kasim both turned to Mercedes and Jasmine as they stood there trying to avoid making any eye contact with them. Cree reached out and pulled Mercedes towards him.

"You're fighting bitches while you're carrying my baby?"

"It wasn't really a fight. I hit her twice, and that was it." She said biting the corner of her lip.

"Cedes, you are pregnant."

"I know that, Cree."

"Then you know that you shouldn't be out here fighting then. You out here risking our baby's life and for what? From what Cortez stated he had everything under control." He stated calmly, but she could see the fire burning in his eyes.

"You're right, babe. I wasn't thinking at the time. My anger took over, and I lost all common sense. It won't happen again." She pulled him down and kissed his lips.

"It better not because next time I'm locking your ass up in the house until our child is born. I dare you to say anything smart about it too." She rolled her eyes, but kept quiet. She didn't feel like going back and forth with him.

Kasim and Jasmine were a few feet away having a similar discussion. "Kasim, smacking a bitch with a pistol ain't the same as fighting a bitch."

"Jasmine, I'm not trying to hear none of that shit you talking right now. You heard what I said." He glared at her.

She stood back a little. "What exactly did you say because I must have missed something? You're my man and I love you, but you do not control me." She said with an attitude.

"Save that fucking attitude for some weak nigga. I don't give fuck about you rolling your neck with an attitude. I'm worried about the safety of my woman and my baby. You know damn well that the shit you pulled today could've gone left real quick. I'm not trying to control you, I'm just trying to make you understand what you did was dangerous and fucked up." They glared at each other for a moment before she finally spoke again.

Jasmine sighed. "When you put it that way I could see where I fucked up. I'm sorry for having you worried like that. It's just, when I saw the condition Kasey was in, something in me snapped. I wasn't trying to hear reason. I have to remember that I have another life that I am responsible for."

"That's all I wanted you to see. Please don't let that shit happen again."

"It won't." She replied.

"Now give me a kiss. I haven't felt those lips all day. I've been feigning for them." He said pulling her closer to him.

"Exactly which pair of lips have you been feigning to kiss all day?" She gave him a raised eyebrow expression.

Kasim laughed out loud. "You a freaky little muthafucka."

"Hey, I'm just curious." She shrugged.

"Bring your little ass here." He leaned down and kissed her lips. Before she knew it he had his tongue down her throat. She had no complaints as she wrapped her arms around his neck.

"Ahem!" They broke their kiss at the sound of someone clearing their throat. They turned around to find

Cree and Mercedes standing there with sneaky grins on their faces.

"Why are you two perverts standing over there watching us?" Jasmine asked jokingly with her hand on her hip.

"Well, it ain't our fault y'all over there putting on a free show." Mercedes commented.

"Whatever, heifer!"

"We were trying to ask y'all if y'all wanted to go grab something to eat and chill. I would've said let's see what my mama cooked, but she probably in there giving Cortez an ear full." Cree chuckled.

"I'm down with that. Let's get out of here before she comes out here and curse us out too. I know Cortez snitching ass told her everything." Jasmine said heading to her car.

"You're going to stop calling my brother a damn snitch!" Cree yelled after her.

"Well, shit he did snitch on us, babe." Mercedes said heading to Cree's car.

"Oh you be quiet because when we get home I got something for your Muhammad Ali ass." He said smacking her on the ass.

"Cree, you better quiet playing." She giggled.

"Naw, I'm going to be doing a lot of playing tonight." He stated while climbing in the car.

The couples met up at a nice spot out in New Jersey. They ate, laughed, and discussed plans for their children's future. Mercedes and Jasmine thought it was too early, but you couldn't tell Kasim and Cree anything when it came to their babies. The day may have started out rough, but it ended on a nice note. Well, at least for three out of the four it did.

Chapter 28

The following day Kasim was still in a sour mood about the information he had received last night. Right in the middle of dinner Spud called him about the activities that Kevin had been up to. Spud told him that he just watched him, Jasmine, Mercedes, and Cree walk into the restaurant. Kasim asked him how he knew where they were. When he revealed that Kevin had been following Jasmine all day, and he had been following Kevin, Kasim almost lost his cool. Cree knew from his facial expressions and body language that something was up. He didn't want to alarm the women, so he waited until the ladies went to the restroom to ask him what was up. After he told him what was going on, Cree was just as mad as he was. Kasim told Spud to continue to keep a watchful eye on Kevin until they figured out a plan.

Jasmine noticed the change in Kasim's mood and wanted to know what was going on with him. After she fixed them breakfast she sat down at the table across from him. "Okay, what's going on with you?" She asked.

"What do you mean?" He tried playing clueless.

She rolled her eyes. "Kasim don't try to play me. I noticed last night a change in your mood during dinner. I see this morning that nothing has changed. So, tell me what's going on? Remember we agreed to stop keeping secrets from each other." She reminded him.

He went on to explain to her how he had Spud keep taps on Kevin. He saw her face frown at that statement. He knew what was coming next.

"Why would you have him following Kevin? Is this because of what happened at the hospital?" She asked with her head tilted to the side.

"I didn't trust him and with the information I got last night I was right not to."

"What information was that?"

"Your little lover boy has been following you around yesterday. Spud said it was the first night he followed you since he's been on him, but there's no telling how long he's been following you before I put Spud on his tail."

"Wow. That's crazy." She mumbled.

"Yes it is. I need you to be more careful and on alert. I'm going to meet up with Spud and see what else dude has been up to." He stood up and walked over to her. He kissed her on the forehead and lips.

She grabbed his shirt when he tried to stand up straight. She brought his lips back down to hers and tongued kissed him. After parting from their kiss she looked him in the eyes. "Remember whatever you do, you're not the only one who will have to suffer the consequences of your actions. We're starting a family Kasim. Me and our baby need you here with us."

He understood her statement, but chose not to respond. He kissed her forehead again before heading for the door. He jumped in his car and pulled off. He honestly didn't know what his plans were for Kevin. He did know that he was getting tired of niggas trying to come claim what was his. First, he had to deal with Davon and now Kevin. At least now Davon got the message after his trip to the train tracks. Now he was going to need to teach Kevin the same lesson. That lesson being that Jasmine was fucking his and anybody that come between that will regret it.

Kasim pulled up on the street that Spud had texted him earlier. He saw Spud's car parked on the corner and parked right behind him. Kasim got out the car and made his way to the passenger side of the car. He opened the door and climbed inside.

"What's up?" He greeted him. Kasim knew something was wrong when he saw Spud's face.

"What's wrong?" He asked.

"I lost him." Spud said quietly.

"What do you mean you lost him? We're sitting on his damn block." He said trying to keep his temper at bay.

"I went to take a piss and when I turned around and headed back towards the car I saw that his car was gone. I crept around his house to see if I could hear or see him, but there was no sound coming from the house. I decided to wait and see if he was going to come back."

"Damn!" Kasim shouted. He wasn't mad at Spud, he was mad at the situation.

"What you want to do now?" Spud asked looking over at him.

He shrugged. "Like you said, we'll just wait to see if he comes back home tonight."

"Okay cool."

"Other than following Jasmine yesterday, what else has he been up since you've been following him?" He asked.

"He hasn't really done much. He's been to the sex store like three times in two days. That fool must be addicted to sex or something. The weird part is I never see him with a woman though." Spud stated.

Kasim didn't say anything after that. He knew Spud didn't know everything Kevin did while working for Jasmine and Mercedes. He wasn't about to tell him either. He hated talking about his woman being a pimp. They hated when he called them that, but what else would they have wanted him to call them.

Spud and Kasim got comfortable in the car as they waited for Kevin to return to his house. Kasim still didn't know what his plan for him was exactly. All he knew was that he had to make sure he got the message to Kevin to stay the fuck away from his woman.

Jasmine did some cleaning around the house that took her about an hour to do. She then sat around the house eating snacks and watching television. It didn't take long for her to get bored with that. She hit up Mercedes and Kasey to see what they were doing. After they told her that they were out with their men she hung up the phone. She mopped around the house until she decided to go to the gym to blow off some steam.

After grabbing her gym bag she was out the front door. She made sure to check her surroundings after the bomb Kasim dropped on her earlier about Kevin. When the coast was clear she climbed in her car and pulled off.

It took her all of twenty minutes to make it to the gym. She walked in the door and ran into a familiar face.

"Hey girl, I haven't seen you here in a while. I see why though, oh my goodness! What are you having?" A chick named Tara that Jasmine used to work out with asked.

Jasmine chuckled. "We wanted to be surprised, so we told the doctor not to tell us." She replied.

"Aww that's so cute. Should you be working out while pregnant?" She asked concerned.

"Girl, you sound just like my man. The doctor said that it was fine for now."

"Oh okay. Well, we can work out together then. Just like old times before you went and got pregnant on me." They both laughed as they headed for the locker room.

Forty minutes into their work out and Jasmine was tired as hell. She looked over at Tara and shook her head. "Girl, I think I'm done for the day. This baby said we had enough already." She chuckled lightly.

Tara laughed as she handed her a towel. "I'm going to do some more squats and then I'll be heading out as well."

"Okay girl, see you later." Jasmine waved her goodbye as she headed for the lockers.

She decided to shower when she got home. Once she grabbed her gym bag she was out the door. She looked through her bag for her keys. "Why the hell didn't I get them out before I walked out the door?" She asked herself.

When she found her keys she unlocked the door from the button on the key chain. She also popped her trunk. When she got to the car she opened the trunk and threw her gym bag inside. She was about to reach for her purse that she had placed in the trunk earlier when she felt à hand grab her around the neck. She was about to scream when the person covered her mouth with their other hand.

"If you attempt to scream I will be forced to slit your throat. That's the last thing I want to do so please don't force my hand." The person holding her captive said.

At that moment Jasmine noticed the knife in his hand. She stared at her purse that held her taser and her gun. She knew if there was any chance she was going to get out of this without hurting her baby she needed one or the other.

"I've been waiting a long time to be this close to you." He sniffed her neck and then licked it.

Jasmine cringed. She willed herself to be strong not just for herself, but for her baby's sake as well. She listened to him talk and realized who it was holding her at knife point.

"Kevin, what are you doing?" She asked with a calm voice.

"I'm doing what I should have done a long time ago. I'm taking back what's mines! I've loved you since the first day I laid eyes on you. You were just as beautiful then as you are now."

"I don't understand…"

"That's your fucking problem! You never understood how much I cared for you. You kept brushing me off. I hated every time you pushed me away I had to do crazy things. I didn't want to trash the club, but you forced me to do it. It was your punishment for ignoring the love I was trying to give you. Well, now I am going to get a taste of what you should have given me a long time ago." He reached for her waist and tried to pull her yoga pants down.

"I'm not about to go down without a fight." She thought to herself.

Without warning she elbowed him in the stomach. When he loosened the grip on her neck she reached in the trunk for her purse.

"You stupid bitch!" He shouted as he grabbed her by the hair and slammed her head on the side of the trunk. She fell to the ground landing on her back. She was knocked unconscious.

"No… no… that's not how I wanted our first time to be baby." He bent down and rubbed the side of her face.

He looked around the parking lot and saw that it was full of cars, but they were still the only two out there. "I guess a quickie wouldn't hurt. Our next time will be special I promise." He said pulling her pants and panties down by her ankles. He then undid the string on his sweat pants and pulled them down to his knees. Kevin then lifted up her legs in the air. He got on his knees and was about to enter her when he heard a voice yell out at him.

"What the hell are you doing?" Tara asked running towards them with her phone in her hand. Surprisingly she was parked a few cars down from Jasmine. From where she stood she could see them on the ground with him holding Jasmine's legs up.

Kevin panicked and jumped up. He tried to run, but fell flat on his face. He had forgotten to pull his pants up. He struggled for a minute pulling them up. After he got his pants up he ran to his car, got in, and pulled off like the devil was on his ass. He would soon find out that he'll have someone on his ass that's even scarier than the devil himself.

Tara rushed over and kneed down beside Jasmine. She had just gotten off the phone with 911. They told her that they were sending an ambulance their way. She pulled up Jasmine's panties and pants and waited for them to arrive.

Kasim and Spud were getting restless sitting outside of Kevin's house waiting for him to show up. He was just about to call it quits when his phone rung in pocket. He pulled it out and looked at the screen. When he saw Mercedes calling him he looked confused.

"What's up, Cedes?" He answered the phone.

She cried into the phone. "Kasim, Jasmine's mom just called me and said that Jasmine was rushed to the hospital. She said that she was attacked."

He felt his heart drop at her words. "Text me what hospital she's at." He hung up the phone without another word.

"What's going on?" Spud asked.

"My baby was rushed to the hospital. Some shit about her being attacked. I'm about to jump in my car and head there now." He said opening the door and getting out.

"I'll follow you there!" Spud yelled out to him.

Kasim rushed to his car and jumped in. He pulled off with Spud following close behind. They paid no attention to the police cars pulling up on the block speeding pass them.

He stormed into the hospital with Spud on his tail. They looked around for any familiar faces. When Kasim saw Cree he ran over to him.

"Where's my baby?" He asked damn near out of breath.

"She's up on the third floor getting checked out. They said when the ambulance got to her she was unresponsive. It took them a few minutes for her to come to. Man, they said that nigga Kevin tried to rape her in the gym's parking lot."

Kasim glared at Cree after the words he had spit out. "Show me the room she's in." He said walking towards the elevators.

"Look man, I'm sorry. If I would have been paying attention I wouldn't have lost him. I would have been there for Jass." Spud said feeling defeated.

"Spud, you like a damn brother to me. I don't blame you for any of this and you not going to either. We're going to find and handle that situation after I make sure both of my babies are okay." He said looking him square in the eyes. Spud nodded his head.

"We might have a little problem with that. The police know it was Kevin from the cameras outside of the gym. They already headed to his house." Cree broke the news.

"Damn! So, that's why all those cop cars were speeding on the street not paying any attention to us speeding off of it." Spud stated in thought.

The elevator doors opened up and Kasim let Cree lead them to the room Jasmine was in. They walked right in and saw her mother Shia, Mercedes, Cheryl, Kasey, Cortez, and Cordell standing around her bed. They cleared the way for him as he walked up to her beside.

Kasim didn't say a word as he kissed the side of her forehead and kept his lips there. Jasmine rubbed the side of his face. "The doctor said the baby is okay." She said softly.

"What about his or her mother? Is she okay?" He asked, now staring her in the eyes.

"The doctor said that I will be fine. I will just have one hell of a headache for a while."

"I should have been there with you. This shouldn't have happened. What kind of man am I if I can't even protect my woman and our unborn child? I don't deserve you, Jasmine." He said on the verge of tears. She had never seen him cry before.

"Can you guys excuse us for a minute please?" She asked everyone that was standing around.

"Sure baby." Her mother kissed her cheek and rubbed Kasim's cheek whiling smiling. She left without another word. Mercedes was the last one to walk out. Before she did, she told her that Zanni was taking a flight out there as soon as possible.

After the door closing sounded around the room, Jasmine placed her attention back on Kasim. She grabbed his hands and placed them both on her belly. "I don't want you to start blaming yourself for something someone else had done. It wasn't easy for us to start a relationship. I had been through some horrible relationships before you. When you came along you showed me that I shouldn't charge you with the crimes of another man. We started building together. This little person inside of me is the result of us falling in love. So, don't ever say you don't deserve me because you worked your ass off to capture my heart. Once you've gotten it you had treasured it."

"I feel less than a man right now. I feel like I could have done something to stop this from happening. I'm trying real hard not to show it right now, but I'm raging inside. I want to find and kill him with my bare hands."

"Kasim…"

He stopped her with one look. A look that sent chills down her spin. "I'm going to kill him Jasmine. No one will stop me from doing that. There will never be a man walking this earth able to say they hurt my woman and my child and live to tell the tale. This is something I have to do, but I promise to be as careful as I can." He leaned forward and kissed her lips.

"Lay with me." She demanded.

He climbed in bed with her as she laid her head on his chest. His hand gently grazed the bandage that was on the side of her head. He closed his eyes tight to keep himself from jumping out of bed and hunting Kevin down. He knew his woman needed him right now. She was his first priority, and he wanted her to feel safe in his arms.

Chapter 29

Kevin was smart enough not to go back to his home after his attack on Jasmine. The police had searched his place from top to bottom and he was nowhere to be found. They had put a cop car outside his place just in case he come back. The things they found inside his house were shocking. He had different pictures of Jasmine all over his bedroom walls. The pictures were of her at the clubs, out with friends, clients, and outside of her home. That was weird, but it wasn't what had shocked and disgusted them. Lying on his bed was a naked blow up doll with a picture of Jasmine's face taped to it. Inside his closet he had two more of them dressed up differently. Each doll had a picture of Jasmine's face taped to it. When the police told Jasmine and Kasim this, they were both disgusted and angry. The detectives that had come to the club awhile back to talk to Mercedes and Jasmine told her that Kevin was the one feeding them information about them running a sex club. They also told her that now that they saw that he was obsessed with her, they can't believe a word he told them. They figured when she kept brushing him off he got mad and started making things up. Both detectives apologized for wasting their time. They promised to search for Kevin and bring him to justice.

A month had gone by and Kevin was still out on the loose. Kasim, Cree, Cordell, and Spud were looking high and low for him and always seemed to come up empty handed. Jasmine noticed that all the guys were on high alert and always seemed preoccupied. She figured that they needed to have one of their family dinners and just enjoy each other's company. She even invited her mother and her husband, but they were out the country on a trip. Cheryl offered to cook the food, but Jasmine told her that all the women would help. She was glad that Zaniela was back in town. She showed up after Jasmine's attack and hasn't left yet. At first everyone thought it was because of Cordell, but she really hasn't given him a second glance.

"I want to go shopping!" Zaniela shouted while they all stood around Jasmine's kitchen coming up with a menu for the family dinner.

"You always want to go shopping." Jasmine laughed.

"So, what's wrong with that? I have two babies to shop for now. I need to get on it before Cortez try to out shop me." She said causing all the women to laugh.

"I want to go baby shopping too." Kasey said.

"Well, why don't we make a shopping trip for next week?" Mercedes suggested.

"That would be great. Have you and Cree decided on a date for the wedding yet?" Cheryl asked her while checking the list again.

"That's what I wanted to talk to you all about today." They all turned and gave her their full attention.

"Well, with so much that has been going on lately, Cree and I decided that our family needed some happy moments. We have decided to have the wedding three weeks from today."

"Three weeks!" Everyone shouted at the same time.

"Yes, three weeks from today. Zanni, you better start making your plans to call off work now." She said looking over at her.

Zanni rolled her eyes. "I'm the boss so I can call off whenever the hell I won't."

"You're really about to make me walk down the aisle looking like a damn whale?" Jasmine glared at her.

Mercedes walked over to her laughing. She rubbed her huge belly. "You look cute carrying our baby."

Jasmine pushed her hands off her belly. "I'm going to pay you back for this watch. I better not hear one damn complaint either." She said now rubbing Mercedes belly bump.

"Whatever! While we're out shopping next week we'll get fitted for the dresses we picked out a month ago."

"I'm walking you down the aisle too." Jasmine said.

"You're not walking me down the aisle. Cordell is." Mercedes corrected her.

Jasmine glared at her again. "You a damn lie. Cordell walking Zanni down the aisle."

"No he's not." Zanni said, but they all ignored her.

"Kasim is going to walk you down the aisle."

"I'll walk down with Kasim so Jassy can walk you down the aisle." Zanni said, but once again they ignored her.

"I thought we were a package deal? We're a damn team mums. That means Cree not just marrying you. I have to give you a way to that nigga. You not about to play me like that dammit! You ain't the only one who invested years into this." She said waving between the two of them.

Cheryl stood back shaking her head with a smile on her face. Kasey was off to the side cracking up. Zaniela was trying not to laugh while she sipped her juice.

"You so damn spoiled!" Mercedes yelled.

"I don't care! You not going to just say I can't walk your annoying ass down the aisle. I have to make sure Cree knows that even after y'all married we still in this together. That means if y'all ever decide to move I need to be at that sit down with y'all. I was willing to share you with him so he better not get on his funny acting shit with me." She said with her hands on her hips.

"I hope Kasim knows all this too." Mercedes said.

"If he doesn't, his ass will find out soon."

"Okay, fine you can walk me down the aisle."

Jasmine frowned at her. "I didn't need your permission. I was going to be walking you down the aisle whether you liked it or not." She looked over at everyone else.

"Can y'all believe her?" She laughed. Everyone else laughed along with her. Mercedes just shook her head and smiled at her spoiled and annoying best friend.

"Come on ladies let's get to the grocery store so we can get this dinner started." Cheryl said heading towards the door.

~Five hours later~

The family was gathered around the table enjoying the delicious meal the women had prepared. On the table sat an array of food. They had fried chicken wings with different flavors, fish steak, fried turkey wings, fried shrimp, homemade three cheese baked macaroni and cheese, collard greens, yellow rice, potato salad, chef salad, fruit salad, corn bread, and Hawaiian sweet rolls.

"By the end of the week everyone will know who's walking who down the aisle." Mercedes announced.

"Couples should already know who they walking down the aisle." Cortez said taking a bite out of a piece of chicken.

"Well, not really because I'm walking her down the aisle. That means Kasim will need someone to walk down."

"I told y'all Kasim can walk down with me." Zanni said.

Cordell looked over at her with a frown, but hurried up and fixed his face before anyone noticed it. "I had you walking down the aisle with Cordell already. I'll just find someone else for Kasim to walk down." Mercedes said looking over at her.

Zanni knew at that moment that Mercedes was up to no good. "Well, change it. You could have Kasim walking down with me and find someone else for him." She nodded towards Cordell.

"Damn, y'all are just going to pass me around like I ain't sitting here?" He asked looking from the both of them.

"It ain't like you ain't used to being passed around." Zanni said causing everyone to pause and look back and forth at the two of them.

Cordell chuckled and placed his fork down on his plate. "Zaniela, do you have something you need to get off your chest?" He asked staring at her.

"Oh this is getting good." Cortez mumbled looking from his brother back to Zanni waiting for her response.

Kasey elbowed him in the side. He glanced over at her and smirked. She shook her head and giggled at him.

"No, I don't have anything on my chest concerning you." Zanni said bringing them back to the conversation.

"You sure about that?" Cordell asked.

"Yeah are you really sure about that because..." Kasey elbowed Cortez again to shut him up.

Zanni glared at Cordell before scooting her chair back and getting up from the table. Without a word to anyone she walked out of the dining room. Mercedes and Jasmine both jumped up at the same time to go after her.

"What did you do to Zanni to make her not want to be near you?" Cheryl asked her son.

"I didn't do anything." He said defensively.

"Naw man, what we just saw looked like a woman who had her heart broken by someone she loved." Cree said looking at his brother.

"Zaniela and I had never been in a relationship to experience those types of feelings." He said staring at the doorway waiting for them to return.

"You don't necessary have to be in a relationship with someone to fall in love with them. Spending time and enjoying each other's presence is a common way for it to happen." Cheryl said as she continued eating.

A few minutes later Mercedes and Jasmine walked back into the room and took their places back at the table. "Where's Zanni?" Cortez asked. He kept looking back at the doorway waiting for her to enter.

"She left." Mercedes said as she picked her fork back up.

"Did she say why?"

"She just said that she needed to leave and put some distance between them." Jasmine told him.

"Distance between her and Cordell? What about us? She not messing with us no more either?" He asked feeling some type of way. They had all become really close over the years. He didn't like having a rift within their family.

"I don't know Cortez. That is something you would have to ask her." She replied.

He looked over at Cordell. "You need to fix that." That's all he said before he finished off his food.

Cordell didn't say a word. He knew his little brother was right. After seeing the way she looked at him, he doubted that he would ever get a chance to fix whatever it was that he had unknowingly broken.

Cree stood at the end of the altar with a huge smile on his face. He couldn't help but think how lucky he was to be marrying one of his best friends and the love of his life. She was stubborn and at times worked his nerves, but he wouldn't change or trade her for anything in the world. He watched as Kasim walked a smiling Zaniela down the aisle followed by Cortez and Kasey. Cordell, who was his best man, had already walked down the aisle with their cousin Brittany. The men were in black tuxedos and the women wore ruby red dresses that stopped at their ankles. The DJ started playing Monica's song *everything*, and the guest stood to their feet.

Jasmine and Mercedes walked towards each other smiling. Her dress was the same ruby red color as the rest of the bride's maids. It was just slightly different. Hers was sleeveless with a heart shaped diamond pendant above her belly. She put her elbow out for Mercedes to wrap her arm around. Mercedes's dress was a beautiful off white, sort of cream color. It flowed down pass her ankles. You could slightly see her legs, shoulders, and arms through the dress. Her little baby bump was growing every day. She was a little happy that it wasn't as huge as Jasmine's yet.

"Are you nervous?" Jasmine whispered as they smiled at all the guest.

"Surprisingly, I'm not nervous at all. I thought that I would be, but I'm not." She replied.

"That's a good sign." When they got to Cree he stepped in front of them.

"Cree, I share with you my best friend, sister from another Misses and Mister, my confidant, and the first female that I didn't want to punch when I met her." Everyone in audience laughed.

"Wait that's a lie, we couldn't stand each other for like two days." She corrected.

Mercedes giggled. "You can't be lying in church mums."

She did a cross across her chest. "The big man knows my heart." They all laughed again.

"Anyway, Cree I'm entrusting you with someone who means a lot to me. I love you like a big brother, but if you ever hurt her, we'll be back in here for your funeral."

Cree laughed out loud hard. "I love you too, Jasmine. You would never have to worry about me hurting her. She means the world to me." He said looking at Mercedes. She was blushing hard.

"Good, well in that case. I give her to you." Jasmine smiled and kissed his cheek. He did the same to her before he took Mercedes hand and led her up the three steps in front of the reverend. Jasmine took her place next to the other women.

Cree and Mercedes stared into each other's eyes as they said their vows. Once the reverend said that he could kiss his bride, Cree grabbed her around the waist with one hand, leaned her back a little, and kissed her as if his life depended on it.

The guest cheered and clapped their hands at the newlyweds. "Aww my second baby is now a married man." Cheryl cried with a bright smile on her face.

Everyone headed over to their reception which was at Mercedes and Jasmine's newly remodeled club Play Time. A few hours in and everyone was still having a blast. Cree and Mercedes would soon be heading off to their honeymoon.

"So, where y'all going for the honeymoon?" Cortez asked them. They were walking around telling everyone goodbye.

"We're going to Bora Bora." Mercedes answered.

"Oh word? Take me with y'all." He joked.

"Fool you tripping. My baby and I about to relax, fuck, sightsee, make love, and enjoy our honeymoon just the two of us." Cree said.

"You a selfish ass nigga." Cortez laughed.

"Call me whatever you want, but before the night is over my wife is going to be calling me king big daddy." He mumbled to him.

Kasim and Cordell, who was also standing there with them laughed. "I bet you won't say that shit to Mercedes."

"He won't say what to Mercedes?" She asked walking over to them.

"Baby, don't listen to Cortez. I think he got into the liquor." Cree said wrapping his arms around her and pulling her to him.

"He better not because I do not want to hear Cheryl's mouth." She said looking over at him.

"I'm a grown ass man." Cortez said in his defense.

"You ain't a legal man yet so don't be getting drunk around your mom. Little punk." She said then jumped at him causing them all to laugh again.

She glanced over at Cordell, who was staring at Zanni on the dance floor with Jassy. She was smiling and laughing while having a great time. He stared at her with a longing in his eyes. Mercedes wished she could help him, but she decided to stay out of it. Apparently, it's more going on than either of them are letting on.

She giggled when she felt Cree rub his hands over her ass. "Wife, I'm ready to go." He whispered in her ear.

"Husband, we can leave whenever you ready baby. I'm trying to see what all the hypes about with the mile high club."

"Oh really?" He smirked at her.

"Yup, so we're leaving or what?"

"Hell yeah!"

"Ahhhhh!" She screamed when he picked her up and carried her towards the door.

"We'll see y'all when we return. Thanks for coming to celebrate our union with us. We appreciate all of y'all." Cree said as he headed out the door. They could hear everyone laughing at them.

"I love you, husband." She said to him.

"I love you too, wife." He replied with a kiss to her lips.

Chapter 30

Mercedes and Cree had arrived from their honeymoon a week ago. They were enjoying the married life. Jasmine was glad they made it back in time for the baby shower. The doctor said that she could go into labor any day now. She needed her best friend there for this experience.

"Look at all these gifts. Zanni and Cortez done had a damn contest of who can buy the most gifts." Jasmine said looking around at all the gifts surrounding the gift table.

"They won't get any complaints out of me when it's my turn." Mercedes laughed.

Cortez walked over to them. "When are we going to start opening up the gifts? I need to show Zanni that she's not going to be the favorite." They looked at each other and then back at him. They knew he was serious by the facial expressions he was making.

"We can open them now so you can stop getting on my nerves about it." Jasmine said.

"I was going to say something smart to your midget ass, but I'm too excited about opening the gifts." He said walking away.

"Aye it's time to open gifts! Zanni, where you at girl? I want you to be right in front to see what the baby's favorite person in the whole world bought them."

"Cortez, I will be in front to see what I bought them. We all know by now that their favorite will be auntie Zanni."

"I'm not about to go back and forth with you about this again. Just bring your ass over here girl!"

"Ouch! Mama what you hit me for?" He asked rubbing his head.

"Stop all that cursing Cortez. Damn you disrespectful as hell." She said glaring at him.

"Y'all saw how she just abused me in front of everybody? I won't be mad if y'all called CPS." He walked away from her before she was able to hit him again.

Jasmine and Kasim sat in front of everyone and started opening gifts. Cortez and Zanni ended up buying a lot of the same things in different colors. Jasmine picked up a small gift and ripped it open. She saw that it was a picture frame. She flipped it over to get a look at it. She sat shocked at what she saw. It immediately slipped out her hand. She looked around at all the faces that stared back at her. She was starting to panic. She didn't even hear Kasim calling her name.

"Baby, are you okay?" He asked. When he got no response he picked the picture frame up and looked at it.

In the picture frame was a picture of Kevin and a blow up doll with Jasmine's face taped on it. The doll had on clothes and underneath it looked like he placed a balloon or something to make its belly look round. At the bottom of the picture he wrote, *'our family will be together soon. I love you, Jasmine. Your man, Kevin'.*

Kasim stood up and looked around the room. He walked over to the trash can and threw it inside. He then walked back over to Jasmine and grabbed her hands. He helped her stand to her feet before addressing their guest.

"Thank you all for coming back I need to get her home so she can rest." He then whispered a few words to Cree before they made their exit.

"How did he get that in there without any of us seeing him?" She asked once they were in the car.

"I don't know baby. He could've had one of the other guests that don't know him bring it in for him." He said as he gripped the steering wheel tight.

"I'm tired of having to worry about when he's going to pop out again." She mumbled.

Kasim looked over at her and placed his hand on her thigh. As he rubbed her thigh he felt moisture. He pulled his hand back and looked at it.

"Baby, did you..."

"Kasim, I think my water just broke." She said in a panicky voice.

He pushed down on the pedal speeding up. He told her to call everyone and tell them to meet them at the hospital. He was glad when the doctor told them she could go into labor any day now that he was smart enough to put a bag in the trunk to always be prepared.

~Nine hours later~

Jasmine watched on as Kasim stood beside the bed holding their baby boy in his arms. He looked just like his daddy with a head full of hair. Jasmine couldn't hold back the tears when she saw a tear slid down Kasim's cheek.

"He's perfect." He said kissing the top of his son's head.

"Yeah, he is. We created a perfect masterpiece."

"Oh what, you not screaming I trapped you?" He smirked at her.

She chuckled. "No, I'm still saying that. I just accept it now." She joked.

"Yeah okay, smart ass."

"Let me hold him while you go get everybody." She reached her arms out to accept the baby.

Kasim handed him over to her and walked out the door. Their family was all spread over the waiting room.

He chuckled at Cortez and Zanni playfully staring each other down. They were anxious to see the baby.

"Well, my boy has finally graced the world with his presence. He's perfect." Kasim announced when he entered the room.

"Oh my God! It's a boy!" Mercedes and Zaniela yelled out in excitement.

"When can I introduce my nephew to his favorite uncle?" Cortez asked.

"Aw that's nice of you to want to introduce me to him, but I can do that myself." Cree said. He then patted Kasim on the shoulder and congratulated him on becoming a father.

"Nigga you ain't his favorite uncle. You and Zanni better gone with all that non sense y'all be talking. Hold up, where Zanni and Cedes go?" He said looking around. That's when he noticed only people left in the room out of their family was him, Kasim, Cree, Spud, and Cordell.

"They left out to go see the baby." Cordell said handing them all a blunt filled with purple Kush.

"Y'all some ghetto ass niggas. You supposed to give out cigars not blunts. Even though they some fat ass blunts." Cortez said inspecting the blunt.

"We don't smoke that shit. We can't smoke these in here anyway. I just wanted to let y'all know we're going to smoke these together to celebrate the life of our newest edition to the family." He said grinning at them.

"I'm down with that. Let's go see my junior." Kasim said leading them to the room.

They walked in and saw Shia holding her first grandbaby. It was a beautiful sight. Cortez walked over with no shame.

"You not going to be a baby hog are you?" He asked. Cheryl shook her head at her son.

Shia laughed. "Maybe. You got a problem with that Cortez?"

"I mean, I know you the grandmother and everything. I do not hate on that, but I'm not just the favorite uncle, I'm his favorite person in the whole world. I think that out ranks the grandmother label."

Shia looked around the room before laughing even harder. "Boy, get over there and wait your turn. You ain't too old for me and Cheryl to whoop your ass."

Cortez walked away with a frown on his face. "Y'all asses going to jail too." He mumbled.

"What did you say? Speak up I didn't catch it." Shia said eyeing him.

"I didn't even say anything. I see where the midget gets her gangsta from though." He said laughing.

"Who is the midget?" She asked looking confused.

"Jasmine." He replied.

"Cortez, I just gave birth to my son. Please don't make me get up and punch you in the face." Jasmine threatened.

"All I want to do is hold my nephew. I didn't come here for y'all to be threatening me."

"Let me hurry up so this boy can hold his nephew. He's going to make me hurt him up in here." Shia said smiling down at her grandbaby.

Cortez started cheesing extra hard. He knew if he got on their nerves they'll give in to what he wants. Kasey smiled at her man. He could be so spoiled sometimes. He leaned over and kissed her cheek.

By the time Jasmine woke up from her second nap, everyone had a chance to hold baby Kasim. He was in his father's arms again. Kasim sat in the chair beside the bed holding the baby while he slept.

"You know if you hold him while he's sleep, you're going to spoil him." She said getting his attention.

"He's going to be spoiled anyway. I want him to have everything that the world has to offer. That's why his parents hustle so hard."

"He has to work for it though." She said.

"Of course. He's going to know what it means to work for what you want in life. Nothing will be given to him for free, but our love."

"Good, that means we're on the same page."

He smirked at her. "Now all we have to do is explain that to his aunts and uncles." They shared a laugh.

"Yeah, Cortez might be the one we have problems with when it comes to that." She said.

"Naw, we might have underestimated Zanni." He laughed lightly.

"Why you say that?"

He undid the blanket that was wrapped around their son and held him up high enough for her to see. "Is… is that a Gucci onesie?" She asked shocked.

"Yeah, auntie Zanni told everybody that her nephew will be in nothing but the best."

"Oh my goodness. They not about to get on my nerves." She smiled.

"I can't wait until we're all at home." Kasim said looking down at their son.

"I can't wait either. Did you tell Kasey that you were letting her have the house?"

"No, I haven't told her yet. I was going to tell her after you and KJ got out the hospital."

"Oh okay."

"Why you ask?" He stared at her.

She shrugged. "I was just hoping you didn't change your mind about moving to my house. That is now your house too."

"I'm going to be wherever my family is."

She smiled at that. It wasn't long before she was knocked back out again. She dreamed of their family at home together making new memories.

Kasim met with the guys outside in the parking lot. They had some important business to discuss.

"I want that nigga found immediately." He said as he stood staring each guy in the eyes.

"I have some of my men out looking for him." Cree said.

"I'm also going to put word on the street that he's a wanted man." Spud said.

Kasim nodded. "When we find him, leave him to me. I have some unfinished business with him."

"What's the plan for him once he's found?" Cordell asked.

"I'm going to make him regret the day he ever made Jasmine his object of obsession." He replied.

"Good. I want to be there when you handle him. Jasmine is like a little sister and I don't like that shit he pulled." Cordell spat.

"I got you. I need this nigga found before my family gets home from the hospital. I don't want her to feel like she can't come and go as she pleases because of this nigga."

"We're going to try to make that happen. If it doesn't happen in that time frame don't trip because he can't hide forever." Cree stated.

"Let me get back up there before Jasmine starts worrying and shit." He gave them all a pound before heading back inside.

He walked in the hospital room and found Jasmine up breastfeeding their son. "Dang, I have to remember that I'm sharing those beauties with my son now."

She giggled. "Well, technically you won't be sharing these beauties for a few months. During that time they will only be his to feed from."

Kasim made a funny face. "Naw that wasn't in our agreement. I knew I should've got my lawyer in on this." He said playing as if he was upset.

"What was the agreement?" She asked trying not to laugh too hard. She didn't want to scare the baby.

"Well, while you were sleeping one night I had a talk with my son. At the time I didn't know if he was a girl or a boy, but I had a feeling it was going to be a boy though. Anyway, he was chilling in your stomach while I was rubbing it. We came to an agreement that when he made his arrival into the world, the two brown beauties would be shared between the both of us. When I felt him lightly kick, I thought that was his way of saying he agrees. Now, I see that I was tricked." He said without busting out laughing like he really wanted to.

"Well, it serves you right. That's what you get for trapping his mother."

"Oh but if I wouldn't have 'trapped' his mother, so you say, then he wouldn't be here." He resorted.

"So, you're finally admitting that you trapped me?" She asked giggling.

"Naw, I don't agree to things that are not true. We both know your ass wasn't trapped. You were just in love with the dick."

"Whatever, Kasim. Come and burp your twin while I fix myself."

"You don't have to fix yourself on our account. We love looking at your breast. Ain't that right little man." He said holding him on his shoulder to burp him.

Jasmine just smiled. She was happy. It was the first time that she was actually happy with a man and didn't have to worry about his motives. She thought about her and Mercedes' lives. Things had changed for the better for both of them. Their lives had been a rollercoaster ride, but she was glad to have gone through everything in her life so far. She would gladly do it all over again if it would still lead to the moment of her watching from her hospital bed, the love of her life hold in his arms the love of both of their lives.

Chapter 31

Jasmine and baby Kasim had been home for two weeks. They were adjusting pretty well except of the late night feedings. Lucky for her Kasim was there every step of the way. The downside was that Kevin still hasn't been found. Kasim was convinced that he had skipped town. They had people sitting outside of all his people's houses just in case he was hiding out there. Still no such luck. That was until Kasim had gotten the call he's been waiting for.

"What's up?" He answered the phone on the third ring. He was in the middle of making Jasmine and himself some lunch.

"I found him." Spud said on the other end of the phone.

"Are you sure it's him?" He asked not trying to get his hopes up, especially after the last time they thought they had him.

"I'm telling you, I'm looking dead at the nigga. He has a different haircut, and he's wearing glasses, but this is him."

"Stay on him. We'll meet up with you as soon as possible." Kasim said cleaning the mess he made up.

"Okay." They disconnected the call.

Kasim heard women voices coming from the living room. He spotted Mercedes, Zaniela, and Kasey in there with Jasmine. Kasey was holding her nephew close to her chest. He wished their mother was here to see her first grandchild.

"I see you got your crew here." He said kissing her on the cheek.

"Yeah, we're about to have a girl's conversation so if you don't mind." Mercedes nodded towards the door.

Kasim chuckled. "Damn I'm getting put out my own house?"

"Sorry, but no men allowed while we talk about y'all kind."

"Well, I know when I'm not welcomed. I was about to run a few errands anyway."

"Well, see that worked out for you then." She laughed.

Kasim kissed his woman and son before heading out the door. He hit Spud up and told him that he was on his way. He then called up Cree and Cordell to let them know that found their rat.

They met up at Cordell's place before heading out to where Spud was waiting and keeping an eye on Kevin. When they were half way to him he called them.

"What happened?" Kasim asked when he answered the phone.

"He's on the move now. It looks like he's stopping at some house on the outskirts of Jersey. I'm about to text you the address it's not far from where he was just at." Spud said. Kasim signaled for Cree to pull over.

"Okay text me the address and call me if he moves again before we get there." He ordered.

"I got you."

Kasim hung up the phone and waited for the text message. As soon as it came through he read it out loud to Cree. They were back on the road again. It took them a little under fifty minutes to get to the address that Spud sent. They spotted Spud car off in the cut. The house sat on a street with about four other houses spaced out on both sides of the street. Behind the house Kevin was in, was a wooden area.

"What's the plan?" Cree asked looking over at Kasim. He looked back when he heard the back door open. Spud got in and gently closed the door behind him.

"Is he in there alone?" Cordell asked Spud.

"Yeah, I checked shortly after he arrived. I think we should make our move quick before he leaves again." He responded.

"I agree. So, here's the plan. You and Cordell go in through the back door. Once you're in find his location, but don't make a move on him. I want you to open the front door for me and Cree. I'm not too much worried about the neighbors. It looked like he had chosen this street because of the privacy. Once we're all inside we'll go from there." Kasim said.

They all nodded and got out the car. Cree and Kasim crept to the front door unnoticed. They waited for the door to be unlocked. When they heard the locks being turned they positioned themselves to rush the door.

"You won't believe what this nigga is up to in here." Spud whispered when he opened the door for them.

Kasim gave him a look and followed them inside the house. Spud stopped and turned to them when they got to the kitchen entry. "What you're about to see may send you over the edge. Remember what we're here to do." He said stepping out the way so that He and Cree could get a good view of what he's referring to.

They stood there and watched as Kevin stood in the kitchen talking to one of those blowup dolls. He had it sitting on the counter while he stood between its legs.

"I can't wait until our family is completed baby. I bought this house in cash so no one could trace us here. Jasmine, I know you love me. You're just afraid of that guy that keeps coming around. I don't like the fact that you having his baby, but I will welcome it into my home.

Anything that's a part of you I will love." He kissed the doll.

"What's that, baby?" There was a pause.

"You want me inside you now?" There was another pause.

"Your wish is my command baby. Jasmine, I can't wait to hear you scream my name." He said pulling his dick out.

Kasim had heard enough. Before Kevin could enter the doll, he rushed over towards him. He pulled the back of his shirt and turned him around. A punch delivered to his face caused blood to spill from Kevin's nose. Kasim sent two more quick punches to his face before Kevin started fighting back. Cordell, Spud, and Cree stood back letting Kasim handle his business.

They went blow for blow. Kasim was quicker with his reflexes than Kevin. While Kevin's punches kept missing its target, Kasim's hits made its mark every time. It was all happening so fast. Somehow Kevin ended up on the floor getting stomped all over. He tried to cover his body, but it was no use. Kasim turned complete savage on him.

Cree stepped in and grabbed Kasim when he saw that Kevin wasn't moving. "We need to get him out of here and dispose of him." He told him.

"He's not dead yet. I promised my woman and son that the man who hurt them will not continue to walk these streets or any other streets." He snarled.

"He will be dead soon. We just have to get out of here. We don't want to leave any evidence in this house." He tried to reason with him.

"We could take him out back in the woods and get rid of him there. What we don't get rid of the animals will." Cordell suggested.

Kasim nodded. He stepped aside as Spud and Cordell grabbed an unconscious Kevin and took him out the back door. He was about to follow behind them, but stopped in his tracks. He walked over to the doll that was now on the floor and pulled the picture of Jasmine off of it. He grabbed his knife out his pocket and stabbed the doll. When he stood up Cree was standing there watching him.

"Let's go." He said walking pass him and out the door.

They walked through the woods putting some distance between them and the house. When they felt they were out far enough they dropped Kevin on the ground. He groaned as he started to come back around.

Kasim didn't waste any time pulling his knife back out. He walked over to him and kicked him in the face.

"Only a heartless nigga would try to rape a pregnant woman. So, what I'm about to take from you, you won't need where you're headed." He spat before he drove the blade into Kevin's chest. He twisted and turned it as the blood started to seep through the shirt. Kevin was fighting to stay alive. Then Kasim did something that even shocked Cree, Spud, and Cordell. He lifted Kevin's shirt and proceeded in cutting his heart out of his chest.

By the time he finished he was covered in blood. He stood up with his heart in his gloved hand. He dropped it on the ground and stomped on it with his right boot. When he was satisfied with his work he stood back and watched as Spud poured the acid he went and got out the trunk of his car all over Kevin's body. That's how they left him. They walked back to the cars. Kasim got in the car with Spud. They pulled off and headed to Cordell's house. Once there Kasim showered. He made sure he got every trace of Kevin's blood off of him. He didn't want to take any traces of him home to his family.

Kasim was fully dressed when he walked out of the bathroom. The men were all sitting around smoking. He walked over to Cordell, who held up a blunt for him. He took three pulls of it and handed it back.

"I'm out fellas. I need to get home to my babies." He said giving them all a pound.

"What happened tonight never leaves this room. We did what needed to be done for our family. When you get home kiss my sister and nephew for me." Cree said giving him a hug.

"I got you." Kasim walked out the door surprisingly relaxed. He thought after what he had done, he would be having crazy thoughts running through his head. Only thing he was thinking about was getting home to Jasmine and their son. He felt now that Kevin was out the way his family was safe. He could be right, but there was always a way for trouble to find them when they least expected it.

Kasim walked into his home and headed straight for his son's room. He opened the door and walked inside. His boy was lying there sleeping peacefully in his crib. Kasim leaned down and kissed his forehead.

"Those errands took you away from us for the whole day." He heard her voice coming from behind him.

He turned to find Jasmine leaning on the door frame with her arms folded across her chest. "Yeah, that's my bad. I didn't expect to be away from y'all that long." He walked over to her. He pulled her close and kissed her lips.

"You seem more relaxed than you were when you left here." She gave him the side eye expression.

"I am more relaxed. I have a good reason to be too." He responded moving forward out of the room with her still wrapped in his arms.

"What got you so relaxed? It better not be another chick or baby Kasim going to be fatherless." She threatened.

Kasim slapped her on the ass. "I don't need another chick when I got you at home."

"Yeah that's what you better had been thinking. Now tell me what got you so relaxed."

They made it to their bedroom. "Jasmine, you don't be running shit but your mouth. You better chill with all that tough talk before I put something in your mouth to shut you up."

She threw her head back and laughed. "I'll bite that muthafucka off too. Try me if you're bad Mr. Davis."

Kasim smirked at her. She stared him in the eyes and knew exactly what was going through his mind. She tried to push away from him, but he held on to her tighter.

"Un unnnn, Kasim stop playing you know we got four more weeks before we can do anything."

"Four weeks is a long time to be in between those soft chocolaty thighs." He licked his lips.

"Well, I don't know what to tell you playa. No sex for four more weeks."

"What about oral sex?"

"Maybe, if you're a good boy." She laughed when he picked her up and threw her over his shoulder.

"Ahhhhhhhh! Kasim put me down and quit playing bitch!" She squealed again when he slapped her on the ass.

"I'm about to fill your mouth with chocolaty goodness." He laughed.

"You're going to be mad too."

"Why?"

"Because I'm going to bite it." She said still hanging over his shoulder.

"Jasmine, if you bite my dick we're going to be fighting like cats and dogs in this bitch."

"Your words don't scare me Kasim. If you put your dick anywhere near my mouth, I'm biting the shit out of it. Afterwards if you want to square up we can. I think I have a good chance at whooping your ass since your dick going to be bleeding and stuff." She was trying very hard not to laugh.

"You wouldn't do that." He said tossing her on the bed.

She leaned up on her elbows. "Why you think that?"

"Because you love this dick. That's why." He said climbing on top of her and tongue kissing her.

They made out for a while before they stripped out of their clothes and got under the sheets. He wrapped his arms around her, pulling her close to him. They slowly drifted off to sleep with smiles on their faces. Kasim figured he would tell her why he felt so relaxed in the morning. He felt as if a heavy weight had been lifted off of his shoulders. His family was safe at the moment and that was the most important thing in the world to him.

Chapter 32

Kasim and Jasmine was excited to finally be able to go out for some grown up time. Baby Kasim was now a month and a half old. He was getting so big. Cortez and Kasey agreed to watch him while they went on their date. Kasim wouldn't tell Jasmine where they were going. He kept saying that it was somewhere special.

Her eyes zoomed in on the logo when they pulled into the parking lot. She glanced over at him and smiled. "You're trying to rekindle old memories?" She asked.

He smirked. "I'm trying to do that and make some new ones."

They got out the car and walked into Barnes and Noble hand in hand. Once they entered the doors, Kasim turned to her. "On this card are directions to the first book I want you to get. Once you find the book open it and read the card that will lead you to the next book and so on. When you get to the last book I will take it from there." He instructed her.

"Oookay." She dragged out. She grabbed the card from him and read it. She made her way through the bookstore in search of the first book. When she found it she flipped through it and read the card that was inside.

"Go to the mystery section. There you will find the book you're looking for." The card read with the title of the book at the bottom. She followed the instructions until she reached the book.

"In the poetry section the book you are looking for will be placed next to a phenomenal woman." She read the card out loud. She looked at the title of the book she'd be looking for.

After she found the book and read the card that was placed inside she headed to the next section. She did this until she had a nice size deck of cards in her hand. She picked up the next book and read the card.

"If our story was ever told, in the romance section is where you would find the book with the title that matches ours." She smiled at the title of the book. She headed to that section and stopped dead in her tracks when she made it there. In the middle of the aisle was Kasim standing there with a single rose in his hand.

"Is that for me?" She asked walking towards him.

"Yes, but you have to find the book and read the card out loud." He said.

"Okay." She glanced on the shelves until she came across the book titled *'Always and Forever'*. She picked the book up and flipped to the page that held the card. She started reading it out loud.

"Since the first day I saw you, I knew I had to make you mines. You were so beautiful even in your workout clothes with sweat glistening on your body. One look in those pretty brown eyes and you had me completely gone. I was ready to stake my claim, but you weren't going to make it easy for me. I knew if I wanted you I was going to have to put that work in to get you. First, you gave me a chance to love you. Then you gave me a beautiful son that I would forever be grateful for. Now I ask you, in the same spot where we shared our first date. If you, Jasmine, would do me the honor of becoming the ying to my yang, the other half of my existence... will you marry me?" Jasmine finished reading the card and turned to Kasim with tears in her eyes. She found him kneeled down in front of her on one knee.

"Baby, I want to spend the rest of my life making you happy. You and KJ mean everything to me. Will you marry me, Jasmine?"

She rubbed the side of his face with her free hand. "I love you too, Kasim. Yes, I will marry you." She announced.

"Yessss! She said yes!" He shouted. He took the ring box out his pocket and slid the ten carat diamond ring out of the box and on to her finger. He stood to his feet and picked her up. After swinging her around in his arms he planted a long passionate kiss on her lips.

Jasmine was so caught up at the moment that she didn't notice all their family and friends surrounding them. Not until they started cheering and clapping.

She looked up and smiled at her best friend. "You all knew about this?" She asked truly surprised.

"Yes, we knew and no I'm not sorry for not telling you either." Mercedes said with a chuckle.

"Heifer." Jasmine said with a small smile playing on her face.

"I'll be that. So, when are we going to plan this wedding... after I deliver right?" She asked.

"Uh hell no! I told you that I was going to find some way to get you back. Your pregnant ass is walking down the aisle just like that." She said pointing to her big round belly.

"You ain't shit."

"You knew that when you became my best friend." She said with a shrug.

"You mean she's going to be wobbling down the aisle." Cortez joked.

Mercedes flicked him off. Cree walked up to him and slapped him on the back of the head. "Leave my damn wife alone."

"Y'all are going to stop hitting my man like that." Kasey said walking over to Cortez and rubbing the spot Cree hit him on.

Cortez looked over at Cree and grinned. "I don't know why they keep abusing me. All I did was kept it honest with them." He said laying his head on her shoulder.

"I know, but you know everybody can't handle the truth." She replied kissing the side of his face.

"Oh please stop." Mercedes rolled her eyes. She walked over to Zanni, who was holding the baby.

"Where the hell Kasim and Jasmine go?" Cordell asked looking around.

"They freaky asses probably snuck off somewhere to have a quickie." Cortez laughed saying it as a joke.

Little did he know, that's exactly what they had run off to do. They couldn't keep their hands off of each other. They had some loving to catch up on since the doctor finally gave the go ahead for them to have sex. Since they had a baby sitter already set up it wouldn't be a problem for them to leave without a word. Kasim decided to take her home and make love to her until her body screamed for him to stop. Jasmine had no complaints with his plans.

Epilogue

~A Year And A Half Later~

It's a celebration with friends and family once again. The crew had all gathered to celebrate the first birthday of Cree and Mercedes' baby girl Chasity. It was also Kasim and Jasmine's wedding anniversary. Chasity had made her arrival into the world a few hours after her aunt and uncle said the words *'I do'*. Their wedding day started out on a beautiful note and ended on one as well. It was a special day for their family. Little Kasim and Chasity had brought a lot of joy into their lives. Mercedes and Jasmine decided not to reopen the secret club. They both now had too much to lose if things ever went sour. Kasim had gone completely legal with his delivery company as well. Cortez and Kasey relationship had grown into something only they could understand. She was his world, and he meant the world to her. They were still in school and doing well. Kasim had given Kasey his old house. She and Cortez had been living there together ever since. They were happy, and that gave everyone around them good vibes. That was everyone except Cordell. He was still walking around jumping from woman to woman. He had slowed down a lot, but not as much as Cheryl would have liked for him to. Then there was Zaniela. She still visited them a lot so that she got to see the babies. When she did visit most of the time she wasn't alone. She was still seeing Jason and to some she seemed happy. To others it was all just a front.

"Come on Chasity; tell Zanni who your favorite person is so she can stop lying to herself." Cortez said to his niece.

"No baby girl, tell your slow uncle that your auntie Zanni is your favorite. It's okay, his feelings won't be hurt." Zanni said.

They were both kneeled down in front of her. She was swaying from side to side with her finger on her lips. Zanni thought it was so cute. She looked and acted just like her mother. Cree really had his hands full with those two.

"Ummm…"

"That's right baby girl, tell her that uncle Cortez is your favorite." Cortez tried coaching her.

"Stop trying to get her to say your name." Zanni elbowed him.

"She's going to say my name anyway. I am her favorite duh." He resorted.

"No you're not. I am."

"You wish that you were. You can keep wishing because that's never going to happen with me around."

"Both of y'all need to let it go. Neither of you are her favorite person in the whole world." Cree said standing next to them.

Cortez stood up and glared at him. "Why are you lying? There you go with that jealous mess again." He shook his head.

Cree ignored him and looked down at his baby girl. "Chasity, who's your favorite person in the whole wide world?" He asked her.

"Daddy! Daddy… daddy… daddy!" She shouted while jumping up and down. Cree looked over at Cortez and Zaniela's frowning faces and smirked. He then scooped his baby up in his arms.

"I can't stand that nigga." Cortez mumbled causing Zanni to laugh.

"Are y'all ready to start opening gifts?" Mercedes asked walking up to them with Jasmine beside her.

"Yeah, I'm ready. Maybe then Chasity would switch to the winning side once she sees what her uncle got her." Cortez said grinning.

"You better not had gotten her anything that makes a lot of noise because it will be going home with you." Mercedes threatened.

"Oh I got her a lot shit that makes a lot of noise. It's all going home with you and Cree. It's my job as an uncle to do shit like that. It's in my application." He joked.

She reached over and punched him in the arm. "Cree, come over here and get your violent ass wife!"

"Cortez, stop all that cursing around these damn kids!" Cheryl yelled out causing everyone to laugh.

"Y'all better leave him alone before he calls the police on y'all for real this time." Jasmine joked.

"Oh don't say nothing to them about it. They'll know what's up when they walking out their house in hand cuffs." He said with a straight face.

"Cortez, you better not send the police to my damn house." Mercedes glared at him.

"What you going to do pimp? Put a hit on me or something?" He smirked. Ever since he had found out about what her and Jasmine used to do, he wouldn't let them live it down. He was faking mad that they didn't tell him about it. He joked that he could have been a millionaire if they had let him work at the club. Cortez eventually chunked it up to them just being jealous for some reason he couldn't even think of.

"Call me that again and you won't be heard from ever again." She smirked at him.

He stood there staring at her for a minute. "Mama! You hear Cedes over here threatening to get rid of your favorite son? If anything happens to me I want y'all to lock her ass up because she did it. Lock up Jasmine midget ass too because nine times out of ten she helped her." He said walking away from them towards his mama.

Everyone broke out into a roar of laughter. Cortez was always the life of a party no matter what kind of party it was. Mercedes and Jasmine then turned their attention to Zaniela.

"What have you been up to chick?" Jasmine asked her.

"Oh nothing much. I'm just living my life one day at a time." She replied.

"That's good."

"How is the marry life treating y'all?" She asked them.

"With me and Cree, nothing has really changed except now a piece of paper saying that were legally married. Chasity has changed both of us a lot though. She's like a miniature me. She gives Cree hell with trying to boss him around. He just takes it with a smile on his face. He spoils her rotten. I hate to see what happens when she gets older and starts liking boys." They all laughed.

"Little Kasim going to be there as her personal bodyguard." Zanni said with a giggle.

"You know he is. Those two are inseparable. Being married feels weird, but great at the same time for me. I never thought that I would be somebody's wife or mother. I love my boys with everything in me. Sometimes they do get on my last nerves though." Jasmine said with a roll of her eyes.

"You weren't saying that last night." Kasim said breaking up their moment. Following close behind him were Cree, Cordell, Cortez, and Kasey.

"Kasim don't start your mess today." She glared at him with a smile.

"Oh I plan on starting a lot of things today. You don't have to worry though I plan on finishing every last one of them too." He wrapped his arms around her waist from behind and placed a kiss on the side of her neck.

"Mannn, nobody don't want to hear about y'all freaky ass plans for the night." Cortez frowned at him.

"Shut up, Cortez!" Jasmine laughed.

He looked at little Kasim in his arms. "Please don't be violent like your mama. You're going to be tall and she's still going to be having short people anger issues." He said to his nephew.

"You lucky that you holding my baby."

"He my bodyguard." They all laughed.

"Zanni, what's that?" Cree asked catching everyone's attention.

"What?" She asked looking confused.

"What's that on your finger?" He asked pointing to her left hand.

Everyone's attention was drawn to the fat rock on her finger. Mercedes and Jasmine walked up on her to get a better view of the ring.

"Okay, I was going to wait to tell everyone after the party. I wanted this day to be about Chasity, Jasmine, and Kasim." She said looking around at them nervously.

"Tell us what?" Cortez asked.

"I'm engaged." She announced holding her hand up.

"To who?" Cree, Kasim, and Cortez asked all at once.

"Jason asked me to marry him before I got on the plane to come here. We had been talking about it a lot lately, but I was shocked that he actually asked me. I said yes." She explained.

They gave her hugs and congratulated her on her engagement. They were happy that she was happy. If they listened closely they would have heard a heart being broken close by. Cordell stared at her finally realizing that he had lost his chance to make her his. It felt as if his heart was being ripped out of his chest and trampled on. The woman he's in love with was marrying another man and there was nothing he could do about it now.

He walked up to her. They stared at each other for a moment while everyone else stared at them. Cordell leaned forward and kissed her on the cheek.

"Congratulations beautiful. I wish you all the happiness in the world. You deserve it." He then walked away never looking back. It hurts too much to do so.

The End...

Other Novels From The Author...

CPSIA information can be obtained
at www.ICGtesting.com
Printed in the USA
LVOW04s1852040416

482086LV00020B/948/P